Albert and the Plague of Miracles

 DAVID KEY

ISBN: 978-1-4269-9757-0 (sc)
ISBN: 978-1-4269-9758-7 (hc)
ISBN: 978-1-4269-9759-4 (e)

Library of Congress Control Number: 2011917759

Trafford rev. 12/13/2011

 www.trafford.com

North America & international
toll-free: 1 888 232 4444 (USA & Canada)
phone: 250 383 6864 ♦ fax: 812 355 4082

This book is dedicated to my family
especially to
my wife Sheila for lots of patience and editing,
my daughter Kathryn for some of the art work,
my daughter Alex who pushed me hard to finish it

and my other children who suffered in silence as I
wrote it and read it many times over.

CHAPTER 1

Not Expected

Believe me Heaven is not all it's cracked up to be. Let's think about this logically. If all the people who had ever been good, poured into Heaven since time began, not to mention those who hadn't been good but had repented in time, then resources and space will very difficult to find.

What would your idea of Heaven be anyway?

For some the picture of an idyllic backwater full of the sounds of nature might come to mind. The singing of the birds, the almost silent noises that most people miss on Earth and some don't even realize are there.

For others the throbbing pulse of the nightclub scene would be better. But which music? Would songs of unrequited love be appropriate in a place, which by definition has no unrequited love?

Many would feel that a good rest would fit the bill, but sleeping for a million or so years could get kind of boring.

The dedicated crafters would find endless time for their hobbies but the stock pile of get well cards where no one gets sick would soon cause a problem.

Those who are naturally competitive would require sport and competition and those that had often lost in life would now like to win, but someone has to lose in any competition and how could that be Heaven? Perhaps Heaven takes away the spirit of competition and everyone is happy just to let death go by, but for how many people would that seem like Heaven?

On top of that, it will probably be fairly hard work lying around being good all day.

Space would be a major problem, how many millions of people with the right immigration papers have been admitted to Heaven by now. There is no sickness, no death, so Heaven now has a major population problem.

How do you run a major population centre with no rules, no workers, and nothing unpleasant going on at all? The answer to this question is that you don't. It isn't possible. What would the career do-gooders do in such a place anyway? What would their idea of Heaven be? The fact is that there is a ready-made Heaven for those career politicians who like organizing many things to do for lots of people. The fact that a multitude of rules and regulations, many of them totally pointless, would have to be dreamed up is only a bonus.

Ask anyone. The place is perfect if a little overcrowded. The fact that it is perfect is actually a problem. Politicians even on Earth don't like to admit that they are wrong. And admitting that you are wrong is even more difficult when the place you are administrating is supposed to be perfect. Especially when most people's idea of Heaven does not include politicians at all.

Let's face it, Heaven is very pleasant but perfect it is not and it has most of the problems that most other places have. It does have sickness and unrequited love and sometimes although rarely it also has death.

They tell me that when you die; if you were good you go to Heaven. If you were bad you went somewhere else, but Heaven is where Albert Archibald Harrison ended up.

Albert was a little overweight for his age and/or possibly a little under tall. Not especially endowed with good looks, sporting a rather severe crew cut in his mousy hair. His eyes however where fairly striking, being bright blue under somewhat bushy eyebrows which were strangely somewhat lighter than the rest of his hair. He was not over endowed with anything in fact. He enjoyed a friendly demeanor and gained friends that way. But being a little shy, this circle of friends was not very large, and the number of friends of the opposite sex that was included in that rather limited circle was down to single figures, in fact a particularly round type of single figure. His portly figure got in the way a little and although he tried he could not enjoy sport and so he got a little fatter and a little more isolated.

They tell you that Angels are what you become when you get here, but that's not quite true either. To be an Angel takes a lot of work and there are many specialties in the Angel world. There are for instance the Angels of Light. These are the ones that produce a nice bright light that people see as messages from God. Their job is to appear now and then to remind people that they should be worshipping and to give an excuse for some necessary but probably unpopular decision that has to be made. There are Comforting Angels who spend long periods in hospitals and other places in times of trouble. There are Guardian Angels whose job is simply to look after a single living person. There are even Angels of Wrath whose job it is to scare people back on to the right path when they are in danger of straying into unsavoury ways. There are Avenging Angels who come in when the Angels of Wrath have failed and something serious needs to be avenged.

Guiding Angels are those who fetch the dying from Earth if there is danger of them being nabbed by the other side. The administration team that backs up all these front line personnel is of course large and varied as well.

There are also the Angels who fly around. Most people think that these are the usual kind of Angel, but they are very highly trained. An elite few, selected for their abilities, honed to perfection. These may be called upon to take on any of the tasks of the other Angels at very short notice. These are the emergency team who, because of the variety of tasks that must be performed are trained in most of the specialties.

Training to be a Flying Angel takes a long long time and is designed to be three years, which in Heaven is both a long time and a drop in the ocean. Some Angels with a really good aptitude have done this training in two years, some and no one knows how they got through selection, have taken longer. The worst ever, took fifteen whole years. This may not seem a lot but when you have the trainers that are available in Heaven and the almost unlimited use of miracles then this period begins to look very long indeed.

Albert Archibald Harrison was only 12 when he arrived in Heaven. Albert was rather surprised to be in Heaven. After all he wasn't expecting to die. He had had a pretty freaky accident in fact. Don't let anyone ever tell you that when your time's up your time's up and it's all predetermined. Even Heaven wasn't expecting Albert. Perhaps I should describe the accident that brought Albert to Heaven.

The day was sunny. The visibility was good. You could see for miles and miles and Albert was standing by a tree in the middle of a park. This tree was a rather old and large Oak tree. I mention this in the interest of completeness only as it could have been any type of tree really.

Albert was watching a football match. To say that he was watching is probably not quite correct. He was watching, but is mind was not strictly on the game. Albert was at that age where he had begun to notice girls. Girls had not begun to notice him but he had begun to notice them. The particular girl that he had noticed lived three houses away. Her name was Jennifer Hoddle. I mention this in passing and again just for completeness, as Jennifer has no further part to play in this story.

The players were about his age and among them were some of his friends. Well actually amongst them was one of his friends because as I had mentioned earlier his circle of friends was rather limited. The referee blew his whistle because a foul had been committed. Boos and hisses where heard from the crowd and comments about the necessity for the referee to see an optician at the earliest opportunity could be heard stated in not so quiet whispers. Albert's attention was brought back to the game. One of the players, in fact Albert's friend had been adjudged to have committed the foul. As, like the majority of the crowd, he did not agree with this assessment he kicked the ball towards Albert in anger, not at Albert you understand, just in his direction. Albert ducked and the ball hit the tree against which Albert was standing and an ominous cracking sound was heard. A branch above Albert but on the other side of the tree began to fall. A cat that had been sleeping on the branch screeched and jumped down running as fast as it could out of the park. Albert moved around the tree to see what was going on just as the cat distracted a golfer who was practising his swing. The ball hit another tree and rebounded hitting Albert between the eyes and Albert slept with the Angels. Well actually as you will see he did not actually sleep but it's a good analogy. It would have taken some amazing predictive power to foresee that train of events so it is perhaps understandable that Heaven had missed this likelihood and were therefore not expecting him.

Albert does not remember much of the trip to Heaven, for him it was not a set of blinding lights and peaceful music. He just went, no guides, no ceremony, no music at all, but then Heaven was not expecting him.

The person they had been expecting, Peter Mitchell Adams, arrived about two seconds later. He was a fast jet pilot in life, but apparently not quite fast enough because little Albert beat him to it. This may not of course have been Peter's fault because as I have explained Albert was not expected at all.

The Angel in charge of assignments had been told that the next person to arrive was to be part of the elite, an Angel of extraordinary reflexes and skill and was only doing as he was told. In this way Albert Archibald Harrison was one of the people selected to be part of this emergency Angel team. He was himself, not sure how come he had been selected; in fact nobody seemed to know that. Any politician in any walk of life could not be expected to admit that a mistake had been made, and a politician in a system that was by definition perfect stood no chance. In this case however a mistake had been made. Several in fact but no one was going to admit it. So selected he was and selected he stayed. Albert was in fact the youngest emergency Angel selected ever. This made him a little bit of a celebrity.

The flying squad of course meant a lot of work. In his first year amongst other things he was to learn the basics of flying and that's not easy considering years spent assuming you couldn't do it. Controlling dirty great big wings is not as easy as flapping your arms and imagine you have arms as well that keep getting in the way.

You have to learn about aerodynamics, flight control, how to go up and how to go down, hopefully not too fast, how to land hopefully without crashing and how to take off. It's all pretty difficult stuff. It's not all about lying around on clouds. In fact clouds are rather cold and damp and you tend to fall through them, pretty insubstantial really and no help at all when flying.

On top of flying practice you had all the other Angel specialties to learn. It was no good flying off to an emergency and then not knowing what to do when you got there.

There are as you might expect several different cities in Heaven. Or perhaps you haven't even thought about it. Heaven is a very big place, but it has an enormous population. These cities don't have the usual type of names. There isn't for instance a London or Paris. A New York in the survey was so good they named it twice, but that still didn't mean there is one in Heaven.

Albert was not given much time to adjust to his new change of status. He was told that he was expected at the Training camp at Cloud Nine at the start of the next week. This was even more confusing to Albert as he had died watching football on a Sunday. His father had always worked on the Sunday being the first day of the week, because his calendar had always started with that day, did this mean that he had a whole week off to get used to Heaven or was he being thrown in to training the very next day? Did Heaven have any concept of time anyway and if so was each day the same length as on Earth and were they called by the same names? It turned out that each day was called the same as on Earth and changed at the same time just to avoid confusion. Even more confusing however was the fact that each day could be of a variable length to accommodate all the things that each individual Angel required to cram into it, or not as the case may be. The first day of the week as one Angel explained when asked was always Monday and was surprised that Albert did not know this from his Bible. "On the seventh day he rested" was all that was said to him as he watched retreating back of the Angel who had responded to his question. Albert had heard of religions on Earth where the Sabbath was on Saturdays so this assumption didn't seem quite fair either.

So how much time had Albert got before being required for training? It was impossible to tell for Albert. He was a novice at this type of thing. Actually he had no time at all before another Angel called for him to guide him to Cloud Nine. Later Albert had time to reflect on this and realized that this was obvious. As time was variable depending on the amount that each Angel had to do, the fact that Albert had really nothing to do, then no time would be required to do it, therefore he was expected at training camp at once.

The training camp for flying Angels was on the outskirts of a city called Cloud nine. It was the only city named after a cloud and no one seemed to know where the ninth cloud was. Perhaps the cloud had been there once but had blown away or had used itself up raining on the land below. Certainly no records could be found for this cloud or any of the previous eight either. "Perhaps it was where they used to throw you off to prove that you could fly," said someone else wickedly (How did they get to Heaven?).

Within minutes, if time had any meaning left, of entering the reception doors at the Training camp, Albert was ushered into a large assembly hall together with several other new trainees. You may have been surprised that several new flying squad Angels were being recruited at once but please remember that Heaven has the choice of several thousand new immigrants every month.

In this group the selected numbered a mere 16 Angels. This was about average for the twice yearly training set.

A voice boomed out suddenly. It seemed to be coming from nowhere but everywhere at once. Albert assumed that this was the voice of God, but it is well known that to assume makes an ass out of u before me and in this assumption Albert was wrong. The voice was that of the head Angel, the Governor of the college. He was none other than Arch Cardinal Angel Seraphus, famous amongst the flying squad for his production of multiple miracles at the scene of a major train disaster decades earlier.

"Welcome," boomed out the voice, "You have been chosen to be part of the elite, and part of the elite you will be. No one here will fail for two reasons. The first is because of the care with which you have been chosen and second because of the fact that we will not allow you to fail." The voice paused for the words to sink in, "I would especially like to welcome the youngest elite candidate ever selected," continued the voice. "I speak of course of Albert Archibald Harrison who joins us direct from immigration. Would Albert please stand up so that everyone will know of whom I am speaking?"

Albert felt the blush rising in his toes and spreading all the way up past his ears. He fought to stop the redness appearing in his face but the attempt simply made things worse. In his effort he also forgot to stand and then was astonished to find his legs and body unfolding themselves without any instruction from him. Moments later he was standing to applause from the assembly.

"Albert seems to be a little shy," boomed the voice, "But we will help him become the superb Angel that destiny has decreed that he should be." Seraphus continued after the applause had died down, "It should be noted that to stop exhaustion and major problems for those who would otherwise have problems with complacency the variability of time is suspended within the grounds of the college and for Angels on college business or exercises. Your skills will be honed to perfection by your tutors during your time here. During your courses you may occasionally be joined by other Angels, who will come here to partake of some special training. These will not necessarily be part of the flying squad but will be made welcome at all times. I am not saying that all of your time here will be enjoyable but I am saying that you will appreciate it—eventually. This college rewards hard work and no one can afford to coast, no matter how good they think they might be."

A door opened at the far end of the room and three impressive Angels appeared with snow-white wings and sporting a ring of confidence that was perhaps a little high. "Follow us", they said in unison and simply turned and left out of the doors through which they had just entered.

The three Angels, it turned out where all tutors at the school and although Albert had not realized it two where female and the other was male. It is interesting if you think about it that this distinction is made at all. What is Heaven's attitude to pleasures of the flesh? The answer to this is actually not much different to the attitude amongst the living.

On going through the doors the students entered a small bright white anteroom. Well Albert thought that it was snow white, it seemed that way to him, but each time he entered it during his time at the college the room seemed to be a different colour. Sometime a subtle shading of the stark whiteness of the room as he had originally perceived it and sometimes a completely different colour, sometimes even, so vibrantly coloured that it hurt Albert's eyes. He also discovered later that each occupant perceived the room in a colour that was totally personal to them.

The three Angels had seated themselves at a table to one end of the room, Albert and the others stood in front of them wondering what was to happen next. There were no other seats in the room so sitting was impossible without simply squatting on the floor.

"I", said one of the Angels in front of them, pausing as the murmurs in the room subsided, "am Symphina, one of the senior Ardon at this college, in charge of the faculty of Messages, Visions and Guidance. An Ardon is the title given to the Teaching staff in heaven and is a title not gained lightly. To my right is senior Ardon Pilotus in charge of the faculty of flight and to my left is senior Ardon Charina in charge of the faculty of Comfort and Miracles. Each of you will be assigned to one of us to act as your mentors. Your mentor group will be like your family while you are in the college."

Senior Ardon Charina spoke next, her voice somehow calming. "Obviously we act as mentors for Angels who have been here for some time and these Angels will try to help you as you progress through the school, as we hope you will do for those who follow you. Generally we do not encourage competition between the mentor groups however some displays developed in the past have now developed into minor competitions to see how well each group is progressing. To help identify members of your own mentor group your tabard insignia will be as follows." Charina paused and waved her hand and to Albert's amazement the clothes, which he had been wearing, were instantly replaced by a long white gown, which fitted him perfectly. Despite its close fitting, the gown or tabard didn't seem to get in the way, "Electric blue lightening is the insignia of the Messenger Group. An emerald Green Star is the insignia of the Comfort Group and a metallic red Wing is the insignia of the flight group. Please remember that the group you are in only reflects your mentor family not your specialism. You will all be expected to excel in all specialist areas."

Looking directly at Albert, Symphina spoke again. "Each of you has been chosen by destiny as one of the elite, no concessions will be made for age or experience you will all be required to live up to your destiny."

Albert noticed the insignia on the Ardon's in front of him, the electric blue on Symphina, the metallic Red on Pilotus and the Emerald green on Charina. Looking around he noticed the glint of the three colours on his fellow students. Looking down he found the startlingly bright blue lightening flash attached to his own tabard.

Albert suddenly realized that Symphina was still speaking. "There are two other mentor groups which you will notice as you travel through the corridors of the college. There is the gold hand of the faculty of healing and the purple crossed swords of the faculty of correction and vengeance. None of you of this intake have been assigned to these mentor groups. We have asked members of your mentor groups to take you to your rooms."

Instantly a door hidden in the wall to the right and two doors hidden in the wall to the left opened and three Angels entered the room. The Angel to the right was wearing the insignia that matched Albert's while the two to the left wore the green and the red insignia. "Please now follow the student from your mentor group. That is all," said Symphina.

There was nothing left to do. The last statement had been a dismissal even if the three Ardons had not moved and the 16 students split, not quite evenly to follow through the appropriate doors. One of the group absent-mindedly tried to go through the wrong door with an effect like hitting a brick wall. The doors from this room would only admit those of the correct mentor group. Albert wondered whether they admitted people wearing the right insignia or whether the doors could distinguish mentor group members by some other means.

Albert followed the correct guide from the room and across a garden bathed in bright sunshine and from there to a building and along a long corridor with doors on either side. Albert was shown to a room off the corridor, which was pleasantly furnished with a large comfortable bed and a chest and a wardrobe built into the wall. A large desk took up the far wall and a further door led to a shower. 'Very nice,' thought Albert as he began to explore in more detail.

The wardrobe contained eight new tabards all sporting the electric blue lightening insignia. The chest was empty, the desk contain a single book, which inside the front cover sported a label—'with the compliments of the Gideon Society'. The shower already contained all the toiletries that could have been needed including a new toothbrush and paste.

Albert was first sent to this nice lady Angel who made him take his tabard off and lie down on a raised couch.

"My name is Therapina," she said asking him to lie down on his front on a couch set in the middle of the room. Albert noticed the insignia of gold glistening on her robe. Massaging something cold into his back she mumbled something that Albert simply did not understand. The sensation was initially pleasant and then after about five minutes it became a little uncomfortable. A little later, downright painful. He tried to wriggle but was told to keep still. His back seemed oddly heavy as though someone was pushing a little on his shoulder blades and the sensation seemed to be getting worse. He tried to look around but this caused him to spin around backwards so that he nearly fell of the bed, (He didn't because he was instantly caught and put back where he was). He decided there was nothing he could do about it anyway and just lay there gritting his teeth. Albert remembered thinking that this was supposed to be Heaven so why was this painful, surely pain was unnecessary in Heaven. More cream was massaged into his back. The pain subsided and Albert felt exhausted—he had no idea why; he had done very little that day. He slept.

The end of his first week came and went before he could stand up without overbalancing. These wings, grown as a result of the treatment, where heavy, they got in the way, folding them up properly was a nightmare and keeping them properly cared for was one of those things that Albert would really rather not do. A feather out of place or a speck of dirt however would swiftly earn a telling off from Therapina who Albert was rapidly coming to the conclusion was not quite as nice as he had thought. In this he was, again, mistaken and later he would come to think of her as one of the nicest members of college staff there.

Lessons on wing care where part of that first week but Albert was so tired that he did not remember almost any of it and so the second week was spent with a tutor learning it all again.

Albert was sure he had seen other people during that first fortnight but he couldn't specifically remember any particular instant. He came to the conclusion that he had been left largely alone with occasional input from the tutor on wing care whose name was Thomus. In this however he was wrong. He had been watched by Symphina on a very regular basis and even a visit by Seraphus had gone unnoticed by Albert.

The fact that Albert had basically forgotten a whole week of tuition had been the subject of much discussion amongst the tutors and administrators of the college. The fact that Albert seemed to be a little slower than the usually expected input was put down to his age and inexperience in his previous life. The fact that a mistake might have been made in the selection was not even mentioned. Seraphus however, had during these discussions, taken a personal interest in Albert and asked about his progress regularly. Phurus head of the Avenging mentor group had noticed the Arch Cardinal's extra interest but had refrained from commenting. Occasional slightly barbed comments about Albert showed that this was jealously regarded. Seraphus' interest and patronage had earned Albert his first opponent.

Impartial observers to this story may have noticed that the reaction of Phurus was most unexpected in Heaven surely Angels throughout Heaven would be above such reactions. The casual observer would be guilty of not thinking about the situation. How good do you have to be to enter Heaven? Does this mean that you have no trace of the petty, or even not so petty jealousies and resentments that manifest themselves during life? Are the people who are considered clever or talented enough to take the top posts likely to be the ones that are devoid of these emotions? Does the entrant to Heaven that entered due to the heartfelt deathbed confession and repentance really leave behind the emotions that caused the repentance to be necessary? The answer to all these questions is a resounding NO.

CHAPTER 2

Flying Class

ALBERT WAS FIRST INTRODUCED TO a formal class at the beginning of the third week.

An impressive Angel hovered above the field that the students had been asked to assemble in for their first group lesson. Her wings barely moved as they supported her without apparent effort.

"I am Soarelle and I am the Assistant head of the faculty of flight and in this instance overseeing the flight instruction of this group". Soarelle paused for the words to register with the group. Soarelle had an awe-inspiring presence, which had silenced the group from the first word spoken. "As flying is such a fundamental part of our work here this initial class in flying will be an intensive course which will be uninterrupted by other classes". Soarelle continued, "Theory will be done in the mornings followed by flight practice during the afternoons. Today however the instructors will be assessing your current capabilities and towards the end of the course the afternoons will be for free practice for the more able students, while the instructors concentrate on getting students that need more help up to the standard required for your initial license. It is expected that each and every student will leave this class with an A class flying license at least." The murmur that this produced was silenced again as she continued after the briefest of pauses. "For those of you who are not familiar with the flying license system used in Heaven I would point out that there are five grades of which the lowest is A and the highest is E. The A license allows restricted solo flying while the E license is very rarely attained as the standard is very high. There are only two E licensed flyers on campus which are Senior Ardon Pilotus and myself. Senior Ardon Pilotus is the only current holder in Heaven of the Albatross Wing, which is highest flying award ever awarded.

Flying did not come naturally to Albert. This came as quite a surprise to the group's teacher Soarelle, who had not expected that Albert would have difficulty forgetting that he couldn't fly. In the past, the rare times she had chosen to teach young people to fly she had found it easy to convince them that flying was simple, and when she had convinced your mind that it was an easy thing to do, that was half the battle. To be fair Albert was not the only new Angel to find flying difficult in fact the flying class included more experienced Angels, who still were finding flying difficult.

The class was taken by several instructors and several older students used as helpers. The class was at this point necessarily a one to one exercise and doing this with just one instructor with a class of 18 would have been much too slow.

Albert's difficulty may not have been entirely Albert's fault, as he did get a little distracted. His mild celebrity status was attracting the girls. As we have stated previously Albert was at that age where he just begun to notice girls. And as most girls dream of being very pretty, and this was Heaven, any of the girls who now had begun to notice Albert were, at least in his eyes extremely beautiful. Concentration was therefore difficult.

Albert's first flying lesson did not go well. Did I say that this was a one to one exercise? Well, in Albert's case this was a one student to three instructors exercise. Albert was a little too round and his wings especially with a novice controller simply pointed upwards behind him, causing him to knock the wind out of the helper who was supposed to catch him if he fell. If he fell? Albert could think of no reason at all why he shouldn't. The use of one helper to catch him soon escalated to two. The wings sticking out of his back seemed totally uncontrollable and really quite weak. Every time he moved the feathers ruffled and felt uncomfortable and Soarelle's trick of remembering to fall upwards instead of downwards did not work at all. Falling up just did not feel natural and Albert just kept on going down.

After several hours of ups and downs (the ups mainly under instructor power while the downs Albert could manage quite nicely on his own), the instructor told the totally exhausted Albert to go and study the rules of flying so that when Albert could fly he would know where he was allowed to fly. Albert was not asked to do this alone as this study was assigned to the whole class. Some of the fledgling Angels had caught on to flying quickly and therefore had time to do some of the studying during the lesson. The majority however had not been that good and would now have to use their own time.

Albert was surprised to find out that he would need to learn rules for flying. He didn't specifically think about it and when he did think about it he had simply assumed that Angels could simply go where they liked. On the other hand even the elite group that was the flying squad was now quite large and it was allowed for other Angels to pass their flying test if they wanted to, so with no regulation Albert reckoned that things could get a little out of hand.

Leaving the class with his whole body feeling as though it had been bashed, dropped, bruised and considerably manhandled (which of course it had), Albert noticed that other students seemed to be leaving the group in a similar state. The electric blue insignia on one particular Angel caught his eye and he wandered in her direction.

Angelina (this was her living name and very appropriate for an Angel) was two years older than Albert. She had naturally blond hair, which hung down as far as the golden belt around her tabard. Her bright blue eyes sparkled as if to try and compete with the electric blue of her insignia. Her slim waist contrasted with the rather rotund figure sported by Albert. Despite being only two years older she was nearly four inches taller than Albert and already jutting out in just the right places. All of this however was not noticed by Albert who was just whacked and had moved in her direction to feel a little kindred spirit.

Angelina spoke first "That was pure hell," she whispered. Albert was not sure whether she was whispering because she didn't want to be heard or because she was so tired that that was all she could manage. Albert didn't even notice at that time that she had the voice of an Angel.

To those who had not thought about this, an Angel who had the voice of an Angel is actually quite surprising. Those who end up in Heaven do not actually change their physical attributes unless it is a specific wish during life. While most girls dream of being beautiful, and this is counted as a specific wish if it is dreamed often enough, most girls do not think about their voices. In Angelina's case she had been gorgeous during life and no change had occurred in that direction during her transition to Heaven. She was one of those rare people who appear to have it all, reasonably intelligent though no Einstein and really pretty but with a wonderful personality as well. She had left behind many boys who missed her but she herself had not even thought about the attentions that had been lavished on her by the opposite sex. She just took friendship as the norm but never taken for granted. She had not yet thought about any romantic entanglements and this had frustrated many boys who had had other ideas.

Albert was so tired that he didn't even look at her as he replied, "I thought I was going to die—several times," he added after a brief pause. Had he looked at her, he like many boys before him, might have been lost in the pools of blue that were her eyes, but he did not look at her and so a lasting friendship that may have been lost in the mists of adoration was started.

The smile that spread over Angelina's face enhancing her considerable beauty was similarly missed. "Bit difficult," she said. "We've already passed that milestone". Continuing to walk back to the quarters for the messenger mentor group and passing through another special door that only allowed the passage of the groups members, the two lapsed into silence. She stopped by the door of her study and living room and smiled again as she said, "I suggest we try this studying together it is probably as difficult as the flying."

"I hope not," grimaced Albert, "but it's still a very good idea to share the burden. How do you suggest we work this?"

"Call here for me in an hour," she suggested. "I will have had time to freshen up by then and we can go to the Library."

Albert didn't know there was a Library but let this go and said that he would be back in an hour. Feeling very tired he found his way slowly back to his room where he showered and changed. This action took him longer than he remembered but then up until recently he didn't have two seemingly huge wings, which seemed amongst other things almost impossible to reach, to worry about and care for. They not only complicated the showering but also the getting clothes on and off. He made it back to Angelina's room with only two minutes to spare and knocked on the door.

Angelina, looking stunning, opened the door. "I do like a man whose is punctual," she said. And this time even a blind man would have felt the radiance of her smile.

Albert was momentarily taken aback but recovered to comment, "It's only polite".

Her smile never dimmed as she replied, "I like a man who is polite as well." She led the way down the corridor and Albert, feeling a little numb, followed. After all he had no idea where they were going.

After several turnings and several doors they arrived at the Library. The room was vast. Albert could not tell how far the shelves went as the effect of so many books may have been misleading. Mobile steps allowed access to books on higher shelves stretching 10 metres above him.

"Impressive, isn't it?" said Angelina, "and this is only one of several floors. The college offers a course in how to get around this Library and how to find the books you need or want. I have spent several days getting to know it as I arrived a little early. The librarian whose name is Bibliolus is very proud of the collection and very helpful if he thinks you are interested in the books. Bibliolus seems to be able to tell you the exact location of any book in the Library and the probable location of books for virtually every subject as well. I don't know how he does it as he can't have read them all."

The magnificent collection appeared to have every book produced on Earth by the living as well as every book ever written by people who had ended up in Heaven.

Bibliolus even claimed that he had managed to obtain books written from the other place but declined to be more specific about what was meant by the other place. Angelina had anticipated the need for books on the rules and theory of flying and had asked for and checked the location of such books on her previous trip to the Library and was able to lead Albert directly to the correct shelf. This however was only the start of the problem. The books on the subject stretched along the shelf into the distance and although the ones written by the living could be ruled out for the purposes of their current research the choice was still bewildering. Angelina suggested a systematic approach starting at one end until they had a book, which seemed to contain all or most of the information required without being too complicated. They could then sit down and go through this together. After about five minutes they each had a book that seemed useful and started to study.

Studying the theory of flying was every bit as hard as studying had always been for Albert. The expectations of being picked as an elite flying squad member would normally have simply piled on the pressure and made it even more difficult but studying with Angelina seemed to take the pressure off somehow and together they got on well. The two read passages from their own books for a while occasionally reading a particularly interesting passage out loud for the other to hear.

The rules of the road when learning to drive a car are difficult enough and even then they change with different countries. Imagine then the problems of doing the same thing in space where you could go up and down as well as right and left. Combination moves such as going down to the right or up and straight ahead had to be learned. No road markings to help the problem due to the difficulty of suspending the paint in mid air produced even more confusion. Add to that the changes with regions when there was no warning that you had just crossed a boundary and you had a subject that was going to take Albert a good time to master. One Angel later said that he had never mastered the problem and he was in his twentieth year of flying. "The best thing to do," he said, "was to keep a sharp look out and expect the unexpected." He had however had several major crashes during those twenty years, so his advice may be considered a little suspect.

The rule that you should give way to anyone who is rising seems fine until you realize that two Angels can be on a collision course when both are rising. Therefore the additional rule that you give way to people from the right sorts out that problem until you realize that if you are flying downwards it is a damn sight more difficult to stop than the Angel that is coming up. On the other hand a stopped Angel on the way up can't get out of the way very quickly being, as it is, more difficult to climb than simply to fall. (Albert remembered being told that it was as easy to fall up as to fall down so this confused him slightly).

Complicated rules applied for Skyways (motorways in the sky) but how did you know where they were? The absence of road markings seemed an ever-present problem. The book said that these were often marked with rows of fine wispy elongated clouds. This seemed to make sense unless you where flying though a cloudless sky wondering where to go next. That is, if you knew where you where already. Albert wondered whether thin wispy elongated clouds always meant the position of a skyway or whether sometimes, thin wispy clouds just occurred with no meaning whatsoever. The problem with thin wispy clouds was that the wind blew them about. Did this mean the skyways kept moving as well? Very confusing.

Angelina found another book, which described the skyway markings in greater detail, and it turned out that the thin wispy clouds were only what the markers looked like to Angels flying on the skyways. They were actually permanent markers, which the living couldn't see at all. This made life easier, but the book went on to say that a grade C flying license was required before using the skyways, so it would be sometime before either of them needed to worry about those particular rules.

Albert found a book entitled "Simple rules for Simple flying" with a subtitle of "The beginner's guide to beginning starting flying", which seemed to Albert a little bit of an overkill for a title but on the other hand seemed to describe his situation exactly. Angelina found a small thin book named "Flying the skies—the Angels' code", which couldn't be that complicated, as it was such a small book.

We have previously stated that to assume makes an ASS out of U before ME and to assume that a small book can't be complicated forgets that this is Heaven and what is small anyway? In this case the small book was considerably bigger and thicker than it looked and the writing in it was considerably smaller and squashed together more than it looked. Each rule which I suppose in itself was simple enough was explained in such terms and with so many unusual and unlikely examples that it became completely baffling.

"Simple rules for simple flying" on the other hand seemed to be quite useful. Angelina worried that it might be too basic but it was the best they could do and so that was what the two of them based their research.

On asking Bibliolus a second copy arrived, to make it easy for them to read together. I say a second copy quite literally as the second was simply a copy of the first. Where the original had a tear so did the copy. Handwritten notes in the original where faithfully reproduced in the second version.

The two sat at a table in the corner and read out passages that they did not understand (quite frequently in Albert's case) or passages that seemed to suggest completely crazy or particularly interesting rules.

"Listen to this," said Angelina. "In the case of a collision on a standard flyway all parties to the collision should remain at the location of the collision and await the ATP. Any craft or single Angels waiting in any queue should move to the nearest extreme edge of the flyway to allow the ATP access to the scene."

"Sounds like a sensible rule," said Albert, "but what is the ATP?"

"Haven't got a clue. I'll look it up. There is a glossary at the back of the book," said Angelina. "Here it is. Angel Traffic Patrol"

"Never heard of them," puzzled Albert, "I wonder which mentor group they belong to."

"I don't think they do. Policing is considered to be administration so they would go to the administration college at Sky House for that."

Albert had failed to consider the possibility that Heaven would actually need police, on the other hand as we have discussed earlier Albert had already worked out that all sorts of undesirables could con their way into Heaven and as we have commented earlier once there no one was going to admit that a mistake had been made. Perhaps thought Albert police only exist to look after the accidents and weren't for investigating crimes at all. As Albert thought this he knew he was wrong to think it, after all Heaven is not everything that it's cracked up to be.

Albert was not really concentrating, so it was with some surprise that he found himself with a rational thought going through his head (Note I said rational not constructive.) "If only the skyways are marked how can you go to the nearest extreme edge of a flyway when you don't know where they are?" asked Albert. "How do you stop yourself falling over the edge?

"There must be someway of knowing where the flyways are," frowned Angelina. "But I can't find it in the book," she complained.

Looking through several books from the vast number about flying that were held in the Library neither Albert nor Angelina could find a mention of any such markings. When they asked Bibliolus he stated that he did not fly and therefore he could not tell them from experience and he also could not remember reading about it anywhere either. Bibliolus was sorry but on this occasion he could not help. It might be interesting to note that this was the first and last time that either of them found a question that Bibliolus could not help them with either directly or by pointing out a book which could be used to research the answer.

With a fair amount of work done on the rules for flying (but probably not as much as would be expected back in class tomorrow) they went back to their dormitories with Albert saying a sleepy goodbye at Angelina's door on his way back to his own room.

The following morning Albert couldn't remember much about the work they had done the evening before and hoped that it would come back to him in class or that Angelina would remember and be able to give him hints. She was already in class when he got there. She looked as sleepy as he did and one of the other Angels had taken the seat beside her. That meant that no hints were possible and as feared when actually in the class he couldn't remember much. Albert remembered wishing to himself that he would not have to answer a question. A BIG mistake. Wishes are like dreams, the very fabric of what Angels are there for. Soarelle therefore knew that Albert didn't want a question and therefore the first person to be asked was Albert.

"Albert", (Albert's heart disappeared somewhere down below his socks), "what action should be taken by a Angel who was not one of the parties involved in an accident on a flyway while waiting for the ATP?"

Albert's heart came back to where it was supposed to be with a sickening but joyous thump. He was going to be able to answer this. "Move to the nearest extreme edge of the flyway thus ensuring access and await the ATP," said Albert knowing that he remembered correctly.

"Very good," said Soarelle obviously impressed with the answer. Soarelle started to ask another question but Albert put his hand up and started to speak. Soarelle's question died on her lips.

"Yes, Angel Harrison," she said with no inflection of annoyance in her voice.

"I was wondering how anyone on the flyways knew where the extreme edge of the flyway was," Albert said timidly thinking that probably every one else knew except him and Angelina.

"A very good question," she boomed out to the class, "Albert, please repeat the question loudly so that the class can hear."

Albert was a little troubled by this. His shy nature did not often put him in situations where it was necessary to be in the public notice. In this case he was also a little worried that he was setting himself up for a fall. There was however no indication in Soarelle's voice that her reaction was not genuine. Albert repeated the question. The silence and the attention in the class suggested, much to Albert's relief, that no one in the class knew the answer any better than he did.

"The flyways are bordered by a barrier that is almost impenetrable to the Angel flyer. This barrier is more felt than seen. Despite its nature it is energy absorbing and if hit feels like a feather cushion, which gets progressively harder the more anything tries to get through it. As each of you gets more accomplished at flying you will find that the position of the edge of each flyway and skyway will simply make itself known to you without it having to be seen. While I can accept that this explanation leaves a lot to the imagination I would ask all of you to leave any further questions about its nature until after you have experienced it in flight. I think you will find most questions will be answered by familiarity. There is a proposal, by the department of flight safety to make these fences visible but this would have the effect of obstructing the view outside of all travellers. Remember that the barriers are by necessity three dimensional and actually more like a tube than a fence."

Albert thought about his own efforts at flying and began to worry about the injuries he might get if he fell or rather bounced about the inside of a tube rather than fell through space. On the other hand each collision would be softened by the energy absorbing feather pillows.

Soarelle continued asking questions around the class with a variety of results. Sometimes the questions were answered correctly sometimes incorrectly and sometimes not at all. In each case Soarelle took it in her stride. Any displeasure she felt, if any, about some Angels obvious lack of study, she didn't show.

At the end of the class she said, "This afternoon the class will be going outside for practical flying practice. I would suggest you get to know your individual flying instructors well as they are a great source of experience in the craft. I also suggest that before this afternoon's practice you pair up so that you can regularly practice together knowing the strengths and shortcoming of practice partners can increase safety quite considerably. I also suggest that many of the class could use some extra study on the flight rules during free time tonight. Thank you for your attention." These last words were obviously a signal for the class to break up. These words it appeared were the last words of most Ardon Soarelle's classes and when she missed them then something was really wrong. Albert got up from his seat almost without thinking and turned to almost bump into Angelina who had immediately come over to see him.

"Nice answer to your question," she said, that incredible smile radiating as she spoke, "I thought that as we seemed to get on last night during study that it might be nice if we paired up as flying practice partners as well."

Albert may have been working without thinking during most of the morning but the prospect of pairing up with someone new scared him a little and so he enthusiastically agreed. In doing so he earned the jealousy of almost all the male Angels in the class, but for Albert this was not a question of romance just a question of friendship.

Meals at the college where always a sort of buffet affair. The array of food was impressive in the canteen and you could have basically what you wanted. Albert who had been a vegetarian for as long as he could remember still had a vast choice of delicacies. He stuck however, to the ones he knew he liked with many a mealtime spent eating a pizza or a pasta meal. He was not, by nature, an adventurous eater. Angelina on the other hand had no particular taboos but while eating with him stuck to vegetarian fare as well. For her, thoughtfulness of this kind was simply second nature. It was not a conscious effort but just a thing that happened. Albert remembered thinking once that he could not blame Heaven for wanting this girl, after all virtually every male seemed to be infatuated with her, but still Albert saw her as a friend and not as an object of adoration. Perhaps that was why she felt so relaxed with him perhaps that was why they could get on so well together.

Flight Practice that afternoon seemed to go as badly as the time before to Albert, but afterwards he didn't feel so bad as he had the day before, he must be getting used to the battering. Thinking back however it did seem that the descents were just that little bit slower and the catches that little bit less frequent and the impact a little less violent. The encouragement from Angelina seemed to help as well although Albert couldn't understand how. Angelina was not having many problems flying at all and she could have advanced to the next class had she wanted, but she chose to stay and help Albert. When Albert commented on this she just said that that was what partners did and they had agreed to be flight partners hadn't they. She asked if he would rather another flight partner but this was the last thing that Albert could have wanted and he told her so.

By the end of the end of the afternoon Albert found that he could slow his descent down a little. He wasn't sure that this was a result of some of the flying theory getting through or just the fact that he could now control his wings enough to spread them out behind him and therefore they acted like a parachute. Supporus, his flight instructor, expressed pleasure in his progress but Albert wasn't sure that he wasn't just being humored. Angelina told him not to be so silly when he expressed this view to her, telling him that progress had been made and that shortly he would be flying around the campus rather than walking. Thinking of the precision flying required to do that made Albert shiver. Would he ever be that good? Somehow he doubted it, but then he doubted he would even get off the ground on his own.

To be fair to Albert he practiced wing control often and did all the exercises that Therapina had suggested. He did feel that he was getting better at controlling the wings and they were certainly getting stronger, but he still couldn't get them to produce any semblance of flight. He knew what they should be doing but couldn't make them do it consistently and when Albert thought he had got it right all that happened was that he fell a little slower, and sometimes Albert felt that even that was just his imagination.

Angelina spent the next few afternoons with Albert in flight practice putting herself into suicidal dives to stay with Albert in some of his more rapid descents. The practice she was gaining and the tricks she was forced into trying just to get out of some of the positions she got herself into was way beyond what she could have got out of the next class. She was fast becoming the best flyer in the group. Pulling out of dives so late that her shoes lightly brushed the ground as she headed skywards again brought shocked and admiring gasps from anyone who watched.

Albert however got very little better. The improvement he was told he was making he was now convinced was simply them humoring him. The older Angels who where supposed to catch him now seemed to resent the duty, when they turned up at all. Albert couldn't blame them he wouldn't like to catch him falling from several tens of metres up either.

CHAPTER 3

Back To School

At the end of the two weeks of intensive flight training everyone except Albert had taken at least one flying license test. All the Angels had been told that they could use the practice field anytime they wished to brush up their skills. Albert was told that he should practice at least an hour a day. He was to call one of the instructors before he went for safety reasons.

Formal class work was to begin on Monday and all of the groups were to report to the main assembly hall first thing on Monday morning.

The whole group was waiting by 9.00am when an Angel they had not seen before walked in through the door that only admitted staff members. He looked quite young with fairly long blonde hair and Albert mistook him for a girl to start with.

"Hello," the newcomer said, "I am your group tutor. If you have any general or administrative problems with your course I am the one you should come to. My name is Humus. As well as your group tutor I will be teaching Angel basics for this year. While this does not have the prestige of the specialist subjects it is still very important. You will learn here how to recognize where help is required as well as some of the history of the Angel world."

"Sounds boring," whispered a voice which did not admit to an owner.

"I found it boring when I did it," said Humus, "I am new here having only just qualified and when I did it wasn't that long ago. I thought that what we could do is to split into groups of four and select a family or group of the living and observe them to see if we could spot any problems and discuss the solutions. I stress the observe, I want no actions taken, actions must be done by fully qualified Angels or at least under their direct supervision. Firstly we will split the group into your working teams."

The teams quickly selected themselves and Albert and Angelina were teamed with woman called Sarah and a man called Jonathan. Sarah was the eldest of the four at around 28 years, rather quiet and subdued but a spark in her eyes showed a hint of the intelligence and passion that she would later bring to the group. Jonathan was the absolute opposite, loud and brash, 26 years of age and Albert wondered how they had come to have him as part of the team. It appeared that he had invited himself and from the way he kept looking at Angelina the reason was not hard to guess.

Humus cleared his throat and the class became quiet. "In the Library annex is a series of rooms which you have yet to be introduced to but they each contain a smaller version of a machine that is used in all Angel dispatch buildings. This machine is called an Omniview. The Omniview is a window on the living world and has powers that may be introduced to you later in your courses. However for our purposes a window will do. During the next two days I will expect each group to spend some time with an Omniview and select a group of the living to study during the coming weeks. I think you will find it better if you select a group containing about five or six individuals such as a family or possibly a business group. Select a group which contains both genders and different personalities. Do not select a group which contains anyone that any of your group has known however slightly during your own lives. I will expect a presentation from a spokesperson for the group in three days as to which group has been chosen and why."

Angelina had caught clues as to Jonathan's intentions and made it plain she was with Albert. This was not strictly true but Albert was both a little pleased and flattered until she later asked whether he minded because really Jonathan was not her type. Albert didn't mind after all it was only for fleeting moments that he saw her as anything more than a very good friend.

Jonathan wasn't as unthinking as both the friends had feared and soon got the hint and settled down to help the group in the project. Jonathan was self-elected as spokesperson for the group's presentation. That was if they had anything to say. They were late getting to the Library annex and there was already a queue for the Omniview rooms which were used for the whole college.

"No point in waiting here" said Sarah, "By the time that queue has gone I hope to be in bed."

Angelina agreed. Albert really hadn't got time to wait, as he was already late for a flight lesson he had previously arranged. Jonathan nodded and the group went their separate ways without another word. Because they had not arranged a new time for the session with the Omniview it became impossible to get together the following day. It was therefore the day following that that the group got together for the project.

"This is leaving this a bit late," said Albert, "The presentation is tomorrow and there is a fairly large amount of work to do to select and then justify our study subjects."

As all the other groups had done their work several Omniview machines were free that evening as the four arrived to view the living world for the first time since they had arrived in Heaven. The temptation to look at what was going on in their own old neighbourhoods was great but resisted.

"We haven't got time," said Angelina, who had been speaking to a girl from one of the other groups, "It took one of the other groups over two hours to find a suitable group. Apparently groups of five or six individuals with different genders and personalities, with something interesting going on to justify the choice are not that common."

"I would have thought that every group of five or six would have something going on," said Albert.

"That's true but researching what is interesting is what takes the time," replied Angelina, "so that Jonathan here has something to say at the presentation tomorrow."

"All the other groups have gone for families," said Sarah. "I had hoped we could find something different. Our presentation and project would then at least be different from all the others."

"It means we can't copy the others," said Jonathan thinking of the amount of work that could be saved.

"Oh good" said Sarah, "Maybe we will learn something". Sarah was obviously indignant that anyone would suggest that they should cheat.

Realizing the mood of the group Jonathan exclaimed, "I was only joking." but Sarah was obviously not buying that. Nobody bothered with a reply.

The Omniview machine was quite complex but the controls were clearly labelled. There was a direction control which allowed the user to select a country, a town, a street etc just like a normal address system. It zoomed in as you typed. The system could go down as for as you liked even to an individual part of a room. A joystick allowed the viewer to roam at will.

"Personally I think we should try England" said Albert "then at least we can all understand what's being said."

"Why not Germany, then?" said Jonathan, "As I am German."

"Because I don't speak German," returned Albert.

"I don't speak English," said Jonathan, "But you all speak perfect German," he retorted.

"I think," said Sarah, "that there is probably a bit of trickery here. I suspect that something in Heaven allows us to hear what is being said by everyone in our own language. I therefore don't think it matters where we decide to look because we will all be able to understand."

It was decided to stay away from countries that any of the group had lived in which ruled out England, Canada (Angelina's home country), Russia (Sarah's home) and Germany just to start with. Albert had never been anywhere and Angelina had only been across the border into America. Jonathon had toured most of Europe and Sarah had been most everywhere. No one had been to Australia so that was the country eventually decided on.

"Pick a big city, like Melbourne or Sydney," Angelina suggested.

"Sydney then," interjected Sarah. "I have always wanted to look at the bridge and the Opera house." Jonathan typed in SYDNEY and the system got confused and did not move. A small message came up saying ambiguous request. Albert noticed a small side panel that had so far gone unnoticed. Pressing a button with the words location by the side the system suddenly showed an overhead view of a big city. Jonathan repeatedly kept hitting a button labeled zoom and the view showed a smaller and smaller part of the city in increasing detail.

"Hold on!" shouted Sarah. "Let's see where we are going."

The Omniview kept going trying to keep up with the many stabs at the button which Jonathon had already actioned. Eventually the view stopped changing and showed a single floor of a building.

The building obviously was not a residence. The corridor that the view showed was long and stark and the only thing showing on the walls was a notice that told of what to do in a fire and a clock on the far wall.

"Looks like an office," whispered Angelina.

"I think so," said Sarah quietly, "The clock shows nearly eight in the evening" The clock, which was digital, declared 19:59.

"Why are we whispering?" whispered Albert "No one can hear us—look." He indicated a panel on the controls which had a clear label saying 'sound'. On the panel was a switch which was labeled microphone and was operated by a key. The switch was in the off position. The key was not present. Next to this switch was a further switch labeled speakers and a volume control. Albert

ALBERT AND THE PLAGUE OF MIRACLES

flicked the switch to ON. Sound from the viewed corridor could be heard. Not that there was much. They barely caught the sound of the clock bleeping as it changed to 20:00.

"We will have to look for another building because it is unlikely we will find anyone especially not a group of people in an office this late in the evening," said Angelina.

Albert had spun the volume control to full and the faintest sound of talking could be heard. "See if you can find who is talking, Jonathon."

Jonathan already had his hands on the joystick type control and was searching the floor as Albert spoke. The ability of the Omniview to move through walls rather than having to search for the doors made this a quick operation and the source of the voices was quickly found.

The man talking was in a business suit about six feet tall with black hair. He was sitting obviously relaxed in one of several large dark blue leather chairs. His speech was precise and measured and held the attention of the other people in the room. "Barry, are you clear what is required of you?"

"Yeah. You've been over it a million times already." The speaker was dressed in a colourful shirt and a pair of loose fitting shorts, his hair was untidy and his goatee beard was not well trimmed. His attitude was that of someone bored to death with the proceedings, one leg hung untidily over the arm of the chair he was sitting in.

"A little more enthusiasm, Barry" said the original speaker, "We don't want any accidents, do we?" Picking up on Barry's attitude he became annoyed and his voice contained an edge of sharpest steel. "Is there anyone else here who thinks this is a waste of time? Michael?" He turned to another suited man on a chair in the corner who looked distinctly uneasy and who shook his head. "Norma?"

The woman at the head of the only table in the room scowled and said "Of course not, Grafton, but we have been over it many times and we should all know it by now." Her voice was silky smooth and showed no trace of fear but the uneasy way she sat contradicted this impression.

"Anne?" Grafton continued ignoring the implied criticism. The shake of the head made by a youngish woman with a figure to die for and long ginger hair falling down her back, was barely discernable. She got up and got herself a drink from a water cooler in the corner. She said nothing at all. "I suggest that we all go back to our organizations and ensure that my requests are actioned to the letter." The last three words, if possible had a note of further emphasis. The assembled participants and the watching group of Angels were left in no doubt of the menace in his voice. "We will assemble here in two days' time and report progress." Without waiting for an agreement or even a reply he turned and left the room through a door behind him.

The Angels watched as the others left through the only other door into the corridor. Some of them were muttering but even with the gain turned up what was said was not decipherable. Norma and Anne left quickly, Michael left with shoulders drooped and Barry left with a somehow false defiant attitude.

"That," said Jonathan, "is our study group. Mixed gender, mixed personalities and as per the request of our Sarah here, it's not a family. In addition we can easily find them in two days to follow up our research and I can go because we have found our group." Jonathan tuned on his heel and left the room despite the protests of both girls.

"Two days' time is a Saturday," Albert pointed out, "Where will we find them when we need to find them?"

"He has left us to write up our reasons for the choosing this group," said Sarah with obvious annoyance.

"I hope he can read the notes then" said Angelina, "Because he's the one who will be standing up and looking stupid"

"We will all look stupid if he makes a mess of the presentation," Albert reminded them.

The three of them spent the next two hours putting together some reasons for choosing the group that Jonathon had just agreed on. The three friends were left with only enough time to grab a quick snack for lunch before Angel Law Class with Ardon Barracus.

The presentation the following day went well with three of the groups giving similar reasons why they had chosen families for their study. The explanations seemed very reasonable when they were presented and Albert began to wonder whether the choice of their group had been a mistake. Jonathan did his presentation quite well considering that he had only had time to read the notes through once just before he stood up.

Humus passed comments at the end of each group's presentation and all were fairly neutral until towards the end of the lesson. "The groups you have chosen to study will be followed throughout the year. You will be doing reports and essays about how various subjects should impinge on your group and what methods should be used to deal with any problems you may find. I would however like to emphasize that this is strictly a watching brief—no actions are to be taken that alert the living group of your presence or interest in them. For this class you will get no formal homework except you will be required as a group to make presentations about your observations weekly." He stood up crossed in front of his desk to sit on the front edge. "The group that has not chosen a family will I fear find it difficult to keep track of their subjects because they may rarely be found in the same location. They might also find that there is more to report on. I therefore do not expect a report on each member of the subject group each week, as long as over the weeks we still keep account of the members of a group. If any of you have difficulty in finding a particular person, come to see me and I will set up a mark for you so that the machine can find him easily."

Humus paused and then continued, "As Albert's group has chosen a set of people who are not likely to be together often I have taken the liberty of doing this already for their group and if Albert or one of his group would see me later I will give them the codes for the mark."

Jonathon was resentful. "Look at the amount of work we have got ourselves lumbered with," he complained, "and all because little Sarah didn't want to take the easy route."

"I believe it was you who decided on the study group," pointed out Albert. "I don't remember any of us getting consulted."

Jonathan went over to Humus and picked up the mark codes and then sulked off to his room without another word. His look aimed at Albert said all that needed to be said.

The others went to their own rooms or to the Library for some of the homework from other classes. Albert went to a special flying lesson. Angelina went to the flying practice field just as Albert was finishing his lesson. He fell quite clumsily from the top ramp into the waiting arms of his instructor and helper.

Albert came off the field complaining that he would never get the hang of flying.

"I don't think you are really trying," said Angelina, "I think you need a major incentive. We are friends, right and you wouldn't hurt me, would you?" She waited for a reply.

"Of course I wouldn't hurt you," exclaimed Albert, unreasonably angry at the implication that he might.

"In that case this afternoon you will fly," Angelina said. "Just turn up at the practice ground after Comforting class as normal and leave the rest to me."

The practice ground was completely deserted when Albert turned up. There was no one there at all. A note on the take off gantry from Angelina told Albert to prepare for flight practice and she would be there shortly. Albert had never seen the practice ground empty before. Someone was always using it even if just for a picnic. Albert did as he had been asked and prepared for flight practice. When he was ready he noticed that he was still completely alone. He waited at the top of the takeoff ramp. Angelina arrived.

"Right," she said, "let's start practice."

"There's nobody here. No catchers. No anybody."

"I know," she said grinning, "I thought that maybe the audience was putting you off."

"The audience maybe, but it's against the rules to practice without a catcher until you have an A license," protested Albert

"I have a C license," said Angelina.

"I know you have," said Albert exasperated. "So you can fly but I can't even try, it would be against the rules."

"Unless you have a catcher who themselves has a C license or above," reminded Angelina, "I will be your catcher."

"You can't," protested Albert, "I'm much too heavy. You would get hurt".

"This morning you promised that you wouldn't hurt me. I won't let you fall so the only way to keep your promise is to fly."

"I can't do this," protested Albert again, "If I leave the ramp, I would crush you as I fell"

"Certainly you will if you don't fly." retorted Angelina. "And if you don't try I will be very hurt. The only way to keep your promise is to leave that ramp and fly to the ground and that is what I expect you to do."

Angelina positioned herself in the catcher's station ready to catch a falling Albert. Albert hesitated on the edge of the take off ramp. He could see no way out of this. The only thing he could think of was not hurting Angelina, but he couldn't see away to do this.

"Anytime today will do," called Angelina from the ground feigning a little impatience.

Albert took a deep breath, told himself to concentrate, flexed his wings twice before spreading them as wide as he could and stepped off the ramp. Albert fell. He saw the ground coming up to meet him. He saw Angelina stepping out to catch him. Letting her break his fall would at the very least cause her serious injury. Albert concentrated stretching his wings even further, angling the wings for maximum effect and awaited the impact, which never came. Albert felt a sensation that he had never felt before. He was going up—on his own. The sensation lasted only a split second until he felt himself sliding backward supported by his wings then his feet touched the ground and he was standing as if he had just stepped backwards off a small step.

Angelina stood in front of him, beaming. "I told you that you could do it."

"I stopped," said Albert, "I didn't fly."

"There's time yet," snapped Angelina annoyed that Albert thought so little of the milestone which he had achieved. "Get back up there and we do it again."

Angelina was there on every practice run that afternoon on their own on the practice field. The only way of keeping from injuring his best friend was not to fall. Albert didn't dream that he could fly but he had to prevent a catastrophic fall at all costs. He had no doubt at all that Angelina would catch him if he did. He knew that she would prevent him hurting himself even if that meant serious injury to herself. That just made it more important that he shouldn't fall. Despite the risk she didn't let Albert quit. She kept sending him back up the ramp to try again. Albert noticed that he could concentrate more easily on not falling as time went on or was it that not falling was easier? Angelina had noticed that the periods when Albert was going up were increasing and that Albert was beginning to control the flight, but she wasn't going to tell that to Albert until he realized it himself. Angelina was no longer worried that Albert would crush her as he fell. Albert was not going to fall. Only once had she needed to touch him and that was just to steady him after he had touched down on his feet. Albert's discovery late in the afternoon that not only was he now controlling the initial fall but he was now rising high enough that he now had to control the fall going down backwards again.

"That's enough for now," announced Angelina. "I think you have done marvelously," she leaned over and gave him a quick hug and a peck on the cheek and left asking him to call for her when he went to dinner.

Albert was over the moon as he left the practice field. He now felt that flying wasn't now as impossible as he had when he arrived just after dinner. The kiss of approval felt good on his cheek. The spring in Albert's step almost made him take off again.

Angelina never offered to set up a private flying lesson again and Albert never knew the effort and the favours she called in to get the first, but Albert could now fly. He got better in his normal lessons and almost a week later Soarelle asked to see him.

"Suporrus informs me that your flying is coming on well and that you are ready to take your class A flying license. I will be examining the test myself. Please report to the practice field tomorrow after classes and we will see how well you do." Soarelle's face wore a smile, which was meant to reassure Albert, but to be examined by the Assistant Head of Faculty who was known to be very strict was not something that Albert was looking forward to.

Knowing that Angelina had already done her "A" class test (Everyone in Albert's class had done their A class test. In fact most had got a B license by now.) Albert asked if she would go through the test with him that evening. Angelina readily agreed.

"It's not that difficult," she reassured him. "You'll do it easily."

"It's not that difficult for you, especially as you already hold a C class flying license," Albert quipped.

"And that's your fault," smiled Angelina. "If I hadn't had to do those fancy tricks to keep up with your flying when we started I wouldn't be able to do half the things I can now."

"Flying," laughed Albert. "You mean falling."

"You did get very close to the ground, that's true" she replied with a small giggle. "I'll see you after tea on the practice ground."

Albert felt much better. He knew that Angelina would check every aspect of his flying and tell him if anything needed changing to pass the test. Angelina had been surprised that Soarelle would be examining. Apparently it was not something that she did personally very often. In fact no one could remember her doing it at all during the previous two years. Angelina had refrained from telling him this, as she did not want him even more nervous in his test. However it had made her even more determined to be thorough during the practice tonight.

Angelina arrived at the practice field more than half an hour earlier than she had said she would. She spent the extra time setting up obstacles to make the practice more difficult. Albert arrived five minutes before the appointed time and looked in dismay at the course that Angelina had set up.

"They don't have obstacles in a class A test," he protested.

"They have obstacles in my Class A practice session though," smiled Angelina. "If you can get through this then the test will be easy and it would be nice to impress Soarelle tomorrow, wouldn't it?" Albert had to agree that it would and prepared for flight.

Angelina's preparations had attracted a small audience to the field, which worried Albert a little until Angelina pointed out that if he was distracted by a small audience; imagine what the effect of Soarelle's examination scrutiny would be.

Angelina could fly. She was now by far the best flyer in the group and some people said that she might be the best student flyer in the college. Some even said that she was better than Soarelle. Those that watched the practice that night where amongst the latter. Angelina flew impossibly tight formations to keep close to Albert while giving him instructions, placing herself in difficult positions so she could watch each maneuver that she asked him to perform. The 'Oh's and 'Ah's from the watching Angels attracted a growing audience but Angelina wouldn't let Albert's attention wander from the task. Every time he made a mistake that might have cost him a fail she made him do it again and she was forcing a standard much better than the A class test. Angelina made Albert fly like he had never flown before. She was not prepared to allow him to fail this test.

It should be noted that the practice field where flying instruction took place had the capability of recording sessions so that students could review their performance. All students are told that every test is recorded and kept so that it may be reviewed in case of any queries about qualifications in the future. It is not generally known however that the recording of sessions on the field could be triggered from Soarelle's office or by remote senders which are part of the normally carried equipment of any Ardon with a remit to teach flying. Neither Angelina nor Albert were aware that Supporus was amongst the audience nor that he had recorded most of the test practice session. They were also not aware that later that evening he entered Soarelle's office. They may have been disturbed by the attention that was being paid to the replay of the session later that night, even without the knowledge that the recording was being watched, not only by Soarelle and Supporus, but also by Seraphus and Pilotus. An urgent request sent to Skyhouse by Pilotus that night, as a result of that viewing, would have both surprised them and worried them had they known of its contents. But as I have said Angelina and Albert did not know, and they went to bed and slept in blissful ignorance.

The format of the flying tests of all levels is not laid out. The examiner can choose any format they like. They can ask the flyer to do any manoeuvre they like but they must include certain items and cannot fail a flyer unless those certain items are performed incorrectly.

The following morning instructors in every class announced that the practice field was out of bounds until the ending of lessons and then it was reserved for tests. This was very unusual but the work of the day soon reduced the comments to subdued enquires asking why. All such enquiries resulted in no response.

An enclosed luxury Skycart arrived with Skyhouse markings. A 'Do not disturb' notice appeared on Seraphus' door. Pilotus and Soarelle were not seen that day. The previous day's practice field recording disc was not in its rack. These facts were not that unusual individually. Together they might be worthy of comment, but nobody noticed. Albert noticed that he couldn't find Soarelle because he wanted to ask if there was any special preparation for the test. Supporus had reassured him that nothing special was required. A single Angel had noticed the Skycart but had not commented on it to anyone else. On its own the notice on Seraphus' door went almost unnoticed. Recording disks where often missing temporarily from the rack.

CHAPTER 4

The Flying Test

THE LESSONS THAT DAY FLEW by for Albert, getting closer to the test that he was dreading. The fact that the test was to be conducted by Soarelle herself had become public knowledge and the subject of many hushed whispers during the day. Many students had wished Albert good luck but Albert had wished that so many had not told him that they wouldn't like to be examined by Soarelle and commented on how strict she was.

During the day Supporus had found Angelina and asked if she would be going down to the field to watch the test, Explaining that he thought Albert needed support and that he always flew better with her there.

The last lesson finished and the time for the test had arrived. Angelina found Albert as they left the Comforting lesson and together they walked down to the practice field. Their progress was much slower than expected, as the whole campus seemed to be going that way. Albert gasped when he first caught site of the practice field. Completely stopped in his tracks, he gazed at the sight before him. He said nothing. He did not move. His mouth had fallen open.

During the day an incredibly complex course had been constructed. Angelina was talking to Albert and only looked when she saw the reaction of her friend. She stopped completely still in surprise before realizing what was going through Albert's mind.

"Don't worry Albert they can't make you do your test though that lot. It must be for some display flying later on."

Angelina was glad that they had an audience during the practice session last night because otherwise the audience that had appeared now would have been certain to put Albert off. The whole college appeared to be there. Angelina steered her way through to the changing area with Albert following. Several comments wishing him luck through that lot were directed at Albert as he went. The changing area had been cordoned off but a smiling Supporus ushered both of them through.

Waiting in the changing area were five people. Albert knew Soarelle, Pilotus and Seraphus but the other two were strangers.

"Come in you two," said Seraphus in his deep but somehow comforting voice, "I would like to introduce to you two of the most outstanding flyers of the Age." Seraphus indicated the two other Angels standing in the room. "This lady was and still is a member of the inter deity fly racing squad and head of the diving eagles trick flying display squad. May I introduce Arch Ardon Avianina." Avianina shock both of their hands as she was introduced. "Over here," continued Seraphus indicating the second stranger. "Is Governor Jetus current holder of the flying speed record over nine different distances and head of the flying licensing commission."

Governor Jetus shook Albert's hand and then did the same to Angelina smiling just a little too brightly.

Seraphus continued, addressing Albert he said, "First I must assure you that the course that you have could not have helped seeing was not set up for your test. We will be using some of the obstacles out there, but only the easier ones. As you know the test is to be examined by Soarelle but I am sure you will not mind if myself and my guests observe the test." The inflection indicated that this last part was a question but that an answer was not really required.

It would have taken an extremely brave Angel to say that he minded in front of that company and Albert was not feeling brave. So he politely mumbled, "No of course not." so softly that no one caught the reply.

Actually Albert minded a great deal. Right now if the ground could have opened up and swallowed him it would have been a great relief. Soarelle pulled him to one side and told him to relax and the test which should last about twenty minutes could start at any time he was ready. Albert spoke in a nervous and small voice, "I'll try not to let you down."

Soarelle smiled and said nothing. She had seen the recording and she knew that he was more than capable of this test after that practice.

No announcement was made of the start of the test. Albert just started to fly.

Angelina told him just before takeoff that the practice last night was really good and flying like that would see him through and she held his hand in encouragement before he started.

Soarelle asked him to fly in a straight line between two posts, which by now was certainly no problem. Next a figure of eight around the same two posts again no problem. The spiral dive around the tallest of the posts he completed quite elegantly although he didn't recall that as part of the official syllabus. Similarly a tight rising turn against one of the obstacles was extra but part of the practice he had done with Angelina the night before. An absolute stop on a signal he completed so well that Soarelle almost bumped into him as she followed giving the instructions. Albert was quite enjoying this now and did the vertical rise followed by a stepped descent before he realized that this was another item not in the syllabus. Albert shrugged and remembered that if he got anything wrong that was not in the official test then he couldn't be failed for it. Albert just flew. He did manoeuvre after manoeuvre some of which he had never done before some of which he did not do too well but all of them he tried. He was not asked to do any really spectacular things. That was not part of Soarelle's plan but she put in things that were more advanced that she had discussed with the others in a meeting they had had that afternoon, just because Albert seemed to be getting on so well. At last Soarelle announced that the test was finished. She merely said that the test was finished she did not tell him whether he had passed or failed.

Albert walked back to the changing area feeling tired. He was met by Angelina who threw her arms around him hugging him and claiming that not even the strictest examiner could have failed flying like that. The two walked back to the changing area together. An announcement was being made so they stopped to listen.

"Good Evening, Students," boomed the voice of Seraphus over the loudspeakers, "I would like to introduce to you two of the most celebrated flyers of our time who have consented to be my guests today."

Albert and Angelina who had already been introduced to the guests decided to continue to the changing area. Albert quickly got changed and then was asked to go back out on to the field where the voice of Soarelle was now asking for a round of applause for Albert's performance.

Angelina would have gone with him but she felt that it was his moment of glory and she held back where she could see him but not be in the way. She did not know that if she had not done this Pilotus would have intercepted her, because he wanted a word.

Soarelle was now speaking over the loudspeakers. "I was impressed with Albert's performance in his test. The test however was a special test with special permissions sought from the flying licensing commission to conduct both an A class and a B class test in the same session. I sought this permission after viewing a recording of a practice session, which showed him as being capable of the standard needed. I am pleased," she paused and then continued, "to award Albert a Class B license in recognition of his reaching the required standard for this level."

Albert was stunned. He looked around for Angelina but she was too far away to speak to. She had a broad smile on her face and was clapping vigorously. When she had finished clapping the announcement she turned to speak to Pilotus shaking her head slightly.

Albert was been given the microphone to reply to the award. Holding the microphone as though it was something without any purpose he stood in silence then raising the object to his lips and said "Thank you very much" he paused, "I don't know what to say" he paused again, "except thanks," he paused yet again but did not let go of the microphone, "especially to Angelina who believed I could do it when even I didn't." He looked around but Angelina was missing. He gave the microphone back to Soarelle who took it from him but also seemed to be looking around expecting something to appear.

Pilotus emerged from the changing area and flew with precision to where Soarelle stood and whispered in her ear.

Soarelle lifted the microphone to speak to the audience. "I now have a special announcement to make which is unique in the history of this college and even in the history of flying." Soarelle paused for just the right amount of dramatic effect. "I have just had the pleasure of examining a student of this college for an examination which I knew he should pass." Soarelle was a past master of public speaking and the pauses where placed in just the right places and for just the right amount of time for any desired effect. "I knew this because I watched the recording of his practice with his friend Angelina last night. As I watched that recording I recognized the feeling of watching a student who, even he would admit was not getting on well with flying, realize some of the potential which he has. He realized that potential because of a bond of friendship that would not let him down, and he realized that potential with the help of a very good flyer. Some of the tricks that Albert's friend Angelina did during that session last night were so advanced that even I would not have attempted them. Angelina on the other hand did them without conscious thought just to help a friend. The recording was viewed by the head of faculty Senior Ardon Pilotus with me last night and has been viewed this morning by our honoured guests, who were asked to come for that purpose. Never before in the history of flying has a flyer so young attempted what is to follow, but it has universally been agreed that Angelina be asked to attempt the Golden Wing Flying Award usually reserved for holders of the class E flying test which in exceptional circumstances can be awarded as part of the golden wing challenge. Our guests together with Arch Ardon Pilotus constitute the required board of advanced examiners and the course was set up in case she should accept the challenge. The rules for the Golden Wing flying test stipulate that the test is attempted by invitation only and with no notice so this evening is the first that Angelina knew about this and she is taking some time to make her decision. It should be noted that failure in this test is to be expected and is certainly no disgrace as only the best flyers are invited to attempt it."

Soarelle, whom was using her voice to build the dramatic suspense, continued. "Candidates can only accept an invitation once every five years, so accepting this challenge before you are ready may mean that a long wait will ensue before it is possible to try again, if of course another invitation is ever made. It is the opinion of licensing board however that she stands a good chance of completing the course and gaining the Golden Wing award. Those that watched the impromptu display last night, I am sure, will agree. So could we have some support for your fellow student."

Albert rushed from the field back to the changing area while the audience chanted "Angelina, Angelina, Angelina". Many people had tried to get into the changing area and had been stopped but no one stopped Albert. Albert was convinced that had any one had tried he would simply have gone through them.

Inside the area Angelina was facing Pilotus and Jetus simply shaking her head and didn't notice Albert enter. Walking up to her he put his hand on her shoulder and said, "You can do it. You believed in me when I thought I couldn't do it and you were right. You have a strength within you that will overcome and I believe in you."

Nothing else was said. She turned and looked into his eyes. He held her hand and the bond of friendship forged then was too strong ever to be broken.

She turned to the examiners and simply nodded.

The announcement was made that Angelina had accepted the challenge and that the test that could last up to two hours would begin in 30 minutes time. Final preparations to the course where made and Angelina was left alone to concentrate. She sent for Albert and they sat quietly together, not touching, not speaking. The atmosphere was pregnant with the fear that both were feeling—Angelina for the test she was about to fly and Albert for his friend. The Golden Wing test was dangerous and many flyers had been injured attempting it. (Did I say many? Well, that is not very accurate because many flyers had not been invited to attempt it. I should have said a good proportion of those that had attempted it had been injured in the attempt.)

Outside the test was being explained to the growing audience. No one wanted to miss anyone flying the Golden Wing test. It was a once in a lifetime spectacle. Pilotus was explaining what was about to happen

"The test has a time limit of two hours and to pass the test it is only required that the flyer complete the course within the two hours without injury of any kind. The flyer will be examined by the medical staff immediately prior to the attempt and then again immediately afterward. The complex course of obstacles requires flying to centimetre accuracy at very high speeds. Sudden changes of direction and stops are all part of the test as is flying in very tight spaces. The course length and obstacles are laid down in the examiners' manual, which is itself a restricted document, but not the order in which the obstacles are put together." Pilotus indicated a huge display screen at one end of the field. "Cameras have been placed throughout the course so that you can see what is going on, possibly better in some parts than the candidate herself." He paused to let that little snippet of information sink in. "Signs will tell the flyer which way to go and which obstacle is next but these signs need to be read at speed and their cryptic content worked out, all while performing other tasks in the test and missing one will slow down the flyer and make the time limit seem impossible. The flyer requires ultimate concentration and consummate skill so I would request that the audience remain silent throughout the test to give the flyer the best chance." Pilotus glanced across at the changing building and continued, "The clock that is on the wall of the changing building we had hoped to set to show the remaining period of the test but it is unfortunately out of order and in any event it is unlikely that Angelina would have any opportunity or chance to look at it. I suggest that knowing the time in the test could only make her rush and or break her concentration, so please refrain from any kind of countdown if you decide to keep track of the time yourselves. I need not tell you that only the official timings taken by the examiners will be used."

Therapina interrupted the silence in the changing rooms. "It's time for a check over, if you please, Angelina". Angelina looked up, squeezed Albert's hand gently and went over to the therapy coach in the corner where Therapina gave her a quick but thorough check over and then pronounced her fit. "You have five minutes before the start," she said and left them.

"Albert," Angelina said, "I have to fly this naturally or I don't stand a chance. If I have to do this by thinking about each move I will fail, but if I treat it like a game then I might just do this. The stuff I did last night I just did. It didn't take any conscious effort. I have to fly the same way now. I'm going to have a problem out there if it is going to be the unnatural silence, it won't work for me, I'm not used to it. Already the silence is a problem and I'm regretting accepting this test."

"Leave it to me," whispered Albert, "Just go out there and fly. I know you can do it"

Albert left the room giving Angelina a light hug and immediately went to find Pilotus. "Can I say something to the crowd?" Pilotus looked perplexed for a moment and then handed the microphone to Albert.

"Excuse me please," Albert's voice was heard over the loudspeakers, "Angelina is about to start a huge challenge and she needs all the help she can get. I am not asking that you be quiet for her as she says that will feel unnatural so could I ask you to support her as much as you can. Don't shout instructions at her or anything she needs to listen specifically to, but otherwise don't hold back." Albert paused, "Thank you."

Pilotus looked astounded. "Are you sure that's the best for her young man?" he said.

"It's at least as good as anything else," said Albert clearly. He was very worried for his friend and went to stand by the door from which Angelina would emerge to take the test.

Pilotus looked at his watch and picked up the microphone. "I would like everyone present to give a big hand for a very brave candidate, Angelina." Angelina stepped out of the changing rooms to tumultuous applause looking nervous and scared.

Albert whispered as she passed him, "Good luck." she stopped and smiled and he said, "Pass or fail you are a winner in everybody's eyes today. You can do it". A tear could be seen momentarily in her eye before she casually wiped it away.

"Your attention please," the loudspeakers announced in the voice of Pilotus, "Could we have silence for the start of the test at least until the candidate has been given her instructions and the Test has started." Pilotus obviously did not approve of Angelina's permission for vocal support.

"Angelina," stated Pilotus still using the microphone. "You must follow the course as indicated by instructions which are contained within it and you must complete it with no injury within two hours from the commencement gong. Medical crew and rescue Angels are standing by to help if you call for it or are obviously injured. You may exit the course at any point, should you wish to give up your attempt, and we would strongly suggest that that is a wise course of events if you find yourself falling too far behind schedule for the time limit. The invitation to take part is a singular honour and to exit the attempt early will be no disgrace. Do you understand these terms?"

"Yes, sir" answered Angelina with no trace of fear or even apprehension. She was over the first nervousness of the attempt and now adrenalin was coursing through her veins and she wanted to get on with the challenge.

"The beginning of the test is a vertical takeoff from the red spot." Pilotus indicated a red painted spot on the ground. "From there to the platform at the top of on the opposite side of the field where written on ceramic tablet are the next instructions. Your two hours will start and the gong will sound the moment your feet leave the ground at the starting point. Do you understand these instructions?"

"Yes, sir," answered Angelina again still eager to start.

"You may start when ready, and good luck."

Angelina almost ran across the field to the starting point, to cheering from the expectant crowd. A test that started with one of the most difficult flying actions, the standing vertical lift was not going to be easy but it certainly was going to be a challenge and she was hopefully going to make it fun. Even if she knew she was running out of time she would not quit. The more of this sort of experience the better. Momentarily she thought that she hoped she felt that way at the end of the exercise.

She stood on the red spot and took her time to remember as much of the layout of the course as she could see from that point. The crowd was completely silent. Facing her first objective, the platform at the far corner of the course she pushed hard with her ankles and knees as her wings came down in a power sweep. Her feet left the ground and she was propelled upward as much on the swelling sound of support as the powerful strokes of her feathered appendages.

She had misjudged her takeoff and was now too high as she headed for the platform. Calmly she chastised herself for the loss of seconds and then noticed a rotating pole, which might just have hit her had she taken the shortest route. She joked to herself that she must have her own guardian Angel. Moments later she had touched down lightly on the platform. A ceramic tablet attached to the back fence of the platform read.—

> Exiting via the door behind you
> A circle of green is your cue
> Let nothing deflect or distract you
> Then you will find your due.

A note underneath stated—Finding a circle of any other colour means you should return here as you have gone wrong.

She didn't understand this but it was plain that she must go through the door behind her. She turned and opened the door. Behind the door she found a tube, which was lined with sharp spikes. These were not long enough to hurt her seriously but plenty sharp enough to cause visible injury if she touched them. With wings slightly folded she flew into the tube. Control of flight was difficult with restricted wingspan but she had done restricted flying in her C license test and she had not found it difficult. This however was a different problem, as she had to do this at speed and with considerable precision. Reaching the end of the tube she found a further door with a handle in an awkward position. Still within the tube she had to adjust her body position while hovering with restricted wingspan. Nasty, she thought, as she did this seemingly impossible task without thinking consciously of the actions needed to do it. Opening the door she passed onto another platform. The platform was edged with lighted spots but otherwise the space was completely dark but while the door was open to the lit tube she noticed a green circle.

The green circle seemed a long way off across the platform. As she watched she saw something move between the circle and her present position. Another booby trap. To avoid this one she must hover and watch for the brief period when she could safely cross. Angelina held the door open for a moment more—long enough to notice that there must be more than one of these moving objects.

She let the door close behind her and the room was plunged into darkness. Specks of light showed her the edge of the platform. She landed and rested for a while wondering how to cope with obstacles she couldn't see. The objects in her path where probably revolving disks or something similar. Small gaps in each disk would allow her through if she timed it right. But this would mean hovering in between each disk, an explosive burst of speed timed exactly right and a complete stop before tackling the next disk. Very tricky flying she thought. She allowed herself the luxury of a few more seconds rest and realized that she could see quite well as her eyes got accustomed to the little light from the luminous platform markers. Once again she had been helped by doing things just a touch sloppily. Able to see the disk not just feel the wind of their passage and hear their turning was much easier. The problem was now only one of precision flying and that had never been a problem. Hovering in the air just before the first disk she counted the seconds before the gap came round again and darted through on the next time. Checking her speed before hitting the next disk. She counted again. Angelina did not notice that the next disk was in fact two disks close together, which only synchronized every second turn. Luckily when she darted through the disks where in sync and she passed though unscathed, but she felt the wind of the passing second disk. 'Concentrate', she told herself, 'don't get sloppy'. She realized that for the third time pure luck had come to her rescue. She reached the green circle and hovered to read the luminous writing on the tablet. As she could not see the floor she would not risk trying to land. The crowd outside could see the floor was a mesh of sticky mats through the special cameras running in the display. Angelina however could not and even though she did not know it, this time her caution had come to her aid. Landing on the mats would not injure her but would delay her quest considerably.

The green luminous writing said
    Go forward ten metres
    Then twenty to the right
    Try higher for three metres
    But you can't use your sight.
    Take care the floor is swept up there

So follow if you dare
Till looking up you see the light
A ten metre vertical flight.
Looking for a circle of bright electric blue
Your quest if you've got this far is almost half way through.

Angelina refrained from looking at her watch. She could check that later. In any case she had forgotten to check the time she started so it would not have helped anyway. In front of her the area was pitch black no way she would see anything here. This part of the test was to see if she could fly accurately distances without looking. She had practiced this many times and she felt reasonably confident. What did the floor being swept mean? She didn't know. Get there and worry about it then, she thought.

Flying ten metres forward was easy even in the dark but she felt her wing tips just touching the ceiling above her. Some Angels may have dropped lower but Angelina was using the light touches to guide her height and she was sure that no damage was being done to her wings that a light wash wouldn't cure. Dropping lower would have mired her in sticky goo, again a major delay. But Angelina didn't know that another obstacle had been avoided without any knowledge. Without turning Angelina used a sidewise sweep of her wing to allow her to fly sideways. She had tried this and knew exactly how many wing sweeps would be need to fly twenty metres. Stopping Angelina had felt the absence of the ceiling above her, as her wing tips didn't touch on the upward sweep. She heard a scraping sound above her. The floor above being swept. She would need to listen for the sweep pattern to avoid the brushes and then to follow in the same direction they went. The brushes seemed to be moving quite quickly and she would have to accurately go up three metres through the brush gap and follow the brushes at speed while looking up to find the light. She anticipated that the light would be only there for a short while so an immediate stop followed by a quick vertical ascent would be necessary Stops on the rise stops while traveling and quick burst of speed all tricky maneuvers when you could see what you where doing but in the darkness almost impossible. Her mind was sorting out the pattern of the noise above her while she thought all that I have just recounted faster than you could have read it.

She heard the scrape above her and reacted instantly, three metres straight up. A change of direction as she followed the brooms, the direction she had already sorted out by the sound. She was so quick that she almost caught up with the broom in front of her. She had reckoned on about four metres between brooms. This gave her no margin for error when coming up through the hatch but now she was up as close to the forward broom would give her fractions more time to stop and fly vertical again. Using a finger lightly touching on the broom in front of her to continually monitor her forward speed she looked up. The course constructors had put small decoy lights in the ceiling and Angelina was almost fooled by the first but then realized that she would be looking for a light that would be big enough to allow her to exit a mere ten metres higher. When the exit came she almost missed it but flying slightly backwards, using all of the four metres of space that she reckoned she had behind her, she flew as fast as she could directly upwards. She felt the following broom clip her heel as she flew upwards and ignored it. She reached the light cautiously and seeing no problems flew upwards in to the bright evening sunlight and to tremendous applause and chants of "Come on, Angelina. You can do it" and someone shouting something that sounded like a rhyme but she couldn't place what was being said. Below her now she could see the electric blue circle she was looking for.

Flying down to a platform upon which she could see no booby traps she read the instructions on the small ceramic plaque.

> Now try to find the Midas touch
> In the tower of a dive of death
> To a tunnel to catch a breath

Struggle forwards till you find
A hand in Midas circle there entwined.

So she was looking for a gold circle with a hand logo in it as the next target. A dive of death is the name of a difficult spiral dive. Difficult to control and even more difficult to stop. But why give her a rest at the bottom? There was bound to be something more to this.

The tower indicated, was to her right and had an opening at the top. Flying to it she looked down the tower, which had a central pole with what looked like a spiral staircase winding down as far as she could see. This would be no uncontrolled spiral. A controlled fall would not be accurate enough. A safe controlled flight would be the safest but would take a lot of time. She would have to fly this as though she was powering down the spiral instead of falling. A power dive in tight space forced into a spiral would mean that she would hit the bottom very fast. She looked down the outside of the tower noted the tunnel exiting at the bottom. Noting the height of the tower and she knew that coming out of this would be a matter of educated guesswork and luck. She was going to try powering down a tight tower in a spiral dive, coming to the bottom at breakneck speed and trusting that she would be going in the right direction to simply power up the exit tunnel when she came to the bottom. Thought about like that it seemed total suicide, so she had better not think about it, just do it. She took a deep breath. Then she dived. Around the inside of the tower she flew gathering speed constantly, stopping at the bottom or even braking was no longer an option. She would fly up the tunnel or into a wall. She knew how far down she had come she knew where the tunnel should be, she pulled out of the dive and flew on. She felt her shoe hit the sidewall but she had made it into the tunnel. She had not tried to brake but felt herself slowing, felt herself stopping. This puzzled her she still should be going forward. She opened her eyes. She now was going slowly backwards in the tunnel because of a strong wind blowing her that way. She now understood the instructions. Forcing maximum propulsion from her wings she slowly forced herself along the tunnel. Passing a certain point switched off the wind and she shot forward towards a wall before a quick emergency stop and found a door above her with a picture of a hand in a golden circle on it. She pushed it open and flew through once again into the daylight.

A ceramic plate next to the door gave her the next instructions—

> Getting tired now as would the best
> Over half way to a well earned rest
> Going this way then that, very very fast
> You will do well if you last
> Looking now for a circle of royal purple hue
> Now what are you going to do.

A door was indicated to a huge enclosed structure and the door was positioned at the extreme right hand corner. Angelina opened the door and peered inside without stepping into the room. All she could see was a bare corridor, which seemed to be built of steel. It ran the complete width of the building, perhaps 200 metres. At the far end Angelina could see an opening. The opening did not appear to have a door just an opening. Angelina stepped into the room to have a closer look and the door closed automatically behind her. To Angelina's horror the wall in front of her started to move towards her. Her only hope was the opening at the other end of the corridor. Flying reasonably quickly Angelina reached the opening in good time and looked through to find another long corridor stretching back the way she had come and the wall was already moving towards her. No time to wait she must go. Flying now faster than before she reached the other end of the corridor to find another corridor going straight up the moving walls making the corridor already seem much thinner. Angelina put herself into a flat out vertical flight and discovered that the next corridor went down. Flying at incredible speeds down corridor after corridor sometimes up and sometimes down, sometimes left and sometimes right and sometimes at a diagonal she often narrowly missed being crushed between the closing walls. The flight was fast the turns where just a blur but somehow she made them all. Emerging from the last corridor into an outside that was just starting to show evidence of dusk. Angelina had not noticed the passage of time she could have been in that nightmare of a course for hours or minutes she didn't know. She looked around and saw a royal purple circle bearing the crossed sword insignia. Below this was another set of instructions.

> Watch me very carefully for instructions to pursue
> Don't take your eyes away, just continue
> Looking for a disk of Red
> The one on which you have already tread

Angelina watched the instruction plate and as she watched it the writing changed.

Go away from me as fast as you can. As she knew she couldn't take her eyes from the instruction plate so Angelina flew backwards. This took incredible nerve, as she trusted that the instruction would not let her hit anything. Always facing the plate Angelina flew in all sorts of crazy directions but always facing the plate. Sometimes the instruction would change so quickly that if she had looked away even for a moment she would have missed them.

Eventually the instruction sheet went blank and then replaced itself with the words—

> If I were you I'd fly towards the setting sun
> Where your task will be done
> By treading once again on a disk of Red
> Having followed where the instructions led

But will your endeavors be in time?
And are you still fit and fine?

The words disappeared as she read them. Looking up she saw the reddening sky of the setting sun and flew off in that direction. Over the course she flew and spotted the Red disk from where she had started an unknown amount of time earlier. Determined to finish as quickly as she could she leaned forward into another power dive pulling up to put a single foot on the red plate.

A gong sounded seemingly in the distance. She had finished. She did not know whether she had passed, she had no idea how long she had taken and she was unaware of the noise around her. She lay down on the grass where she landed and totally exhausted she slept.

Albert rushed to her side thinking her severely injured knowing that no matter what had gone wrong she would have finished. He noticed a missing heal on her right shoe. He was pulled away by Seraphus, while Therapina knelt to check out her charge. "No broken bones" she announced "but I need to make a thorough check in the hospital". Helpers rushed on with a stretcher, which appeared to be made of clouds that cushioned her every place it touched and she was carried by willing hands to the hospital. Albert never left her side.

No announcement was made the following morning except to say that Angelina was still sleeping and no matter what pleas were made as to the outcome of the test all that would be said was that an announcement would be made when Angelina was up and fit to be told.

Angelina herself woke during the evening having slept for a solid 24 hours and found Albert holding her hand. He had been awake during those same 24 hours and it looked like it. She squeezed his hand and told him to go to bed and she would see him in the morning but he wouldn't go. Therapina made up the next bed and ordered him into it. He protested that he wasn't one of her patients and she couldn't force him. Therapina simple wrote up a set of bed notes with the illness stated as complete exhaustion and said, "Now you are" and ordered him into bed. Albert slept.

Pilotus arrived 30 minutes later having heard that Angelina was awake. Angelina declined to see him and asked him to come back in the morning. All other visitors were treated in the same way and Angelina's request not to see anyone was vigorously enforced by Therapina.

A veritable deputation therefore arrived together the following morning. Jetus and Avianina were still guests of Seraphus. Pilotus and Soarelle came as well. Albert was now sitting up in bed.

"How are you feeling, young lady?" asked a very concerned looking Jetus. Avianina looking equally concerned said nothing. Pilotus smiled but the smile was somehow false. The only people who seemed at ease were Albert and Angelina.

"How did I do then?" asked Angelina.

"Very well I would say," said Jetus.

"Extraordinarily well I would say," said Avianina. "Anyone finishing the course at all would have been doing very well. I said that it was set too hard when it was built, but you lot wouldn't listen."

"Did I pass or did I fail?" Angelina was exasperated by their evasion.

"The fact is we don't know," said Pilotus. "Therapina has refused to complete the required medical examination until you where at least rested. When that has been completed we will make the announcement.

"Now that Angelina has slept I will complete the formalities," said Therapina coming into the room. "If all the visitors would kindly vacate my ward, I will bring both my charges up to the main hall when I have finished."

The visitors were almost pushed out of the room by Therapina. Angelina leaned over towards Albert and asked "Did I do it in time?"

"The clock on the changing room wasn't working," said Albert, "and only Jetus and Avianina kept official timings and they are refusing to say anything until the result of the medical."

"So currently, two people know whether I made it in time and no one knows whether I will pass medically."

"You should know whether you are injured or not," said Albert. "Does anything hurt, do you think you got injured?"

"Everything hurts, but I think that's only stiffness and I took a couple of minor knocks but I don't think I did anything that counts. On the other hand I don't know whether I remember it all or even if, with so much going on, I would have felt any minor injuries."

"We will have to wait and see then but I suspect that many people took unofficial timings and though I have not spoken to virtually anyone if you had been obviously out of time I doubt that the reaction to your finish would have been quite so loud," stated Albert, "It won't be long before we find out now."

Screens were placed around Angelina while she was given a thorough check up and examination by Ardon Therapina, helped by a nurse who proudly wore the golden hand of healing. The examination was completed about 25 minutes later and the two dressed and were led up to the hall where the whole school had assembled.

Governor Jetus asked to speak to Angelina in private as they entered the hall. They spoke for several minutes about aspects of the test though Angelina's questions about passing or failing were left unanswered.

Both Albert and Angelina were shown to seats at the front of the hall and Seraphus stood up to speak. "The day before yesterday the flying license commission saw fit to invite one of our students to attempt the Golden Wing challenge. I believe it is true that nobody is yet in possession of the full results of that test although the information will be given to the examiners of the test shortly. It is however a great honour for the college to have the youngest ever Golden Wing candidate as a student. I am however also proud of the young Angel in question and her friend Albert for showing what real friendship is about. Whether the challenge was passed or failed the achievement supported by that friendship will always be a very memorable and proud moment of my life. I would now like to invite our Head of Flight Faculty to give us his appraisal of the event."

Pilotus stood up. "I have reviewed the tapes of the challenge several times and would not like to go too much into the methods used or the quality of flying that was displayed. I will however make the following general comments. Angel Angelina allowed herself time to think during the challenge. She did not rush in to the flying without thinking about the problem in hand. She came up with one unusual solution which while very risky actually came off. She, in my opinion conducted herself with utmost courage. I will say no more. I do not currently know the results of either criterion for passing the test so I need to hand over to the chief examiner for a more detailed assessment."

Jetus stood up. "I am now in possession of both parts of the results." He paused for effect, "I would like to make certain comments about the conduct of the test. There were five stages to the challenge, the first of which the candidate approached with caution. Her again understandable caution waiting for her eyes to accustom themselves to the dark lost even more time and as a consequence she was six minutes behind time at the first checkpoint. A further minute was lost in the second stage due again to her caution making certain that she knew the position of obstacles before moving. In stage three she elected to throw caution to the wind and attempted a course of action that I considered foolhardy. I originally considered that this had been done to make up time. Her power dive down the tower could have resulted in serious injury but as it was she succeeded in flying the start of the tunnel so fast that she saved almost nine minutes and considerable energy getting through to finish the stage. Her stamina and her saving of energy allowed faster than expected flying in both the latter stages where she saved a further three and two minutes respectively over expectations. The test was finished in a time of one hour and 52 minutes and 33 seconds." The hall erupted into cheers.

"Quiet, please. Quiet, please." Jetus continued, "This is not only well within the allotted time but is an all time record by 42 seconds." Quieting down the hall this time took several minutes before Jetus could continue. "I considered however that the reckless flying in the third stage was not within the spirit of the Test and should disqualify the candidate." A silence of disbelief spread across the hall as Jetus continued, "I have searched the rule book however and I find that they do not give any provision for such a disqualification. I have this morning also discussed this flying with the candidate and believe her assessment of the risks to be more sound than I originally thought and even if a provision for such a disqualification existed I would not now have used it. In short I admit that my assessment of this part of the test was wrong. Medical evidence then had to be collected about any injury sustained especially as the recording shows two incidents, which may have caused injury. A complete medical examination was ordered and completed and found no injury of a type that would give grounds for a failure." Most of the last words could not have been heard by anyone further than two inches away as the college had erupted into spontaneous celebrations. The announcement had not yet been made officially but this was a mere formality. A student of their college had passed the Golden Wing challenge.

Seraphus himself appealed for silence and after a several requests succeeded. "I would like to ask our other guest examiner up to say a few words and to present the award itself to the successful candidate. I ask you to once again to welcome Avianina." A more restrained applause greeted Avianina as she took the microphone. "I would like to invite Angelina up onto this stage to receive her award and while she is making her way up here I would like to apologize to her. I believed that the ordeal was too much for someone her age. I believed that the challenge was too much for someone of her size and strength but I was wrong. I would like also to disagree with some of the assessment of my fellow examiner. I can find no fault with Angelina's performance except understandable small errors in flight. Her decision to power dive the tower was correct and courageous. I doubt that I would have had the courage to make that decision and carry it out. I tried to have this event cancelled, as I believed it was too dangerous. I was wrong. I now welcome up onto this stage a flyer who has earned by courage and skill my respect as a matchless flyer. Will you welcome, the new Golden Wing Record Holder and the youngest ever recipient of the award, Student Angel Angelina."

Many words were probably said on the stage that morning but the incredible noise of the applause for Angelina made then inaudible. Angelina accepted the award and a recording was made of the event no doubt to grace the accounts of the history of the college for many years to come.

Albert had been there to see the award given and had clapped as loudly and as vigorously as all the rest, but he left early as he felt it was Angelina's triumph and he didn't want to get in her way. She missed him later in the evening. The party was in full swing and they would never miss her now. She went to find him and found him reading happily in his room.

"I wouldn't have done it without your support," she said, "I had already told them that I wasn't up to it when you came and believed in me."

"I know," murmured Albert a smile on his lips, "but I knew you could do it given a reason. And that reason had to be that you believed it too. I just helped you realize that."

"Thank you," was her only reply and was probably the right one. She left with tears in her eyes wondering what she had done to deserve such a good friend.

CHAPTER 5

Group Therapy

THE COLLEGE WAS BUSY FOR the group of Angels. The subject classes they were expected to attend numbered six as well as flight practice. The group had Angel Basics every morning and a different subject each afternoon. On Monday afternoon Navigation was taken by Ardon Soarelle who was very strict and gave out lots of homework. Tuesday and the Stage One Miracles class, was the responsibility of a small strange Angel who was the only Angel any of them had ever seen wearing glasses. His name was Ardon Steven. This in itself was strange because the rank of Ardon brought with it the right to change your name and most chose a name which had something to do with their work.

Ardon Steven explained when he was asked. "I am quite content the way I was when I died and have never bothered to change anything, including getting my eyes fixed". As he said this he pushed his glasses back up his nose.

Angelic History with Ardon Anticus was on Wednesdays. Ardon Anticus looked so old that most of the students thought he could teach from personal memory. He may have been old but he had certainly had his eyes and ears fixed. He never missed anything. The passing of notes or the slightest whisper brought quick responses and instant extra work for the offender.

Angel Law and the Rights of the Living was a dry subject that could have dried a thunderstorm and was made even drier by the mono tone in which it was taught. The tutor was Ardon Barracus who was obviously very knowledgeable on the subject but could make a midnight party with ice cream and loud music and dancing sound boring. Angelina however strongly professed that the Rights of the Living was a fascinating subject and listened attentively to Barracus while most of the rest of the class had fallen asleep. Barracus did not seem to notice.

"How the hell do you keep awake?" said Jonathon one day, "I fall asleep in his lesson the instant he starts talking."

"You fall asleep in anyone's lesson," retorted Angelina.

It was true that Jonathon had once earned himself several hours extra work for falling asleep in Anticus' lesson. He had explained to the others that it was after an especially hard night with one of the older girls. No one knew whether to believe him but everyone knew that it was not possible to get away with sleeping in a lesson supervised by Ardon Anticus.

Comforting was with Judith, the nurse who had helped with the examination of Angelina after the Golden Wing Test. Judith was patient and never seemed to require much of the class but always seemed to get a lot out of them anyway. Comforting was the favourite subject of most of the male members, mostly because it was easy to fall for the pretty youthful teacher. Surprisingly perhaps it was a favorite amongst the girls as well.

Humus still took them for Angel Basics, which was supposed to link the others together into a cohesive course. He continued with his project work with the selected living subject groups dragging in seemingly random parts of the other subjects. He emphasized at least twice every time he was with them, which was not that often as it turned out, that the living groups were to be observed. ONLY observed, nothing else. He didn't seem to realize that to do anything else would in any case have required a key which none of them had any right to be given.

At the beginning of the first week following the presentation of the living group choices Humus asked for research and a group presentation on the rights of the living where observation was concerned. "I will expect the work to be presented in class on Friday."

"We haven't covered all of that yet, sir," complained Angelina, who was the only one who had taken enough notice in Angel Law to realize this.

"That is why I called it research," answered Humus. "I have spoken to Barracus and he says you have covered most of the material and the rest is easily found in the books on the subject in the Library."

Soarelle was called away to a faculty meeting that afternoon and the navigation lesson finished early. This allowed some extra time for research and most of the students headed for the Library.

Jonathon followed Angelina, Sarah and Albert to one of the Library study rooms complaining all the time about the amount of work that would be required.

"If you had paid attention in class," said Angelina, "there wouldn't be so much to do". Looking down at her notes she continued, "We need to look at four different aspects to this problem. Observation in public places, at work, within relationships and in privacy. I'll take whatever the rest of you don't want to do."

Jonathon who had taken not the slightest bit of notice in class was open mouthed with surprise "This is supposed to be a group presentation. We should work on it together."

"And have you skive off again while we do all the work?" said Sarah. "I like the idea. I'll take observation at work please."

"I'll take the public places, then," said Albert. Albert had at least been alert enough in class to hear the subject mentioned and realized that this was perhaps the easiest.

"That leaves you with—relationships or privacy," said Angelina to Jonathon. "Which of those do you want?"

"How do I know? I don't really want any. I think we should work on this together."

The rest of the group said nothing and waited. The silence became too intense for Albert and eventually he said, "I'll do the actual presentation this time." Walking over to the flipchart in the corner of the room he wrote 'The rights of living individuals concerning observation'. Underneath that he wrote the four categories and by the first he wrote "Research by Sarah" by the second he wrote "Research by Albert". He hesitated and then by the others he wrote "Research by" and left the names blank.

Jonathon looked miserable. He knew he would have to work at this one if everyone would know who had produced the input for each section. If he didn't do the work he would look very bad. He scowled at Albert and said, "You can't do that. It's supposed to be a group effort."

"It is. I'm just marking out some of the group's effort." Albert had no intention of using that particular opening to the presentation but wanted to see Jonathon squirm for a while and maybe get some work done.

"You don't really think this is a good idea, Sarah?" said Jonathon more in a state of desperation than in any expectation of support.

"I don't see why not," came the reply that he had dreaded but expected.

"I'll take the next one down, then," Jonathon said in what was almost a growl. He had not even realized what he had chosen until Albert wrote the names on the chart. Walking into the main Library he went to the law section and placed all the books he could find on observation on the desk around him. If he was going to have to work on this on his own, which he thought was unfair, he was going to make it as difficult for the others as he could, to get them back for what they had done.

Back in the study room the rest of the group looked stunned at the reaction.

"He has got easily the most complex," said Angelina, "I hope he copes all right."

Albert began to feel a little guilty about his ruse until he saw what Jonathon had done with the books. "Look at that," he exclaimed peering through the open door. Albert went over to Jonathon, "Can I have a book on public places, please?"

"Sorry Albert. I need information from all of these, you will need to wait until I have finished". Albert was annoyed about this but it was obvious that he was not going to change Jonathon's mind.

"Well, I will look forward to your submission for the group presentation," said Albert. "It ought to be really detailed." Albert walked away while Jonathon realized that he had landed himself with even more work than ever if he was to avoid looking foolish and petty.

Albert returned to Angelina and Sarah and recounted his discussion.

"No matter," said Angelina. "I have two books about living rights in my room that I borrowed earlier. If we work together we should find plenty for the presentation." Albert carried the flip chart pad and pens and the three returned to Angelina's room, where they worked for nearly four hours. Most of the information came from Angelina's notes and memory, which turned out to be remarkably good.

A living person's rights concerning observation while in public places were virtually non existent An Angel was not allowed to bring the attention of other members of the public to the actions of a subject. Sarah didn't think that counted anyway as it was not strictly observation.

"I can't think of anything else," said Angelina, "and there doesn't seem to be anything in the text books either."

Albert wrote on the flipcharts he was preparing 'Subjects' observation rights in public places are extremely limited' and then wrote the rule about alerting others to any actions for completeness. "We need to look at rights while at work now."

Although Sarah had volunteered to do this part the three of them worked together, with Albert writing points on the flip chart as they talked. There were not many rights at work either.

"Much the same as public place observations," said Sarah, "Quite a lot about what you can and can't do with information gained during the observation, but almost nothing about what can or cannot be observed."

"I can't remember many rules about observation in any category but we haven't finished the subject in class yet," said Angelina, "I have done some further reading and found very little extra."

"There is a small amount about what can be recorded in this book," said Sarah lifting a book so that the others could see. Albert took the book and laid it out on the table in front of himself and Angelina.

"There is a point here on recording relationships. Kisses and Sexual details are not supposed to be recorded unless as evidence of unfaithful acts and then only if this is the point of any surveillance and only as much detail is recorded as is necessary for that evidence," Sarah said.

Albert read from the book in front of him and Angelina. "When kisses and other intimate actions are occurring the subject should be given privacy from observation, except that when monitoring a subject for a particular purpose where constant surveillance is necessary, periodic viewings are allowed to ensure the subject has not tried to evade such surveillance. Such purposes should be documented and approved prior to commencement of any observation."

"That is supposed to be something Jonathon comes up with," said Angelina "I wonder if he will."

"Here's another," said Sarah. "Acts of personal toilet such as showers and baths should not be viewed without special license obtainable from STARHOUSE. Such a license will only be granted in exceptional circumstances." Sarah paused reading ahead a little. "And there is more 'Viewing subjects in a personal situation is strictly not allowed for the purpose of the gratification of the viewing Angel'. If Jonathon finds that one I bet he will be disappointed."

"I bet he would be, but I doubt he will find it," said Angelina, who was by now fed up with his attentions.

"I think you're right," said Sarah. "That would mean him doing some work."

In this assessment however the girls were wrong. Jonathon had found all the points that they had found and laid them out carefully for inclusion in the presentation. He had also included some work on the consequences and penalties of transgression of the rules. He had felt quite guilty after they had left and had worked hard to put together something meaningful.

Albert spoke next, reading from the book in front of him. "Viewing of the living partner of an Angel is not encouraged but is often allowed by special request."

Jonathon passed his work to Albert the following morning. The girls were astounded and apologized for thinking that he wouldn't do it.

"I deserved it," Jonathon said. "I haven't really done a lot. I've been a bit of an idiot really."

Sarah agreed with him and was obviously suspicious of his apparent reform but the other two accepted his apologies without reservation. Angelina made it plain however that she would accept no more romantic advances. This was immediately echoed by Sarah.

"OK, I've been put in my place." Jonathon grinned and held out his hand which was covered by that of Albert and Angelina and though a little more slowly and hesitantly by Sarah.

The presentation the following day went reasonably well although Albert was nervous and started a little hesitantly, stopping and looking at his notes too often. Most of the groups had much the same points except only Jonathon had researched the penalties involved.

Humus picked up on this "The penalties have been properly reported by Albert's group and can vary considerably between a light telling off to suspension of duties. The famous case where an Angel was expelled from Heaven was not thankfully a member of this college." He paused, "I hope we are all now better informed on this subject and we can continue with our research on the selected living subjects. I will not require any of you to attend these lessons for the next week. Instead I want you to write up a personality profile of the subjects within your groups with the aid of the Omniview machines. I require the work to be handed in as a group project folder in six days' time." Humus walked around his desk and sat on the front edge. "Do not forget the rules that we have talked about today, as any infringement will NOT be taken lightly. I will be talking to each group separately about their projects the next time we meet. I will then be reading some of the work to the class to show how the work should be done." He paused for effect, "or not be done." He paused again, "Make sure your work does not come into the latter category." Humus pushed himself off the desk "Thank you." He left the room without even a glance at the class.

Albert, Angelina, Jonathon and Sarah met in one of the Omniview rooms several minutes later. Angelina had booked the room for the rest of the morning so they could at least find the members of the group.

"Bet we can't find them together again." said Jonathon.

It had been several days since they had first selected their living subjects and had missed the meeting that was supposed to have occurred.

"Forever the optimist I see." quipped Sarah who was regretting even if very slightly her earlier reservations about him.

Jonathon had, since the incident about the observation homework, pulled his weight in the group and even though that had been only two days ago the four were acting more as a team and the beginnings of a friendship amongst all four of them were becoming apparent.

Jonathon had received the mark codes from Humus in an earlier lesson and typed the first into the machine. The group was astonished to find the Omniview go directly to the same meeting room as before and even more surprised to find the five members all there. An additional person had joined the meeting.

Grafton was again talking, his voice was exceptionally quiet but had lost none of its menace, and in fact the softness of his voice seemed to increase the tension. "The delay to the project is unacceptable." The glance he gave to the newcomer could have withered weeds. "Failure is not something we expect or will tolerate. I assume you will not be making the same mistake again."

The object of Grafton's wrath obviously did not know what to say and was both nodding and shaking his head at the same time. "Yes—err No" he stuttered.

Grafton didn't seem interested in the answer anyway, "You will NOT be making that mistake again." Grafton had slowly walked around the room as he was speaking and ended up behind the quaking man. As he spoke he pulled from his jacket a silenced pistol and fired it twice through the heart of the helpless victim. "You will not be making any mistakes again," he mumbled walking back to the desk and leaving the body where it had fallen. Turning to Barry, apparently untroubled by the murder he had just committed, "I expect you can deal with that problem," he said indicating the corpse. His tone left no doubt as to the consequences of non-compliance. "This incident has cost us weeks of planning. The job will begin again."

"You don't seriously think we can continue," said Norma her silky voice tinged with an edge of astonishment, "His death will cause many questions and investigations, surely there is no chance of success now."

"He will not be found." Grafton's glance at Barry carried its own threat, "A missing person will be forgotten especially with false trails to suggest he might have gone overseas. By the time we are ready again it will not be a problem. I expect a report from each of you as to how your particular part of the enterprise has been compromised by events for the next meeting. Do not write it down. I want no documentary evidence of any kind." His glance took in everyone in the room, "We will meet again here in three days' time. Don't be late." Grafton walked out of the room.

Anne had said nothing, she had not moved and she looked shocked as she, shaking uncontrollably, stared at the body on the floor. Michael was trying to comfort Anne without any visible success and Norma was simply trying to stand, her fear making her legs feel like jelly.

Albert suddenly realized that Sarah was no longer standing either. She had fainted as the gun had been fired. Jonathon noticed at the same time as Albert and got to her quicker as he was closer. Angelina had already run from the room for help.

Ardon Supporus was the first of the tutors to reach them. Therapina arrived shortly after and Seraphus himself about a minute later.

Therapina organized getting the now reviving Sarah over to the hospital wing while Supporus went to fetch Humus as the group pastoral tutor. Seraphus himself, after asking the three remaining of the group if they were OK, did a complete debrief starting with Albert. Albert told the story as best he could and what he missed out was filled in so completely by the phenomenal memory of Angelina that Jonathon had nothing to add at all. The debrief was still in progress when Humus arrived with Supporus. A complete list of the settings of the Omniview machine was taken and the recording of the debrief was taken for inclusion of a permanent record of the incident. Therapina returned with Sarah following, Sarah had refused to stay in the hospital insisting that she was OK. Therapina, ignoring protests proceeded to check pulses and blood pressures of the others before telling the whole group to go and rest at least until morning. A note was signed excusing them all from lessons for the rest of the day and Therapina personally escorted them back to the dormitory block.

They all went back to Sarah's room where she explained that she had only a small graze to show for her fall and that otherwise she was fine.

"I can't believe I fainted like that."

"It was quite a shock," said Jonathon. "It surprised the hell out of me."

"You didn't fall over for no reason though, did you?" said Sarah.

"I'm not of such a delicate disposition, either," said Jonathon smiling.

"Delicate!" Sarah almost shouted before she noticed his smile, "Sorry Jon, I am feeling a little sensitive about it."

"No problem," said Jonathon covering her hand, which was holding the arm of a chair, with his in a reassuring gesture. Albert noticed the gesture and was surprised that Sarah allowed it to continue as long as she did before moving her hand to move some hair from around her face.

The little group spent the next hour discussing the incident amongst themselves. Sarah said she wasn't sure she wanted to continue with the study of the living group but Albert didn't see a reason not to, Angelina was on Albert's side but thought that it was unlikely that they would be allowed to.

Surprisingly Jonathon supported Sarah. "It is obvious that some of the group aren't tough enough." Sarah again took the bait before realizing that Jonathon was having difficulty suppressing a laugh.

Humus however had already discussed the matter with Soarelle and Seraphus and the group was told the next morning to select another group for study. Angelina and Albert both said that it wasn't necessary and that it would mean much more work but Humus was insistent that the decision was final. Humus suggested that the group split up and join the other groups so that the initial work would not have to be redone but none of the four wanted that.

With help from Humus another group of living subjects was found. A six strong band of singers was selected. Humus suggested that it was a good compromise as it was not a family, which the group had attempted to use as an excuse for keeping the original set, but easy to find together. The band of singers was called Inertia and consisted of four girls and two men. They sang a rock / country mixture and none of the four minded the music. The leader of the band was a girl with a shock of blonde hair which was showing black at the roots and went by the name of Honey. Angelina could not see how she played the drums as her hair obscured almost everything with wild gyrations in the passion of her playing. Both men (David and Metro) played guitar as did a raven-haired beauty called Jewel who obviously made a couple with David. The violin player who helped sometimes with vocals was called Clare and this left Marianne on full time vocals.

The group worked hard on the new subjects. Despite being allowed extra time the group decided to try and hand the personality essay in with the work from the rest of the class. Jonathon had surprised Sarah by working at least as hard as anyone. His work had been detailed with much of the work being done in his own time in one of the Omniview rooms. As a result the work was handed in by Sarah on time the following Thursday lunch time.

The Angel Basics class the following Monday morning was eagerly anticipated by everyone. Most of the class was wondering what would be said of the incident especially as details were sketchy as the four had been quite tight lipped.

The only mention however, was to note the change of subject group by Albert's group. No reason was given and discussion was not encouraged, even direct questions were ignored or rebuffed.

Humus took his usual place on the edge of his desk. "I am impressed with the general standard of these essays. Generally it is obvious that a great deal of time has been spent in observation. There are however some points which could do with further discussion."

Humus spent the rest of the morning going into details about the various groups' work. One group was warned that they were close to infringing observation rules and that they should be more careful in future.

Each group had been given wall space on the walls of the Angel Basics classroom for a semi permanent display of their project work as the work progressed. One group had discovered a feature of the Omniview that enabled pictures to be taken and had displayed these on the wall.

"I would be watching that one closely as well," Jonathon muttered mainly to himself as he noted an incredible looking girl in one of the pictures."

"Jonathan!" exclaimed Sarah.

"Sorry. I hadn't realized that I was speaking out loud," he said, embarrassed.

Sarah glared at him "Men!"

Individual sessions with each group followed. Groups not in conference with Humus were asked to create presentations on the rules governing the production of miracles and a discussion on how the rules might be applied in general terms to their subject groups.

Humus, having seen each of the groups in turn, assumed his usual position propped up on the front of his desk. "I thank you all for some good work. You have shown me that I was right to trust you to get on with your studies with a minimum of supervision and we will therefore continue in the same manner." Humus paused to allow the mumbles to die down ignoring the "You mean you can't be bothered to teach us" comment he could just about hear to his right. "I will expect a presentation folder from each group handed in by Friday lunch time on what miracles might be welcomed by members of your subject groups. Why these should or should not be performed and what rules apply in each situation."

Groans and mumbles permeated through the class as the amount of work this could mean was noted.

"I will be here in class for anyone who requires to ask any questions or require any guidance during any of the normal lesson times." Humus waited to see if any questions would be forthcoming. "Good afternoon." He left without another word.

There was almost no time before lunch so any work would have to wait. Jonathon had about an hour before Soarelle's Navigation class and had yet to do his homework.

"You are an idiot," said Sarah, "Of all the classes to forget homework for." She shook her head in a knowing yet pitying manner which somehow managed to avoid being patronizing.

Jonathon was obviously a little panicked. "I thought I could do it one evening but something else always came up."

"I bet it was something to do with girls," said Sarah.

Jonathon looked hurt momentarily. "I suppose I deserved that," he said, "but no, I haven't seen anyone at all this week. It was other homework and things like that."

"Come off it Jon. Everyone else can get their homework done, including Soarelle's. What have you been up to?"

"Sarah, I just have other things to do OK. Is Soarelle's work very difficult?"

Albert and Angelina had caught up with the others by this time and Albert caught the last statement. "A real swine. It took me ages to work out."

"That's because you made some wrong assumptions at the start and had to start again," said Angelina softly.

"The work's not that bad," said Sarah, "as long as you start right, but it does take a fair amount of time to get neat, so you had better get cracking." Sarah paused, thought about it for a few minutes. "Let's go. I'll come and help."

Albert looked at Angelina in surprise and saw the same thing mirrored in her face, but neither said anything until the other two were out of earshot.

"What's up with her?" said Albert.

"She must have mellowed," Angelina replied, "A lot."

Albert and Angelina went to lunch, it was a little early but they had little else that they wanted to do.

Neither Sarah nor Jonathon made it to lunch. They worked on Jonathon's homework in his room and only made it just in time for the lesson. Albert and Angelina said nothing to them or each other but both individually thought they could see a difference in the manner in which they were interacting with each other.

Navigation was not that difficult, just quite detailed. It had not yet been complicated by three-dimensional problems as Soarelle had concentrated on just navigating across the ground to start with. Some people found that difficult enough. Albert had got to grips with the theory and so he found the lessons fun. He found he could understand the differences made by wind drift and planetary rotation easily and was usually first to finish any problem and then often helped the others in the class, but he was still likely to get lost during practical flying.

One of the problems with Ardon Humus' project system was that it created four small groups, which seemed to stay together and not mix too well. Soarelle had noticed this and had deliberately organized different groups for her class. Albert found it difficult to force himself to help others in his new group before finding Angelina. His feelings he realized had grown for the girl despite the two years between them.

Outside of Soarelle's class Albert's group would usually be found together again and if split then invariably Albert could be found with Angelina and Jonathon would be found with Sarah. The turnaround was complete for Sarah she could now be seen holding hands with Jonathon in corridors and on walks together. Jonathon was not seen with any other girls.

Late that week Sarah came to Albert with some disturbing news. Two days after the time she had helped him with his homework she was looking for Jonathon and had found him in an Omniview room observing the original living subject group

"We have been given another group," said Albert. "Why would he want to do that?"

"He apparently asked what was being done about the murder and the obviously nefarious plot that was being hatched and didn't get a satisfactory answer," said Sarah. "He was just told that he shouldn't concern himself with it."

"That's a stupid thing to say to Jonathon. He would simply concern himself with it more."

"He did," said Sarah. "He found that the group had been observed for less than an hour and then just left."

"So nothing's being done," said Albert surprised.

"Nothing by the authorities anyway." replied Sarah.

"So Jonathon thinks he will do the work for them. Still he can only observe."

Sarah was silent for a while, looking concerned.

"Don't worry Sarah he can only waste his own time. Let him if that's what he feels like doing."

Sarah looked up having made a difficult decision. "He has a key to the controls. Someone left one in the microphone switch the other day apparently."

Albert now looked shocked "Whoever lost that key will know where they left it and therefore know from the booking sheets who has it. He will get into an awful lot of trouble." Albert thought for a while, "Do you know where he is now, Sarah?"

"I think you will find him in one of the Omniview rooms. Every time I've seen him recently that's where he has been."

"OK. We need to speak to him." Albert stood up. "Perhaps the group should be together. Can you find Angelina and meet me in the Library?"

When Albert entered the Library several of the Omniview rooms were in use but only one had a closed door. He guessed correctly that that was where he would find Jonathon. Opening the door quietly Albert slipped into the room. Jonathon was watching the Omniview's broad top so closely that he didn't notice Albert enter. On the desk beside him amongst the books Albert could see a small brass key. He stepped over and picked up the key before Jonathon noticed he was there.

"Hello," said Albert now examining the key in his hand. The key was strangely shaped, seemed primitive and had no branding or writing on it at all.

Jonathon reached over to switch off the Omniview guiltily but then realized that this was pointless. Albert had obviously already seen what he was watching. "That's mine," Jonathon said holding out his hand for the key.

"Is it?" replied Albert tucking the key into his pocket and closing the flap. "And where did you get such an object?"

"I made it," said Jonathon "Now give it back."

Albert now knew why the key looked so strange, it was a copy made by hand from the original. The reason there hadn't been a college wide search for a missing key was because no key was missing. Jonathon had found the key, copied it and returned the key to its owner or more likely simply left it where he found it. Albert made no move to return the key. "Does it work?"

Jonathon was taken aback by the unexpected response. "What do you mean? It's just a key."

Albert reached into his pocket and retrieved the key. "Does this work in the machine?"

"Yes," said Jonathon now realizing that Albert was aware of the key's purpose. He paused thinking for a while and then decided that there was no point in not co-operating. "I tried it in the microphone switch the day I finished it. The room I was viewing had no one in it." He paused and chuckled "Unfortunately a passing security guard heard it and spent 10 minutes looking for intruders. I hope he just thought he had an over active imagination."

Sarah and Angelina arrived. Albert slipped the key back into his pocket.

"What the hell are you playing at Jonathon?" Angelina cried. "Sarah here is scared you will get the whole group into trouble. She says you have a key."

"Keep your voice down," hissed Jonathon.

Sarah went to the door and checked the main Library. Only two people were there and they were engrossed in a book in the corner and did not seem to have heard. She quietly closed the door and gave the OK sign to the others.

"No one knows I have a key. Except you lot, and anyway" Jonathon paused "Albert has it now."

Albert patted his pocket. "Why are you watching this lot, anyway?" he asked, "We have been given another set of people who might be more boring, but they don't go around shooting people."

"Nothing was done about that murder you know. They watched for less than an hour and then just left it saying that it will all be taken into account in the final reckoning."

"Sounds reasonable to me," said Sarah.

"What if we could prevent another murder?" reasoned Jonathon, "With the key we could simply warn Grafton we were watching when he was about to fire and maybe that would be enough."

"I think that would be a very bad idea," said Sarah. "The trouble we could get into doing something that might not have any effect at all."

"Who left the key, anyway?" asked Angelina who had been listening with care and growing concern.

"I don't know," said Jonathon "I found the key in the microphone switch lock and took some impressions in a block of soap from the toilets and then put it back. I wasn't going to hang around to find out who fetched it."

Angelina was thoughtful for a moment. "If someone was going to use a key to speak to the living they are not likely to want to be disturbed, therefore they are almost sure to book a session. Which Omniview room did you find it in, Jonathon?"

"Viewing room two," said Jonathon. "I've avoided it since. It was the night of Soarelle's navigation class."

"So let's go and book a viewing room for our project tomorrow." Angelina left the room and walked over to the librarian's desk. On the pretext of booking a session she looked back at the records. On returning she was visibly shaken. "The session before you was booked by Senior Ardon Phurus."

Albert gasped realizing the full significance of the statement. "If that key belongs to Phurus then it is a full master key and will operate the full intervention panel as well as the microphone switch." Turning to Jonathon he said, "What have you done?"

Angelina had time to think. "You have missed another important point," she said. "Senior Ardon Phurus has several Omniview machines in his department, so why did he come to the Library to use the ones down here? The machines in Vengeance and Corrections are fully audited and the records regularly checked, while these are only used for viewing so nobody bothers with them unless something extraordinary happens. I bet he was doing something that he didn't want anyone else to know about and I also bet he erased the logs, but down here no one would notice the gaps in the records."

"Especially as he must have wanted to speak to the living or he wouldn't have got his key out at all." puzzled Albert.

"I think you are letting your imaginations run away wild," said Sarah getting a little concerned about where all this speculation might be leading. "He was probably just checking a reported problem with the machine."

"Nothing reported in the booking log," said Angelina, "and anyway he wouldn't need his key for that."

"It doesn't matter why he was here, or even about the key. What I want to know is why did the original discovery of the murder not create a bigger investigation and why was it dropped so quickly?" said Jonathon. "I wonder who was in charge of the investigation?"

"Is all this speculation getting us anywhere?" said Sarah now getting very troubled by thoughts of the group standing against Senior Ardon Phurus in some sort of accusatory tribunal. "You can't go around suggesting ulterior motives for Senior Ardons. It could get us into so much trouble, and in any case I don't see how the key whoever left it and the murder are connected."

"Did anyone suggest telling anyone else?" said Jonathon looking around in a mock search.

"Look," said Angelina. "No one outside this group must know about the copy of the key and no one is to know that anyone has continued to view our original living group against instructions."

"It's not against instructions," Jonathon stated forcefully, "We were asked to study another group but no one actually told us we couldn't look at the old one as well."

"That's splitting hairs," said Sarah.

"I think he has a point," said Albert. "We weren't told we couldn't we were simply given another group."

Both Angelina and Sarah were surprised that Albert had stood up for Jonathon and were about to comment when Albert continued. "I also think that there is something going on here that stands discrete investigation, there are just too many things that don't quite add up."

Sarah looked at Angelina for support, but Angelina was now nodding slowly deep in thought. "What do you think we ought to do?" she asked, "Whatever we do we must be very careful."

"I think we are OK as long as we are reasonably discrete," said Albert. "The only thing that could get us in serious trouble is the key, the rest we could put down as simple curiosity."

"You don't think that poking into the business of a Senior Ardon could get us into serious trouble, then?" Sarah was worried. She had gone to Albert in the first place because she hadn't wanted Jonathon in serious trouble and now he seemed to be getting encouragement instead of the put down she had hoped for.

"What do you suggest we do now then?" asked Angelina "Even if something fishy is going on I don't see what we can do about it."

Sarah nodded thinking that at last something sensible had been said.

"It won't hurt to do a little investigation," said Albert. "We could try three things for a start. Firstly we could try asking how the case into the Grafton murder is going. It may not have simply been abandoned, and it would be nice if we could discover who is or was in charge as well. Secondly we could keep an eye on Grafton's group ourselves. It would take some time but it might well be worth doing. Thirdly," Albert paused looking around at the others to view the reaction to what he was about to say, "we could see if the key works."

"That is too much," said Sarah "There you are on very dangerous ground. How can you sensibly consider it?"

"I told you that I have already checked it," said Jonathon, who had until this time simply waited for the outcome of the argument.

"You have tried the microphone switch," put in Albert. "Microphone keys are commonly given to more advanced students but does the key work the intervention panel. If this key is a master key then it should give access to all the functions of the Omniview. If it does not then we would know that this was not copied from Phurus' key."

"NO!" Sarah almost screamed. "You can't be serious." Luckily no one else was now in the Library at all. "None of us has even seen an intervention panel let alone knows how to use it. Even if we knew how to use it doing so would certainly get us into serious trouble."

"Opening the panel will probably trigger an alarm," said Jonathon.

"We could check that," said Angelina though not very enthusiastically, "Omniview Five is currently switched off and completely powered down for repair so if we tried the key there it probably wouldn't set off an alarm."

Albert stood up and led the way across the Library to Omniview room five. All of the others followed, though Sarah was a little reluctant.

When all the friends were in the room and Albert had checked that the door was closed the group had a look around the defunct machine.

"Looks like they have almost finished the repair," said Jonathon.

"Will you keep your voice down?" hissed Sarah. "We certainly shouldn't be in here."

The group was quieter after that. The machine looked completely finished but the main power cable was still disconnected from its floor-mounted block. Jonathon noted that the block contained wires that were certainly not for power and surmised that they would be for any external logs and alarms. Albert did not hesitate. Removing the key from his pocket he put it into the lock which would open the intervention panel and turned it. The panel opened on a spring-assisted hinge and stood up leaning backward slightly. Inside there were several switches and to one side was what at first glance appeared to be a pencil. On the other side there was a button coloured red which had a guard over it to prevent any accidental use. The label under this button read 'Direct Intervention extreme caution'. In the center of the panel were five smaller panels labeled

Shield
Energy
Push
Restraints
Dumb

Each of these smaller panels had several controls within them. Each of the panels had a switch labelled on or off and a switch labelled Global or Wand. The first four panels had a slider switch labelled strength and the Shield panels also had another slider, this one labelled Opacity and further label which stated Transparent at one end and Opaque at the other.

A further five buttons across the top of the panel were simply numbered and none of the group could hazard a guess as to the use of these.

"I suppose that this is the wand," said Albert picking up the object that looked like a pencil and discovering that a cable was attached to the end opposite the tip, which was long enough to reach completely across the top of the Omniview but recoiled smoothly as length was not needed.

Jonathon was carefully examining the door of the intervention panel. "As we suspected the panel door is alarmed." Taking a small piece of gum from his mouth he carefully jammed the small electrical contact in the closed position so that the alarm would no longer function.

Sarah was horrified. "You can't do that, Jon. If you, we, got caught we'll be . . . ."

"Who's going to know?" interrupted Jonathon. "Nobody ever opens this panel anyway." Jonathon pointed out the dust apparent on the inner controls, "Even maintenance didn't bother with it."

"I don't like this one bit," whispered Sarah who had realized that she had momentarily spoken too loudly. "Let's get out of here."

"I think she's right. We have found out everything we came to find out," said Angelina.

Albert carefully replaced the wand in its cradle and closed the panel. Ignoring Jonathon's hand he placed the key back in his own pocket. Jonathon's mouth opened as if to say something and then closed as he thought the better of it. The group left room O5 after checking that the Library was still empty. Jonathon retrieved his books from room O3 and the group followed Albert back to his room.

CHAPTER 6

Investigation or Treachery

"WHERE SHOULD WE START?" SAID Albert, "Who is going to do what and when? The first thing is to find out what is happening to the official investigation and if possible who's in charge because if that is still being dealt with we need not bother with anything else at all."

"I'll try that." said Sarah. "Then perhaps we can forget all this nonsense and get back to normal."

"I don't think we should use the Omniview on our own when looking at Grafton's group," said Angelina, "We need a lookout and an extra witness would not go amiss if anything needs reporting to higher up." Everyone nodded in agreement.

"I think we wait for Sarah to report and then take it from there," said Albert.

Sarah, because she had fainted, probably created less suspicion asking about the case than anyone else. It was natural that she should be curious. She found it very difficult to gain any information because no one seemed to know anything. Throwing caution to the wind she decided she would approach Seraphus directly. Just walking into his office however would cause questions to be asked, so she waited near his office so she could make the question as casually as possible.

"Excuse me, sir. "she said as she contrived to be simply passing in the corridor. "I was wondering what is happening with the monitoring of our original group after the shooting."

"You need not concern yourself about that, my dear," Seraphus replied, "The investigation team considered the shooting to be a one off spur of the moment killing. It will simply be left to the final reckoning. Phurus who conducted the investigation himself assures me that no further action needs to be taken."

"Thank you, sir."

The conversation was reported minutes later to the rest of the group.

"A spur of the moment killing. Unlikely to occur again. No chance." said Jonathon, "Grafton did that without as much as a flicker of remorse. It wasn't the first time he had done that, nor, I would think will it be the last."

"Another mystery involving Phurus," pointed out Albert. "I wonder when we will come across another. My mum always said things come in threes."

As it happened they didn't have to wait long. That evening Angelina saw Phurus enter the Library. She quietly followed just in time to see Phurus disappear into Number Two Omniview room and close the door quietly behind him. She sat in a corner where she could watch without being easily seen and got on with some study work for Healing class. Some time later as she watched the Omniview room door slowly open. After a quick check Phurus left quietly but with some considerable speed closed the door after him just as quietly and speedily and walked out of the Library. Angelina, leaving her books where she had put them, slipped into the now vacant Omniview room.

The settings on the system had been neutralized. This was a standard rule when leaving an Omniview system and Angelina had not expected anything different. Nobody however looked at the logs. Had Phurus thought to erase them? Checking she found that the time during Phurus' stay had been carefully deleted. 'He's being very careful,' she thought. Checking further she discovered that he had not quite been careful enough. Phurus had set a log mark so that deleting the record would be easy, as he only had to delete back to a mark instead of searching for particular scenes. The log mark he had set after he had set the coordinates and so only the record of what he did was lost. The location could still be found. Sydney, Australia.

Angelina reported her evening to the others during Angel Basics the following morning.

"The mystery deepens," said Albert, "I bet all of this is part of the Grafton incident."

"It could be that Seraphus was just trying to be nice to me and the investigation is still continuing," said Sarah not really believing this herself.

"He's covering up something," said Angelina. "Otherwise he would use the machines in Corrections. The question is what do we do about it? We can't go to Seraphus as we have just suspicions and we would just get called paranoid or something. No one else in authority is going to listen either, not about someone like Senior Ardon Phurus."

"We need to keep an eye on Grafton's crew," said Jonathon. "If he's getting help from up here for some nefarious intent then someone ought to keep an eye on things. No one else is going to believe us without a lot more then we currently have."

"Remember, no one is to do this on their own," said Albert. "We might need witnesses and if anything important happens someone will be needed to fetch the others or help while the other continues to watch."

"I'll work with Jonathon," said Sarah immediately. "You and Angelina seem to go together somehow."

Albert looked at Angelina who looked back, both of them thinking that Sarah was taking every opportunity to be with Jonathon.

The following day after flight practice all four of the group made for the Library. Angelina had pre-booked an Omniview room as it had been decided to start their investigation as soon as possible. Angelina had booked the now fully operational

Omniview room five and the group gathered around the unit as Jonathon dialled the requisite coordinates.

The office where the group had been found on previous occasions was empty but turning up the volume resulted in voices being heard through the door, which had provided an exit for Grafton on the first viewing. Jonathon adjusted the coordinates so that the other room could be observed.

The room was much better furnished. A leather settee had been placed along one wall. A large desk occupied the center of the lush red carpet with a high backed executive leather chair provided seating for the user. In the chair was Grafton, his back turned to Michael who was speaking. He did not appear to be listening, but then appearances can be deceptive.

Michael was outlining some plans. "The shipment will be met off the plane before customs by our courier. It has been arranged that he will arrive on another flight scheduled to land about 10 minutes prior to the shipment. All luggage from Asia will probably be searched quite thoroughly but our courier will have come from New Zealand so will probably be waved through. We have also managed to obtain an Auckland security seal, which will be attached to the bag before customs. The shipment itself has been sealed in an airproof bag which has been taken to a clean room and carefully washed. This has then been sealed in another bag to prevent any chance of the drug dogs detecting the drugs in the luggage. The drugs have then been surrounded by the chemical powder that is on the import documents. If the courier is searched then the drugs should not be found. We have also taken the precaution of employing this courier through several third parties and no trail can be tracked back to us so that if the drugs are detected the courier is expendable."

"The shipment however is not expendable the drugs are being used as payment for some of our other dealings. Its loss would negate considerable investment," said Grafton turning on the swivel of his chair to face Michael. The searching look that fixed on Michael seemed to reduce the man in size. "Thank you, Michael." The words were polite but the tone was sneering. "As your couriers are expendable it would not be a shame if they simply went missing permanently. After the delivery is complete please book them a nice holiday to Neverland."

Grafton had casually ordered the murder of two more people. Jonathon looked at the others. "Told you," he said, "Grafton would murder again even if he doesn't actually get his own hands dirty with the deed this time."

Grafton had now turned to Norma who was almost lying on a settee and quickly pulled herself up to as close an approximation of attention as you can get while still seated. "I trust your part of the operation is going smoothly."

Norma stood up, her demeanor was of confidence but she did not hold Grafton's eyes for long. "The deal is set up, although I have not actually seen the merchandise. Transport is ready to ship to a remote desert facility in Africa where biologists are ready to prepare the correct cultures."

"Ensure nothing goes wrong this time," Grafton's tone was less sneering this time, but still did not hold any respect for the woman towards whom it was directed.

"Mr Shett," Grafton snapped out the name. Barry, who looking out of the window, hitched himself off the wall against which he had been leaning and turned to face the occupant of the black chair. Barry simply waited without speaking his black untidy hair seemed to be totally out of control.

Grafton spoke again. "I trust my special order is available."

"Not yet," said Barry, "but then getting the parts for biological weapons safely out of anywhere was never going to be easy."

"I did not ask whether the job was easy or not. I am aware of the difficulties. You are here because you claim to have the skills and the contacts to overcome such difficulties." Grafton's anger was plain to see, "I hope my faith in those abilities was not misplaced."

"The items will be ready in time, but until you tell me where they are to be delivered I cannot give you an estimate as to how long it will take to get there."

"Let me take care of that. You only need to have obtained the devices and I will arrange transport." The sneer in Grafton's voice had returned in full measure. Turning his chair slightly Grafton took in the whole room with a glance. "Thank you for your reports I will contact you when I require anything further." He turned his chair to face the window as Barry passed him on the way to the door. Anne was the first to leave and if she had had anything to report this had been before the viewing friends had arrived. The room quickly emptied leaving only Grafton in a thoughtful mood.

"That was a fine display of leadership." The voice dripped with such a level of sarcasm that Grafton could only dream of getting close.

Jonathon adjusted the view of the room so that even the most extreme corners were visible. No one else was in the room. Grafton however had ignored the sarcasm and did not turn towards the intercom which the four had noticed on the desk.

"What I do with my operatives is my concern not yours." Grafton had somehow injected the words with a menace which showed that Grafton did not fear the speaker.

"It is when your actions cause problems for me," replied the disembodied voice, "That unnecessary killing the other day could have done untold damage."

"It caused me no problems." Grafton's voice had now taken on a casual tone which somehow was even more menacing. "Any problems you have up there I am sure you can deal with. My job is to provide you with Earthly vengeance and yours is to ensure me of a place up there when I've finished and to keep your lot off my back."

"If anyone but a bunch of students had seen your stupid actions the other day, then-"

"But it was a bunch of students and you coped with it," interrupted Grafton.

The truth had occurred to Albert and his shocked and almost silent exclamation, "Phurus." seemed to echo around the room. Sarah looked at him not knowing what he was talking about.

"The voice we are hearing is Phurus via another Omniview machine," Albert continued. "He could be next door now."

The four sat in silence somehow not daring to move or speak. The Omniview speaker had remained silent after Grafton's last speech and the effect had simply emphasized the tension in the room. Grafton had not moved in his chair and was still staring out of the window. More than five minutes must have passed.

Angelina broke the silence. "I bet he is in O2," she said, "If he always used O2 then if anyone noticed the gaps in the logs he could just say that it must be faulty and then fix it before anyone else could say anything else. If all the machines showed gaps the explanation wouldn't fit. I'll book us another session tomorrow." Angelina left the room and returned a few minutes later to report that Phurus had once again booked Omniview room 2 for some exploratory maintenance. She had also noticed that he had already left as the door to Omniview 2 was left open.

"Do you think he can detect the fact that we were looking in?" said Sarah with a worried expression on her face.

"I don't think he would have given that last speech to anyone if he thought anyone was listening in," pointed out Jonathon.

"I wonder whether it is possible to detect someone viewing through one of these machines," said Albert thoughtfully. "I will make some discrete enquiries."

Albert's idea of discrete could be said to leave something to be desired. During Angel Basics the following morning when someone asked Humus a question about the rules for viewing living subjects Albert stood up and asked whether it was possible to detect a viewing anyway so how could you get caught.

Humus thought that it was a good question. "A detector was built in the past," he said, "but did not work if the Omniview was in view only mode. If any of the features of the Omniview Interference panel are invoked then a detector was built to detect that. The detector was only an experiment which I believe was abandoned years ago as pointless, after all we know when we are using the system and why would we want to alert the living of that fact? There are of course particularly tuned living individuals who can detect the Omniview even in viewing mode but as this is only apparent as a vague feeling of being watched. It can be largely ignored. I believe that the Angels on the project thought that it could be tuned to detect the Omniview in view mode as well but the project was stopped before this could be done. If you are really curious you could ask Senior Ardon Phurus as I think he was part of the development team." Humus paused. "however sometimes random checks are made of the logs to check you lot are sticking to the rules, so don't think you can get away with anything." Humus smiled.

After the lesson Sarah came up to Albert and said, "How could you just come out and ask that? In the middle of the class. Everyone will know we're up to something now."

"I don't think so," said Angelina who was the only person close enough to hear Sarah's voice, "I think it was rather clever really. No one would expect someone who was getting up to something to ask a question like that and Albert didn't have to try at all to work the question in casually."

"The point is," said Albert, "that we now know that no detector works while we are in view mode, so we are safe when we watch."

"Well we have another session booked for this evening," said Angelina, "and if we all go to each session then all of us will end up in trouble as we won't have time to do other work. So who is on duty tonight?"

"Jon and I will do tonight," said Sarah, "but I don't think we can do it every night or things will be noticed. We will have to try and see if we can get a sort of schedule so that we know when significant meetings are to be held. I haven't a clue how to do that though. I think Grafton is much too clever to go writing things like that down and then leaving his diary around for us to look at."

"I think we are simply going to have to accept that we will miss quite a lot of what goes on," said Angelina. "I'm not sure what we are going to do with the things we find out anyway. I just don't think we can afford to let Grafton or Phurus get away with what is obviously something more than a little doubtful."

During the periods over the next two weeks when the friends had time to watch, no notable incident occurred and the friends were starting to think that the worst was over. Phurus was not known to contact Grafton again and no significant meetings with Barry, Anne, Norma and Michael were observed either. Grafton's everyday business as an importer and exporter of the most innocent looking cargo continued as though nothing untoward was happening.

An investigation into Phurus' background to find out upon whom he might have reason to exact Earthly revenge, which had been started by Angelina had run into several dead ends. "I can't ask directly," explained Angelina, "that would be bound to get back to Phurus and cause suspicion."

A trip to the Library to do some work for the History of Angels class, saw Sarah on her own in a corner surrounded by books. The shadows cast by a desk lamp almost completely hid her identity from all but the most intense of gazes. Phurus emerging from Omniview room Two, could not have recognized her. Phurus' mood was obviously one of rage and Sarah was convinced that he was past the concentration needed for any sort of recognition even if she had been standing in front of him. Sarah gathered her personal belongings quickly and ran to fetch the others.

Jonathon was the first she found and he told her to find Albert and Angelina and meet him in Omniview room Five. When they had arrived Jonathon had already started the machine and was searching for Grafton.

"Grafton is likely to be the only person capable of creating that sort of rage in Phurus," he said, as a note of explanation to what he was doing. "I doubt if any of the others even knows of Grafton's ability to communicate with here."

The Omniview system easily located Grafton despite the fact that the friends did not risk the setting of a tag. "A tag might be noticed as it appears on the tag list for all the Omniview rooms," explained Jonathon the first time it was suggested. It was also noticed that Phurus didn't set a tag on him either not that the friends would have risked using it if he had done so.

Sitting behind his desk Grafton was obviously deep in thought. It must have been a pleasant thought as a smile lingered on his lips. His desk was littered with official looking papers many of them stamped with receipt dates. In the corner was a newspaper with the headlines ringed in red pen. Jonathan adjusted the Omniview so that the paper could be read. 'Government denies anything stolen in raid.' The story went on to explain about a break-in at a top-secret laboratory. 'A spokesperson said that the potential burglars had been disturbed and had left empty handed.' The spokesperson went on to deny rumors that the laboratory had been working on antidotes for some really deadly bugs, and went on to joke, "that is if you discount the director's cold."

The notes handwritten on the paper in red seemed to differ with the spokesperson's statement. Jonathan brought the friends attention to a particular note further down the page which stated. 'Release systems available in two days' and just underneath that, the note 'phial to be in China in three days.'

The silence was broken by a light tap on the door and Grafton's smile disappeared instantly. "Come." the voice was precise and icy cold. The door opened slowly echoing the lack of confidence which the person on the other side of the door was feeling.

Barry entered and nervously started speaking. "The virus phial has now left the country disguised as a perfume bottle and surrounded by some strong perfume and should be in China on time, if not early. We have declared everything to customs and all of the bottles will work properly if tested, even the one with its deadly payload."

"I expect nothing less, Barry." The smile on Grafton's lips was more akin to a sneer as though the last thing he expected was Barry to actually perform, "It only remains to get the release systems in place and then we will be able to release the virus at the most opportune time."

"When do you expect that to be and who are we going to ask to pay the ransom?" asked Barry plucking up the courage from somewhere to ask the question that he had been burning to ask since he had got involved with Grafton's plan.

"I pay you to do the jobs I ask of you and you are assured that you will be well paid. I do not expect to be quizzed on the details of the planning and I will try not to tax you too much by asking your opinion or for your input." The statement dripped with more sarcasm than any of the watching group could ever remember hearing, "Suffice it to say that the action we take will be at the opportune moment to satisfy the needs of our sponsor together with other needs to which neither you nor he need be aware. I thank you for your news and be sure to tell me when the delivery systems I asked for are in place. You may leave at anytime."

The last statement was not meant to be ignored and the tone left no doubt that the mentioned anytime was anytime now. In fact, instantly. Barry wisely did not ignore it or wait to discover how far he could push Grafton's welcome.

In Omniview room Five the silence was complete. Albert broke the silence first. "This is getting out of hand. Obviously Grafton is planning things that even Phurus is not aware of."

"We have to tell someone," said Sarah, "The release of a virus on Earth could kill thousands."

"OK," said Jonathon, "I am with you on the last statement but who would you tell, who would believe you and how would you explain spying on a Senior Ardon? Especially as the Senior Ardon in question has done a fairly good job so far of covering his tracks."

"We know what's going on," exclaimed Sarah.

"True," continued Jonathan almost without breaking his flow of speech, "but we stumbled on this by accident and then have continued looking. What evidence have we collected that is not going to end up being just our word against Phurus?"

"Then," said Albert with determination, "we are going to have to collect some hard evidence or prevent Grafton executing his plans ourselves."

"Aren't we taking on too much?" asked Angelina quietly, "This is likely to mean tangling with Phurus directly before the end and some serious interference in the living world as well. Surely we can't do this on our own."

Jonathon had listened to the exchange carefully. "I agree with all of you," he said. "We cannot allow Grafton to succeed, we also cannot take this to anyone else at present, but trying to take on the might of Phurus and Grafton is likely to end in tears or worse. We have to watch and try to collect evidence that will allow us to bring in the college authorities. If we get caught before we can manage this we are likely to be in serious trouble as what we are doing right now is against the rules. We have the tools to interfere if we need to but if we get caught using a interference key or if anyone discovers we have disabled the alarms in this Omniview room then we will no longer be able to do anything. We need to be careful."

Sarah looked worried but she had now come to trust the instincts of the man that she had initially detested. Angelina looked at Albert and noted that none of the determination had left his expression. She held out her hand to the others and as the friends joined hands, in a silent pact they had agreed to see this mystery to a conclusion together.

Grafton was now working silently on the papers that lay on his desk, quietly scribbling notes and slowly moving documents to the out tray in the corner of his desk. The newspaper had now been consigned to the wastepaper bin at his side. Angelina suggested they return to her room, as it didn't look likely that any other drama was likely to occur that evening.

Angelina lay on her bed and Jonathon sat on the edge of her desk while Albert took the study chair and watched Sarah take the easy chair in the corner.

"We need to watch the others," said Albert, "Does anyone here realize how lucky we have been to see some of the things we have seen? Twenty minutes later and we would have seen nothing."

"I'm not sure that that would not have been a better idea," said Sarah, "Do you realize what trouble we could be getting into? Albert suggested only a few minutes ago the possibility of actually interfering in the living world. We have no idea what the repercussions of that would be."

Albert caught the twinkle in her eyes that showed she would have it no other way in time to stop him making any comment. Jonathon did not even look, he was now confident in his ability to read the girl that he had growing affections for. Angelina looked at Albert and caught the hesitation and smiled.

"We have been lucky, haven't we?" she said. "But we obviously missed too much of this plot and I agree with Albert we have to watch the others as well. Perhaps we should work during the night when no one else is about. Grafton's group is about eight hours out of sync with Heaven so some significant things could happen during our night."

"When would you suggest sleeping?" questioned Sarah the twinkle still evident in her eyes.

"We would need to take it in turns," continued Angelina, "During the night I don't think we need to be in pairs as no one will be around and we will only be watching and recording."

"That sounds a bit dodgy to me," said Jonathon tentatively, "If anything happened then someone on their own would be unable to do anything but watch and anyone caught by someone in the Omniview rooms at night would be sure to be in trouble."

"Well just watching and recording is better than nothing," said Angelina and encouraged by Albert's nodding head continued, "I will get up early in the morning and take the first watch. If I get up at midnight then it should be at eight in the morning there and something may be happening."

"I don't think it is likely that anything will be happening that early," said Sarah thinking that getting up early for her was going to be pure hell.

"I wouldn't have thought anything would be happening the first time we saw them either," said Albert, "If you remember that was almost eight at night for them."

CHAPTER 7

Breaking and Entering

THE EXTRA TIME SPENT WATCHING Grafton's exploits with early morning stints in the Omniview room was taking its toll on the group despite that midnight had slipped by agreement to two in the morning. Although they had only agreed to do one morning in four each, it was rare to find any of them alone during their time in O5. On Sarah and Jonathon's sessions they always arrived together and although Angelina and Albert often started on their own the other always arrived within the first hour. The watching however returned almost no reward at all. Confirmation that the deadly cargo had reached China had been observed. The knowledge that the release systems had been built and were available as needed was also obtained. This information was gained by listening in on telephone conversations in Grafton's office. Barry, Norma and Anne were observed some of the time but nothing to do with Grafton's enterprise was ever discovered.

The friends met one evening, in Sarah's room following a particularly boring session with Anticus.

"This is getting us nowhere," said Angelina.

"We haven't learnt a lot," agreed Albert, "though I don't think we should give up. We still don't know what, where, why or how Grafton is planning."

Jonathon agreed with Albert, "We know enough to make me think that to give up now would be letting Grafton get away with killing a lot of people."

"Let's take stock of our current position," suggested Albert, "We know that he is planning to release a virus and that it will be released somewhere in China. We know that the smuggling of the bug has been completed and that the method of release is available. We know very little else." Albert paused to see if the others had anything to add but nobody spoke so he continued. "What we have to learn at all costs is where and when the release is to take place. Anything else is unimportant. I don't see how else we are going to do this except by continuing to watch."

Sarah who had been sitting quietly in the easy chair, mumbled almost too softly to be heard, "We would still have to be extremely lucky to find out by simply watching."

Despite this statement the group was in agreement that giving up was simply not an option. The four left to go to their own rooms quite early. Sleep was something that all had been short of. Albert's room was the furthest away and rounding a corner he almost ran into two final year students coming the other way. They were too preoccupied to mind and kept chattering as they stepped aside to allow Albert to pass.

"Much nicer day tomorrow," one of them said.

"Always nicer when Phurus is away," smiled the other.

"Yeah," replied the first. "And away for two or three days this time."

The reply was the last thing Albert heard as the two disappeared into a study room. The impact of what he had heard passed him by until early the following morning.

It was Angelina who was watching early the following morning in Omniview room Five. She arrived a few minutes before two o'clock in the morning and Albert arrived about 30 minutes later to keep her company.

"Any activity?" asked Albert as he entered.

"No one there at all yet," replied Angelina. "Most mornings there is no one in the offices at this time of the morning. They seem to work very strange office hours." The glow of the Omniview machine cast a strange glow on her face and emphasized its beauty as she spoke. Together they watched silently for a few minutes.

"I ran into two final years yesterday," said Albert, more to break the silence than any other reason. "I overheard them saying that Phurus was away for two or three days. That should make the college a more pleasant place."

Angelina looked at him with eyes wide "That means that his room will be empty," she said, "Perhaps we can find some evidence that we can use in his room."

Albert looked a bit panicked. "You can't seriously think you can break into his room without being caught," he exclaimed, "The Ardons' rooms are in a separate block and there is no excuse to be even in the building. You wouldn't even get to his door, especially as his room is about as far away as possible from the entrance."

Angelina shook her head. "His room is at the end of the long wing right next to the back stairs. The back stairs door is almost never locked as it is a fire exit so that gives us a way in and out without passing anyone."

"Us!" exclaimed Albert, "You might be that crazy but that doesn't mean that I am."

"Just a calculated risk," said Angelina quietly, "We need the evidence and I didn't think you would let me go alone." She smiled the sort of smile that would melt any other person but Albert was not so easily led.

"Well calculate it then, and when you have finished, you will realize that the odds are way against you. The door to his room may be at the end of the wing near the back stairs but that also makes it at the end of a long corridor where several other Ardons' have their rooms. Any of them or anyone who was visiting them could spot you trying to break in and then there is the noise—that would be sure to attract attention. Once inside, if you got that far you would need to search quickly but silently without leaving clues that you had been there. Assuming you got away with all that you still need to get out again correctly locking the door behind you. All of this just on the off chance that Phurus keeps incriminating evidence in his room. It can't be worth the risk."

Angelina somehow smiled again despite the slightly worried look in her eyes. "Got any better ideas?"

The room was silent as the two, deep in thought watched the office displayed on the wide top of the Omniview machine.

"I haven't," was the reply some minutes later. Nothing else was said.

During the morning lesson Angelina mentioned the idea of searching Phurus' room to the others. Sarah let out an audible gasp but managed to turn it into a yawn so that it did not attract too much attention. Jonathon almost choked on the pen that he was chewing at the time. During morning break the four friends found a quiet corner to talk.

"Thinking about it," said Sarah," There is no other option."

The statement surprised Angelina but she saw the opportunity and elaborated. "We have to find out more information and we have to take action. We cannot continue to rely on luck to help us stop a terrible Earthly tragedy. I personally don't see why a supposed mentor should be allowed to get away with such horrible behaviour either."

Angelina's mind was made up and Albert could see that appealing to her emotions was not about to change it. "How is this to be done then?" he asked, hoping that a viable plan could not be worked out.

"Phurus' room is on the top floor right at the end of the corridor of the Ardons' wing," said Sarah, "That puts it very close to the flight practice area. We could at least do some reconnaissance without straying too far. The stairs at the back are open so it should also be possible to fly almost to the door, though it would be a tricky flight."

"The flight wouldn't worry me," said Angelina, "I hadn't thought about flying in. I could use the whole thing as flight practice and as long as I wasn't caught in Phurus' room I might get away with it even if I was spotted."

"I could fly lookout almost without leaving the practice ground," said Sarah, "I could use a whistle as a warning of someone coming up the back stairs."

Jonathon was now as worried about the enterprise as Albert or more accurately he was worried about the girls. "I don't think this is a good idea," he said. "To use flight practice as an excuse it would have to be done in daylight and anyway the chances of Phurus leaving anything lying around for you to find is simply not worth the risk."

Albert agreed but Sarah echoed Angelina's words of the earlier in the day, "Got a better idea?"

The break had ended and Jonathon reminded the group that they had time to think about this as Phurus was away for at lease another complete day and they could talk it over tonight. The friends returned to their work.

During lunch the girls went to a display of Angelic art in the main hall and the boys disappeared to the Library.

The display was unsurprisingly Heavenly and it gave the girls chance to talk on their own.

"The boys are never going to agree to this," said Sarah.

"Let's not give them a choice then," replied Angelina, "Meet me on the practice field after Angel Law class today. There is a speaker coming from one of the other colleges this evening and the seminar in the main hall should keep most of the Ardons busy and make the venture a little safer."

Angelina made her way to the practice field straight after class, avoiding giving any excuse to the others as she left. She didn't want to mention that she was going anywhere near the practice field as she knew that would make Albert suspicious. Sarah went with Jonathon as usual and waited for him to take his usual shower before quickly making her way to the waiting Angelina.

"Nice timing," said Angelina. "I have been practicing some tricky dives to give my excuse a little more weight if I am caught.

I have watched nearly all of the Ardons wander up to Main Hall so this should be easy."

"I wouldn't go that far," said Sarah, "Breaking into Phurus' study is not likely to be a case of just walking in. A thorough search without noise and without leaving it obvious that you had been there is also not likely to be a picnic either. Have you worked out where you want me for this enterprise and what you want me to do?"

"I think that an audible warning may be too obvious and the tree at the end of the block will make close flight dangerous, so I thought that if you did a circular flight over the far practice trail you could see the back stairs from everywhere. If I keep checking, if I can't see you I will know that all is not well."

"Sounds OK to me but you will have to look pretty often and please remember that someone may arrive down the corridor from the front entrance that I will be unable to see." Sarah touched Angelina's hand and continued, "Be careful."

Angelina kicked hard off the ground going up in a steep climb. She had decided to go high where she was less likely to be seen and then come down in a steep suicidal dive ending in a duck under a large branch between two trees, a slight rise with a quick change of direction should see her at the top of the back stairs. With any luck the back stairs door would be open and her manoeuvre would not have been spotted by anyone.

The flight was not a problem for Angelina. She landed on the wall of the stairs in just the right position to be able to take a quick look through the open door to see that the long corridor was empty. Her wings folded behind her as she stepped off the wall and entered the building where, if spotted, she would find it difficult to explain her presence.

The door immediately to her left was the door to Phurus' study and Angelina's hand reached out and tried to turn the handle. It turned. Surprised Angelina gently pushed and not surprisingly the door did not give at the pressure. The door was locked not by the usual privacy latch on the door handle that would have not let the handle turn, but by some other method. A quick inspection revealed a small keyhole just under the handle. This was not going to be easy but on Earth she had often gone to places where her brother had not wanted her and she thought she could get this open. All she needed was a little time. She set to work immediately with a small pack of tools that she had brought with her consisting of some common items hastily modified to her nefarious purpose.

Angelina's hope that her spectacular high-speed dive had not been observed was however in vain. Judith the nurse had seen what she thought had been a fall and was now coming to investigate expecting to find an injured flyer near the tree, which Angelina had so skillfully dodged.

Sarah had seen the danger and had disappeared from the far training trail. She knew that this warning would be useless until Angelina was actually in Phurus' study, as the corridor boasted no windows. Flying fast Sarah managed to intercept the hurrying nurse landing about two metres from the surprised nurse. "Did you see that dive?" she asked.

"Was that you?" replied Judith, "I thought that at least I would be patching up a few broken bones."

"I seem to be alright," Sarah stated, smiling.

"It was really stupid to do something like that," said the nurse now starting to relax a little. "You are lucky not to have hurt yourself".

The nurse was concerned but Sarah didn't believe she knew how to be angry. The problem which Sarah needed to solve now was that although Angelina would have heard the two talking and would be warned of the danger, Nurse Judith lived in the Ardons' block and would almost certainly use the back stairs from here. Angelina would have nowhere to go so Sarah had to give Angelina time.

Angelina heard the discussion at the bottom of the stairs and knew her only hope was the successful conclusion of her work on the little lock in front of her. She worked without haste but renewed determination feeling the clicks of the lock's levers. The conversation below did not distract her and she opened the door and silently closed it behind her shutting out the continuing discussion as she did so. Working quickly and almost silently Angelina then relocked the door behind her.

Finding herself in a room that was scrupulously tidy and exceptionally clean Angelina knew that that made her task both easier and more difficult, easier to search for the documents or items that she had to look for and much more difficult to leave so that her presence was not to be noticed when Phurus returned. She went first to a filing cabinet in the corner of the room. The lock was quickly defeated with the same small tools that she had used on the door. The cabinet contained many files which were labelled with student names. Angelina ignored all of those as she was looking for something personal to Phurus. The filing cabinet however only had three files in them which did not relate to students and those had only teaching notes inside them. Suddenly a noise at the door alerted Angelina to the presence of someone outside. She doubted whether she had been heard, as she had been as quiet as she could. She froze and listened. 'A key being fitted in the lock,' she thought and before the thought was complete she had looked around and moved towards the only hiding place in the room. Angelina was very glad that she had thought to relock the door as she entered the room.

"Phurus said that if I needed it I could take the book on Omniview interference etiquette from his shelf," said a woman's voice.

"I am surprised he gave you his keys," said another female voice. Some one sat on the desk under which Angelina was hiding and the desk creaked under the weight.

"I wonder where it is," said the first female. "He said it should be in plain sight."

"Probably on the bookshelf then. What does it look like? I will help you look."

"Thank you. I believe it is quite large and has a red spine and is about 3cm thick."

Angelina was now sure she must be discovered. With two people searching the room surely they couldn't help finding her.

'Is that it up on the top shelf?" said the second voice. The only part of the woman that she could see was her feet and they stood on tiptoe reaching to a high shelf. Suddenly the floor in front of the desk became the resting place of several thin tall looking books and the voice gave out several very un-lady like and even more un-Angel like expletives.

"Here is the book you are looking for Sophie," said the second voice.

"So it is, thank you, shall I help you pick those up?" said the first voice.

"No, this won't take long." And a hand swooped down to collect all but one of them which fell open such that Angelina from her hiding place could see that it was a scrapbook. In an instance a second hand caught the open book and lifted it out of sight.

The sound of the door opening and closing was a relief to Angelina, even more so when the sound of the key turning in the lock from the outside reached her ears.

When she got up Angelina was almost panting. She had been very careful with her breathing and holding herself like that had left her a little breathless. Finding a chair from the corner she used it to stand on to reach the top shelf on the wall in front of the desk. Angelina spread the four retrieved scrapbooks out on the desk. The books contained clippings and photographs mostly of people and places that she didn't recognize. Angelina leafed quickly through the books not noticing anything she felt like taking the time to read when about midway through the third book she found a picture of a destroyed town which included the headline 'Engineer dies attempting to save his family in Flood disaster'. A small portrait picture of Phurus was set into the text.

'This I need to read,' thought Angelina to herself.

Leigh Pathos, chief engineer for the Tai Wong Valley dam in China that so disastrously collapsed, died while trying to help people in the path of the impending flood. Several people say that they owe him their lives and that he is a hero. These feelings are however tempered with the fact that had he lived he would almost certainly be facing charges over his supervision of the way the dam was built. Ironically the engineer was trying to get to his family to warn them when he stopped to help others. His family survived but his son was seriously injured and doctors do not expect him ever to walk again.

Questions are being asked throughout the world as to the design of the dam structure which was being built and whether this disaster can be put down to bad materials, bad workmanship or bad design.

Angelina read several other articles that afternoon and the time disappeared as she read. Her knowledge of the events which lead to the death of Phurus expanded giving her some insight into why Phurus would want revenge. She even felt some pity for the man. "This is difficult to read" she found herself thinking and then realized that the light was fading from the sky and she would now have a problem getting out unseen. She dared not put on a light in the study, as that would almost certainly be noticed. Putting the scrapbooks back on the shelf and replacing the chair she moved to the door and listened. The corridor outside was obviously busy. Sounds of people in the corridor speaking to others could be heard. Escape was impossible she would just have to wait.

Sarah had not noticed Angelina leave and was sure that if she had left unseen then she would have come to find her. The seminar over, the Ardons returned to their rooms and the fact that most of the lights were on in the building was testament to the fact that the corridor was a very risky place to be. Sarah began to get suspicious that Angelina had been discovered and was right now being questioned by Seraphus himself.

In the fading light Sarah knew that her current job of keeping lookout was now useless. Flying directly to the messenger group dormitory she quickly found Jonathon.

"I think Angelina is in trouble," Sarah said as soon as she had closed the door, without realizing that Albert was sitting in the easy chair across the room.

"Why? Where is she?" exclaimed Albert now looking worried. Sarah explained the events of the afternoon.

"I haven't seen her come out," said Sarah, "and the corridor is bound to be too busy now. She had only meant to be a few minutes she said that she would be back before the seminar finished but that was ages ago."

"Slow down, Sarah," said Jon soothingly. "Let's look at this logically. Phurus is not back for another 24 hours so she should be safe in his study until the Ardons are asleep. We could go and keep an eye out and alert her when the coast is clear."

"If she is still there." Sarah was almost in tears. "She could have been discovered and then waiting around would be of no use to her and could start people asking questions about our involvement."

"She has not been discovered," stated a worried Albert. "It's just a feeling. I think she is still safe. If she has been found then we would already have been questioned because we are almost never apart. Hanging around near the Ardons' block however is likely to bring attention to the problem. I am not suggesting that we don't help but just that we have to be very careful and we have to have ready-made excuses in case we are noticed."

The depleted group was silent for a while.

"Where is the assembly area in the case of a fire in that block?" asked Albert suddenly.

Jon thought for a while and then said, "There are two I think, one at the front and one around the side between the block and Admin"

"That's what I thought," continued Albert. "The back stairs can't be seen from either of those positions so if we can set off the fire alarm the corridor will be as busy as hell while the fire marshals check all the rooms before reporting to the assembly areas. Angelina will then have several minutes before anyone is allowed back in which to escape."

"The marshals will find her when they check Phurus' study," Sarah pointed out. "So that would be a bit pointless, don't you think?"

"They wouldn't check Phurus' room, Sarah," said Jon thinking through the idea. "They know he's away. They would check if the door was unlocked but not otherwise."

"One of you go to the back stairs as quietly as you can. I doubt that they will be much used tonight and in the dark you should be able to remain unnoticed in amongst the trees. When the marshals have left go up and alert Angelina. Leave the rest to me." Albert left the room.

'Stay here, Sarah. I don't want you in trouble and we might need someone to cover for us here". Jonathon closed the door as he left Sarah alone. She was a little panicked and was glad that she had been asked to remain here but that didn't stop her being worried about her three friends.

Setting off an alarm in a block that you have no valid excuse to be in at all without being discovered doing it was not going to be easy. It crossed Albert's mind that he could go and ask some question of Humus but then how would it be that it could not wait for the lesson tomorrow? Albert had left the other two with no clear idea of how to accomplish this and had simply ambled towards the Ardon's Block. He found himself crossing the path between the student dormitory and the Ardon's Block, before he realized that he still had no excuse to be there. Altering his course slightly he passed down the path towards the medical block. At least he could claim he had a headache if stopped. At this end of the Ardon's block was a kitchen in which the staff could prepare coffee and the occasional meal and as Albert passed he noticed that it lay in darkness but a large window was slightly open. 'Kitchens are bound to have fire alarm points,' thought Albert. Glancing around him he spotted nobody watching and darted into the shrubs, which intervened, between the path and the building. Listening carefully he reached up from his hiding place and tried to push the window open wider. The window would not budge. In the dim light Albert noticed a catch, which would prevent the window opening any further, and stood up a little for a better look. Studying the latch he realized that he could not release it but just as he was about to look for another option he noticed a small box outline on the wall to the side of the window. It was the fire alarm. He realized that he couldn't reach through the window but a bent stick might just do the job. Feeling around in the bushes that were hiding him he found a stick that had a branch close to the end. Breaking off the end would give him just what he needed. Keeping as low as he could he pushed the stick through the window and in the dim light manoeuvred it into position and pulled back. Nothing happened so he moved the stick forward a little and pulled it back sharply. Something gave way and sirens started howling. Pulling the stick back out of the window, a brief check showed that it appeared intact. He immediately headed at a run towards the medical block. He might need an alibi and his fictitious headache still seemed like the best option. Carrying the stick with him he disposed of it into thick shrubbery some way down the path.

Albert was waiting in the foyer of the medical block when Nurse Judith came through from the wards.

"What is all the noise about?" Judith said as she caught site of Albert.

"Sounds like a fire alarm," said Albert, "I came to find a cure for a headache so I will keep away from that, anyway." Albert's tone was grumpy as he might have been if he actually was suffering a bad headache. The grumpiness covered up the breathlessness, which had been caused by the run to medical.

Judith was immediately sympathetic. "You just wait here and I will get you something for that." Judith left through a door and returned moments later with a glass of something clear. "Drink this. It will get rid of a headache in minutes."

Albert was prepared to suffer for the cause, took the glass and bracing himself he took a sip. The mixture was very pleasant tasting and Albert thought that he would pretend to have a headache more often. "How long will this take to work?" he asked the nurse.

"I have to go and see if I am needed wherever the trouble is," said the nurse. "If you come with me the headache should be gone by the time we get out of the front door."

This would be useful to Albert he could go and look curious and be seen walking up with the nurse from medical giving him an easier alibi.

Jonathon had barely made his hiding place beside a bush near the back entrance when the commotion started. Looking up he noticed the curtain move in the window of Phurus' study. Daring to step into a position which would hopefully make him visible from that window, if someone were watching, he stuck his thumb up. He could not be sure that he had been seen by Angelina or even that she was looking but felt that the gesture cost him nothing. Stepping back into the shadow of the bush he waited. People poured out of the back stairs but this was expected and not what he was looking for. Normal procedure should be that the fire marshals would check each room starting at the other end of the corridor and then exit by the door that he was watching closing the door behind them. The door would not be locked, as fire drills always left doors unlocked for safety purposes but the fact that the door was closed would signify the building empty. Evacuation should take less than three minutes and the marshals would double that as they checked the rooms. The procedure was finished in record time but to Jonathon it seemed like an eternity before two staff members emerged closing the door behind them and disappeared around the corner of the building. Jonathon raced for the steps and went up them three at a time. Throwing caution to the wind he wrenched the fire door open and knocked hard on Phurus' door. "Angelina." he said in a voice loud enough to carry into the room but not he hoped too far to anywhere else. The sound however seemed to echo around the empty corridor. He was however rewarded almost instantly by the sound of the door opening and Angelina emerging with a little more caution than he had shown.

"Thanks, Jon." she said as she bent to the task of relocking the door with her little toolkit. The door was locked again in a matter of only 30 seconds and the pair left through the door through which they had both entered, though their actions had been separated by several hours.

The group, now together in Jonathon's room were eager for information but Albert wouldn't hear of it. Angelina has been through too much. "I can see, even if you can't, that she is tired. Let her sleep we will hear about it all in the morning."

CHAPTER 8

Reasons for vengeance

Before the four could get together the following morning an assembly of the school was called, and the fire alarm in the Ardon's building was the subject of much debate. Assemblies were not a daily affair and except for the beginning of term were very unusual.

"A fire alarm point was broken in the Ardon's kitchen last night," boomed the voice of Seraphus. "An investigation is being undertaken to find out what happened but as there was no traces of it being touched by someone it is likely that this was simply a failure of the point. I would like to thank all that came to enquire if they could help but point out that this is both unnecessary and could end up putting yourselves in danger in the event of a real fire."

Seraphus whispered to Therapina sitting on the dais next to where he was standing and continued. "No injuries were reported last night and the evacuation procedure went well but in the event of a real fire it was considered that students could have been lost without any one being aware of the fact. With this in mind I have decided that in the event of a fire alarm in any building the alarm will be sounded in all buildings and all staff and students not assigned as fire marshals should immediately present themselves at the respective assembly areas. Thank you"

As the students filed out of the assembly hall a Senior stood at the entrance and as Albert passed she pulled him aside and asked quietly if he would accompany her to Symphina's office.

As they approached Symphina's office he noticed Nurse Judith waiting on the seats outside.

"I was asked to wait for you and then go in," said Nurse Judith as he approached. She got up and knocked lightly on the door.

"Come in."

Symphina looked up from the mountain of paperwork on her desk as the two entered and, smiling, indicated the two chairs off to one side of the room.

Albert's mind raced. The smile had seemed genuine but somehow he didn't feel reassured. He had not seen anyone until he was with Nurse Judith, but that didn't mean that someone hadn't seen him. What excuses could he dream up if he had been seen?

"You may be wondering why I have asked you to come and see me." Symphina's eyes scanned the two intently as she paused, "It is in relation to the fire alarm in the Ardon's block last night. It was noted that you were seen just after the alarm close to the block and we wondered whether either of you had seen anything suspicious."

Nurse Judith answered at once "We heard the alarm from the Medical block where I was helping Albert here with some medication for a headache. I thought I ought to see if I was needed and Albert came with me. I personally saw nothing at all of note."

Albert was pleased with this response as it gave him a perfect alibi by implying that they were in the medical block together before the alarm had been sounded.

Symphina turned to Albert. "Did you see anything or anyone which you thought even slightly strange?"

"I came up the path from medical slightly behind Nurse Judith. I think she would have seen more than me and I saw nothing at all out of place." Albert wondered whether he should push his luck and decided that this would probably help anyway. "In assembly Seraphus said it was a faulty point, do you think it was deliberate?"

"Just checking all the possibilities, that's all," said Symphina. Her manner was dismissive but Albert didn't believe her, he detected reservations in her tone.

Nurse Judith voiced a statement that Albert had decided would be too much from him. "Why would anyone deliberately set off the alarm anyway?"

"I have no idea," said Symphina, "As I said, just checking all the bases. Well thank you both for coming to see me." The statement was not a thanks but a dismissal.

Albert and Nurse Judith left the office and Nurse Judith whispered to Albert as they left, "I wonder what is going on, that sounded rather serious."

"No idea," said Albert truthfully but his thoughts were going through each step he had made the previous night. Had he slipped up and left clues to his presence? Had the others done anything which had been noticed since? Had anyone been spotted where they should not have been?

The rumors of sabotage rather than the accidental failure of a faulty part were rife by the time Albert got to classes. Angelina caught Albert as he entered the Angel Basics Class. As usual Ardon Humus wasn't on time and she whispered in his ear, "What is going on? We heard that you had been asked to go to Symphina's office."

"True. She asked whether we had seen anything strange last night apparently we were spotted after the all clear had been given. They must suspect that something was decidedly up last night."

"Well, it was. Thank you." She leant over and kissed him lightly on the forehead.

Humus came in moments later and took his normal pose on the edge of his desk. "Quiet down now please." He waited while everyone found their seats and were paying attention. "It is suspected," he paused for the subsidence of a slight murmur, "that the disturbance at the Ardon's block may not have been entirely innocent." Another pause "The point in question has not been used for several months and it is strange that the point should have failed last night without some external encouragement. I would ask that if any of you has any information, has noticed anything slightly strange, however small that they communicate it to me as soon as possible. I will be in my office. Please carry on with your assigned group projects." Humus hitched himself off the desk and left the room leaving behind a background of fervent whispering.

The four friends decided that an Omniview room would be the safest place to discuss matters and they all left for the Library and found that Omniview room Five had not been booked for the following two hours. Sarah did the paperwork for the group and they knew that they would not be disturbed until the end of that time.

"How come they suspect you did anything?" said Jonathon in a hushed voice to Albert.

"I don't know whether they do. They simply wanted to know whether I had seen anything strange as I had been seen along with Nurse Judith while the evacuation was underway."

"Jonathon and I have been talking about this," said Sarah, "and that explanation won't wash. Many students and ancillaries went over to see if they could help but not one of them has been asked to see Symphina."

"Did they ask you why you where there?" asked Angelina her eyes showing the worry she was feeling. After all if she hadn't been in trouble then Albert would not have needed to create the diversion.

"No they didn't and I didn't have to lie either as Nurse Judith explained that we were coming up from the Medical block where she had been treating me for a headache. Symphina seemed to assume that I must have been there when the alarm went off. Nurse Judith doesn't know I wasn't so I think that will hold up. Symphina did seem a little surprised at the alibi though it was never questioned. I suppose that they would be quite sure that

Judith would not be in on any untoward goings on and that would mean that the alibi would not be questioned."

"Something however alerted them," mused Jonathon. "Something has made them suspicious. I wonder what it could have been."

"I suggest we forget about it," said Albert, "I have been through everything that I did last night and I can't remember anything that I did that could have caused this fuss. Anyway I have been given an alibi and that should be enough. The question now is did the venture produce fruit or was it all a waste of time?"

All eyes turned towards Angelina. "It would appear that our Phurus had a murky past. He was the chief engineer at a dam that collapsed catastrophically. Apparently many questions have since been asked about the design and of the workmanship at the Dam since Phurus died. Phurus has been blamed for the collapse. I found several articles which would suggest that Phurus did not seem to have as much authority over the work as he has been blamed for and it would seem that the design was approved by a committee of engineers organized by the Chartered HydroPower Engineers Association. They have said that Phurus changed the designs and the material specifications without permission or approval and that the design as built would never have been safe. It has even been mooted that he was skimming money off the top and that is why he was allowing the use of sub-standard materials. He does appear to have been slated internationally. The notes that Phurus has written along with the cuttings that he keeps in scrapbooks would suggest that any changes to the design were approved, sometimes against his advice, but the approvals were a result of pressure from financial backers and it was much the same with any material changes. This does seem to be glossed over on most reports with only small articles suggesting anyone at fault other than Phurus. In Phurus' notes it would appear that he blames himself as well. He told the backers that the changes were not wise but did not push as hard as he should have and he blames himself for being so weak. Despite this it seems to me that the Chartered HydroPower Engineers Association and especially the financial backers have made him a scapegoat. Several documents have apparently disappeared and possibly several people made permanently silent to perpetuate this impression."

"I can't imagine Phurus being described as weak," said Albert, shivering slightly. "He seems fierce to me."

"Perhaps he asked for more determination when he came into Heaven," quipped Jonathon.

"It still doesn't look like a good reason for murderous revenge to me," said Sarah. "Surely he can take a bit of abuse now he's dead."

"I haven't told you about the worst bit of it," said Angelina. "Phurus has a son whom he was rushing to help when he was killed. He stopped to help other people and never made it to his family. The family was however rescued but not before his son was injured and became crippled for life. The family however has to move every few months, as they are hounded by people when they discover that it was his father that caused the death of several thousands of people in the disaster."

"I can certainly see why he is mad about that," said Albert, "It almost makes you feel sorry for him."

"We now know why he is after revenge so maybe we can now find out who the target or targets are," said Jonathon, "We know that the deed is to be done somewhere in China, but where and to whom?"

"The people whom he blames more than any others are the Chartered HydroPower Engineers Association," volunteered Angelina, "Perhaps then if we tap into the Internet system we can see what they have been doing recently."

The Library boasted access to a very large number of systems from Heaven and almost all the systems from Earth and although there were many restrictions as to what private information systems could be accessed and under what circumstances, the Internet had no restrictions to it at all. The Internet was not even a monitored source and therefore the interest of the group on the Chartered Hydropower Association was not noted. The four friends where very careful that no one was in a position to view the screens that they were using either as even a casual mention of the subject of their research getting back to Phurus would immediately arouse suspicion.

The Chartered Hydropower Engineers Association had, only two months earlier, had a major conference in China at the site of a newly completed dam. The dam had created a reservoir of huge proportions and had spawned a tourist industry which had included a large hotel with state of the art conference facilities. The report that Sarah had found went into great lengths to describe the superb facilities and also mentioned that the association had booked the facility again for their annual conference which was to be held in only two weeks' time. Further research by Jonathon revealed that the dam hotel complex was the subject of heavy investment for the Association as well.

"The perfect target for someone with a grudge against them," said Albert, "Get the hotel and the organization at the same time."

"The next conference is due in two weeks' time in that time we need to confirm whether or not this is the target—how the attack is to take place and try to stop it occurring," said Albert, "We will need an awful lot of luck to sort that lot out."

"Or an awful lot of time," said Jonathon.

On the following Monday morning the four again met in O5 for another Angel Basics class which Ardon Humus had avoided. "I wonder what Grafton's doing now," said Jonathon. As he spoke he spun the dial of the Omniview and typed in the required information to find Grafton. He was expecting the machine to come up with coordinates that were somewhere in Sydney but the coordinates on the readout continued to change rapidly as though tracking something moving very fast before revealing Grafton sitting in a seat, his head supported on a cushion. His eyes closed as he lightly slept. "Grafton's going somewhere. He's on an airplane." He paused, "I will see if I can find out where he is going."

Drawing the view back a picture of a plane of the Australian National Carrier Qantas was revealed. The coordinates still changing rapidly showed that the plane was somewhere over the Pacific. Going almost anywhere from Australia would require a trip over the pacific so that didn't help.

"We need to keep an eye on this and find out where he is going."

"I would bet that he is traveling to China," said Angelina, "Further I bet that he is going to the Hotel at the dam."

"It will take several hours to get there, anyway," said Sarah. "So we can at least get a little other work done. I suggest that we check again in few hours and find out where he is then."

The four friends used the machine to complete the assignment for the week with their new group and then went to lunch.

The friends caught up with Grafton again several hours later when he was found in a taxi moving towards the Hotel at the dam. A small aluminum camera case and an attaché case where on the seat beside him. He was watching the scenery as the taxi travelled the road. A paper lay on the seat unread. The bumpy road would have made reading it quite difficult anyway.

"I suspect that he will just be checking out the lie of the land for the conference in a fortnight," said Jonathon. "I would think that he would simply go to bed when he gets there and any action will happen tomorrow or even after that. I suggest that we all go to bed as well and see what we can find out tomorrow."

The friends were however surprised the following morning when once again before class they met in Omniview room 5. Grafton was not difficult to find but the rapidly moving coordinates and the simple expedient of expanding the view confirmed that Grafton was already travelling back to Sydney on a plane.

"Bet we missed something important," said Albert. "We know he went to the Hotel or somewhere very close to it but he obviously didn't stay even one night."

"He had to be going to the hotel," said Angelina. "That road doesn't go to almost anywhere else. What he did there is the important thing now. He could have just taken some pictures for later study, he had a camera with him in the taxi."

"Could be." Sarah almost sighed the words. "But how can we tell?"

"Any camera that he is likely to have would be digital," said Jonathon, "So any research will be back in his office on his computer. He would not risk having photographs developed and discovered later. We will have to watch him to find out what photographs were taken for some clue to his next move. I will stay and watch here and you lot can cover me for Humus' lesson if he notices that I am missing which I seriously doubt."

Sarah brought Jonathon a snack in O5 before Angel Basics where Humus noticed instantly that Jonathon was missing.

"We have left him doing some living group study for us," explained Angelina not untruthfully, "We thought that would likely be the work that is to be done this session anyway. One us can fetch him if required," she continued hoping that this would not be necessary.

Humus appeared to think about this. "Very commendable commitment to the work for your group however in future please ensure everyone attends the start of the session. The work we were going to do this morning I will now do tomorrow. This morning it would be useful if you could continue with your projects, concentrating for the week on any spiritual actions and beliefs exhibited by your subjects and how they conflict with everyday life."

Angelina wholly doubted that there had been any other work scheduled for that day but was grateful that the four friends could now officially research their unofficial group together with a good excuse for using the Omniview machine.

When they reached Jonathan, Grafton was still in the plane.

"Nothing going on out of the ordinary at all," said Jonathon in response to the looks of his friends, "He has chatted unconcernedly to the hostess and taken only soft drinks. There is no sign of nervousness nor excitement."

"He wouldn't be worried about anything. I don't believe that he has a conscience at all," said Sarah taking the seat next to Jonathon.

"He is not going to get up to anything on the plane anyway," said Albert. "So we might as well get the research done on our official group. I suspect that finding evidence on spiritual influences is going to be a long drawn out process."

Albert's words turned out to be prophetic. Angelina noted a cross hanging from a necklace around Clare's neck. This was probably not for show as it was usually hidden from plain view but other signs of belief were not to be so easily found.

Occasional viewings to see how Grafton's flight was going on were swift and the group quickly returned to view the group Inertia until Grafton's plane landed.

The four watched intently as Grafton left the plane and went through the normal formalities of immigration control, picked up his luggage and then proceeding through customs. None of the four noticed any nervousness or hesitation in any of the processes. Grafton hired a taxi outside of the terminal and instructed the driver to take him to the office. Leaving his overnight case with security in the foyer he used the elevator to the seventh floor and sat down at his desk to work through the papers in his in tray.

"All boring stuff," said Jonathon. "I don't see how that helps us at all."

"Not worth watching," agreed Sarah, "but then we must expect most of this to be boring I suppose."

CHAPTER 9

The flight plan

LUNCHTIME WAS GETTING CLOSE AND the four went to the canteen together discussing the coming navigation lesson with Soarelle that afternoon.

Soarelle as usual was in class by the time the four entered together despite the fact that they were not late. Navigation charts were already laid on each of the tables along with some specialist tools and instruments. Jonathon whom had taken some time sailing during his time on Earth recognized some of the items. "A pair of dividers and a set of Captain Field's Parallel Rules. I know how to use those so this will make life easier."

Jonathon leaned over the table to take a closer look at the chart. Some of the symbols were familiar and some were new to him. Many of the familiar depth markings were present in the oceans and he wondered why these would be necessary in an air navigation map. He was looking around for a key to the symbols when Soarelle began to speak.

"Thank you, class." She waited for the hum of voices to settle and the attention of everyone in the class to be fixed on her. "We are today going to look at real navigation charts which show current information and in the full detail required for the planning of long distance flights. By the end of the day I will expect a full flight plan to be ready for my inspection. The plan will show directions, expected speeds, expected times of arrival and departure, flight levels for a long distance flight. Your homework will be to create for me a similar flight plan for which I have obtained special dispensation for you to fly, in groups of four, at the weekend. I will not insist on your current class groups as the flights require flyers who are confident in each others' flying and are reasonably close in ability"

A murmur of excitement was quickly hushed as Soarelle continued. "The flight plans should be designed to take into account the flying abilities of the weakest member of your group, they should be planned so as not to take you near any Earth flight paths and should be set at levels where you are likely to meet little or no other traffic. The use of standard flashpoints will be allowed, in fact encouraged, but all such use will be prearranged and approved through me."

Jade Jones who was still exceptional pretty despite her 35 years of mortal age put her hand up and at a nod from Soarelle said. "Flashpoints, miss, I don't think I've used one before is there anything we should know about them?"

"A good question, Jade. A flashpoint is a transport node which enables Angels to travel long distances very quickly. When it is used a Flash of light dissipates some of the surplus energy of the flight. When a message is being delivered to the living the recipient often describes the appearance of a flash of light. On some occasions this is a deliberate manifestation and designed to create an impact with the person to whom the message is to be delivered. Sometimes however due to the urgency of a message it is because a moveable flashpoint has been setup to allow the delivering Angel to go directly to the point where the message is to be delivered."

"Does that mean that we are allowed to go anywhere in the world," a feminine voice enquired.

"I would insist that the areas you visit are not greatly populated and that no one attempts to visit any relatives or people that they knew during their lifetime, however with that in mind I have no hard and fast objections as to your choice of destination."

Bradley Symons deep voice asked, "What happens if we get lost, miss?" Bradley was naturally cautious and that caution had actually contributed to his death, as he had been too slow to turn out of the way of a fast moving train.

"The exercise has several built in safeguards, Bradley. Firstly your flight plan will be monitored and will have several checkpoints, if any of you fail to check in within a certain time of your planned arrival search Angels will be sent out to find you. Secondly you will be flying as a group and severe punishments will be meted out to those who leave their group, and finally each Angel will fly with a trace unit attached so that we can track them if necessary. We will be able to tell if people are straying from their assigned course possibly before they themselves know that they have strayed."

Bradley smiled, his cautious nature satisfied but some of the others noted that any errors in navigation would be very quickly known to the monitoring angels.

The class continued with theory of a flight plan and an explanation of some of the symbols on the charts. Break came and went with all the groups continuing to work and the time crept past 5 o'clock before someone noticed.

Soarelle stood up "Homework will be collected by Ardon Humus on Thursday morning first thing. Those allowed to test their plan with a flight at the weekend will be informed by me at the start of your comforting lesson with Nurse Judith on Friday afternoon. Those allowed to go will be excused lessons from break onwards for their preparation. Thank you, class." With that Soarelle left the room to a hum of excitement.

David Peters, speaking a little too loudly to his group, was worried. "I would like to do this flight he said but I spoke to one of the Angels on last year's course and he said that the plans have to be really good otherwise no flight."

"Do you have any details or hints David?" asked a member of another group.

"No but apparently only two groups out of six were allowed to fly in the first exercise last year."

Albert glanced at the others to check that they had heard the conversation his face showing altogether more anxiousness than could be explained by the exercise. 'We must get on that flight,' he mouthed at the others. Albert's finger held briefly to his mouth showed that he didn't want to discuss this further until they were alone.

The four friends left the classroom and went to the Jonathon's room, it being the closest.

"The virus has already been planted," said Albert his voice showed a little panic. "Grafton will not be going back and a lot of people will die. We have to stop him."

"Hang on," said Sarah "We never saw anything out of the ordinary, what makes you think that the deed has already been done?"

"You're right," said Albert. "We never saw anything out of the ordinary but I realized during class that we didn't see anything ordinary that we should have seen."

"The camera," said Angelina and Jonathon together.

"Precisely. He had it with him on the way there but not on the way back. He is much too efficient to have forgotten it so he must have left it there deliberately. Our only hope of stopping a disaster is to find the device before it goes off and our only hope of doing that is to search the hotel."

"Can't we use the Omniview" said Sarah.

"Either way we would be lucky to find it", said Albert, "but the Omniview doesn't smell and can't track inanimate objects. In addition to that even if we found it we may need to dismantle the device to stop it and I don't know whether that can be done with the Omniview."

"We could plan a flight close to the hotel as it is in a remote area but too close and we would be suspected if the virus release was stopped or if some interference was discovered," said Angelina, "Our flight plan couldn't actually include the hotel anyway as it is sure to be rejected by Soarelle. That would make it impossible to do anything as any variance from an approved flight plan would quickly be detected and the Angel authorities on top of us before we could move far."

"Would that be a bad thing?" said Jonathon. "At least then the alert would be out."

"Only if we found the device before the authorities found us," Albert said, "and that would be incredibly lucky. We need more time than that so we need to be able to get close, but not too close on our flight plan and then to enter the hotel without the monitoring systems but with time to search."

"A cute trick." said Sarah, "If the monitoring system stayed still it would be noticed instantly. If the monitoring systems were taken off and given too one of the group the consistency of close flying would be noticed later if it was ever investigated. It can't be done. The time has come to tell Seraphus. This is way over our heads."

"Tell Seraphus what?" said Angelina quietly, her sympathy obvious for a worried Sarah. "There is nothing we could tell him that we have any evidence for, on the other hand I can't see that we can do anything directly either."

"I have thought about this," Jonathon almost whispered, "and I think it can be done. Firstly however we need a flight plan that will get us within about 10 minutes normal flight time of the hotel that will be approved by Soarelle and that in itself will not be easy."

The friends worked in the Library that evening gathered around a large chart of China. Large portions of the maps were almost devoid of significant population so the reasons for picking that map should be easy to explain away if asked, however the construction of the dam had created quite an industry around it and the immediate area around the hotel was now an area which would be certainly rejected by Soarelle The friends were trying to work in landmarks to make navigation easy so that the flight would not seem too ambitious but getting within 10 minutes of the hotel at any point seemed impossible.

"We need to loop the hotel," observed Jonathon, "so that whoever goes can get back without having to catch up and whoever flies the plan won't have to slow down suspiciously."

"That would mean flying to the north on the way out and the closest I think we could get would be about 12 minutes away," said Angelina. "As the two fastest flyers myself and Albert would have to go. The only way of getting a path to loop south would be to continue East for about 40 minutes and then looping through that valley to the South."

"The problem with that is that the flight time is too long without a check point and we have to consider Sarah as our weakest flyer," said Jonathon.

"I could make the flight," retorted Sarah, "but a check in would mean that we would all need to be there."

"Leave the check point out and see if we get away with it, "said Albert.

With some minor changes to the plan to allow more time for the two searchers and to increase the likelihood of the plan being accepted the flight plan was finished.

The evening had turned to night and the day had changed an hour earlier. The four now tired left for their own rooms to sleep.

The four were busy for the intervening couple of days until the flight plans would need to be submitted—presentations still had to be made for Humus as well as work for the other subjects. The four tried to use the work, unsuccessfully, to drive the flight plan from their minds when they weren't actually working on it. In Angel Basics on the Thursday morning Ardon Humus asked for any submissions of flight plans for Soarelle. Jonathon handed in their plan with the others—one group had failed to complete their plan but Humus asked for the incomplete one as well. Nothing else was said and the normal class work continued.

Ardon Barracus had obviously been told about the forthcoming exercise and concentrated his lecture on the rules of flight. Angelina as usual paid attention but Albert and Jonathon could not keep their minds off the forthcoming adventure. They had long ago assumed that they would be going, for to wait to be told officially would have left too little time for preparations.

The whole class was early to Comforting Class. Nurse Judith was in her normal position at the front but made no attempt to start the lesson. The bell went that signified the start of afternoon classes as Soarelle walked swiftly into the room.

Soarelle spoke briefly to Nurse Judith and then turned towards the class. "The standard of flight plans submitted was, as I have come to expect from this group, of a very high standard. One group handed in an incomplete plan and therefore has no chance of being allowed to fly it. However the quality of the work was such as to be allowed a second chance." Soarelle paused briefly as the mixed sounds of surprise died down. "Another submission, though well presented was we felt too much for the whole group of flyers and will need amendments to be done to allow a sufficient margin of safety. These two groups will be allowed to resubmit their plans for a possible flight the weekend after next." This time the murmur was quieted by a sweep of her hand. "The other three groups will be allowed to fly the plans they have submitted although a couple of extra checkpoints may be required.

"Congratulations are therefore in order for the plans submitted by the following people on behalf of their groups. Jonathon, Jade and Bradley. The flights will be flown at all times with a tracking unit and a cloaking unit in case of accidental exposure to the living. Nurse Judith has kindly agreed to allow those groups flying this weekend to be excused immediately so that the requisite equipment can be obtained from stores and final preparations can be made."

Soarelle turned and spoke to Nurse Judith but no one heard what was said and then walked from the room.

"Better and better," exclaimed Albert as soon as the group was out of earshot of others. "An early chance to check out the equipment, and to find a way around some of the restrictions. In addition the use of cloaking devices could make the whole search much easier."

I was worried about that," said Angelina. "At least if we get to the hotel we will not be seen while we search."

Jonathon was looking at the returned flight plan which had a few minor amendments. "As I feared they have put a check point in at the end of the loop that will cause a major problem."

"I wonder if they would accept a member of the group checking in for the group," said Albert. "In any case the whole mission is off if they don't, so I say we risk it."

Sarah was the least sure but agreed to play her part. "We could try it on one of the earlier check points to see if there are any objections," she said without much enthusiasm. She was a little scared but did not want to admit that to the others.

"Sarah will carry Angelina's Tracking Unit and I will carry yours, Albert," said Jonathon. "That should allow you two to fly to the hotel without any interference or problems from the monitoring."

"I've been thinking about that," said Albert. "The tracking system is very accurate and it is possible that they could tell if two tracker units were flying in too close a formation especially if Sarah went to a checkpoint and she was carrying Angelina's unit. It would be obvious that Angelina wasn't where the tracker said she was. We somehow need to vary the tracker units' positions relative to one another especially during the part of the flight where we are not there. I suspect that if we are successful Phurus will scrutinize the logs carefully."

The four were quiet for a while and then Jonathon said, "It is obvious that I must carry both of your units. I think I have an idea but I would like to try it out before I say anything. I will go for a light evening flight on my own this evening to see if it works."

"Don't be out too late," said Sarah, "Remember we have a hard flight tomorrow and briefing is at 9 o'clock in the morning."

"I'll be OK, don't worry."

Jonathon went out on his own for a flight later after dinner. His pockets bulged a little. A little over an hour later he returned saying nothing but his smile told of a successful trial.

CHAPTER 10

Mission In Flight

ALBERT FOUND HIMSELF AWAKE EARLY his mind full with the day's flight and the problems that could occur, the trouble that both he and the others could be in if anything went wrong. The loss of life that was likely if they failed in their mission and a mind troubled with what to do with what they found, if they found anything at all. The window showed a dusky sky and the clock showed just after 5 in the morning. He should try to get some more sleep but he knew that sleep would not come. Albert got up and showered and dressed. His flight gear was ready and waiting but it was much too early to actually get into it. He found and read his flight rules book, thinking that the last thing they needed is to be picked up for some flight infringement in a place where they shouldn't be.

About six a light tap on his door, not loud enough to awake him had he been asleep found Angelina at his door and together they checked the flight plan and the plans they had of ignoring it.

"We should leave the others as soon as we leave the second checkpoint. That will give us more time for the search," said Angelina

"And more time to be discovered," pointed out Albert. "We would fly directly over populated towns and although we would be cloaked from mortal eyes we are also more likely to be spotted by other Angels ministering to their charges. If we leave here, where we scheduled a rest point on the flight plan," Albert pointed to a point on the chart, "we will be able to get to the Hotel without over flying any towns and we will lose only about five minutes in the flight. We should be able to rejoin Jonathon and Sarah just before checkpoint four which being to the south will once again give us a clear flight without over flying populous areas."

"It worries me that we might be required to sign in individually at the checkpoints."

"If we are then our adventure is finished before it has begun and we will have to report our suspicions to the authorities without any proof and risk being thought of as crackpots or worse," replied Albert.

The discussions and the planning took the time and Albert and Angelina had to rush breakfast, so as not to be late for the briefing. They were even too late to see Jonathon and Sarah who had breakfasted together and then managed to miss each other in the corridors. The four friends saw each other for the first time that morning at the briefing and then too many people were around to discuss nefarious plans.

"Thank you, Angels," said Soarelle's voice. She waited the extremely brief period it took for the eleven Angels and several staff to give her their full attention. Addressing herself mainly to the Angels but somehow managing to include everyone in the room, "The navigation exercise is the first realistic long distance flight without supervision and I therefore urge you to extreme care. I notice that all of you have mounted your transponders on your wrists and to make it a safe as possible each transponder group will be monitored constantly. If any transponder wonders too far from the other within a group then a rescue squad will be sent out immediately. If a group starts wondering from their chosen flight plan then as long as this does not seem to result in the group flying over dangerous territory the group will be allowed to find its own mistake though of course some marks for the exercise will be lost. This is the limit of supervision so if you get into trouble it could take us several minutes to get to you so once again respond to the responsibility we have allowed you and take very great care. If in doubt take the most cautious approach." Soarelle spoke to a member of staff who whispered something in her ear. "We have given each of you cloaking devices which we don't expect to be necessary because of the routes that you will be taking. I must remind you that these devices are portable devices and are not designed for continuous use. Use them only when in immediate danger of being sighted by the living and remember that the devices power sources will only allow their use for a period of around 20 minutes total during the flight." Soarelle paused again and looked around the room taking in all the faces of the new flyers in a glance. "Any questions?"

The room was silent for a while most of the groups eager to get into the air or to the Flash Point transfer room. Sam Spenik a clever flyer from the group who had elected not to use the flashpoints asked, "About the checkpoints, miss? Do we all need to sign in or will one of the group do?"

Sorrel again whispered to one of the other staff and then answered the question. "As we are monitoring the transponders and will be able to tell the whereabouts of the rest of the group, one should do. However," she paused, "we have not given these instructions to the Angels manning the checkpoints, and they have already left, so they may insist otherwise. In that case please abide by the wishes of the Angel in charge of the checkpoint."

The room was once again silent. Soarelle looked around and nodded to Humus. "Right, Phurus has been assigned to look after Sam's group. Nurse Judith will look after Albert's group and I will look after the other group. Will you please follow these tutors so that they can do a thorough safety check before you fly off."

Nurse Judith beckoned to Albert and his group as she left the briefing room to a small annex. She was very detailed in her checks and made ticks and notes on a clipboard as she checked off every item. Albert was processed first as she checked the security of the fastening of the cloaking device on his right wrist even taking down the serial number of the unit as she checked. She then removed the transponder from his other wrist and fastened it with a security seal to his flying suit jacket. As a nurse she questioned him about his health and any pains or worries he might have. Finally she checked his flying suit for the warmth it would need to give at altitude and to ensure that it did not interfere with his wing or other limb movement. She went through each flyer with the same detail taking Jonathon next then Angelina and finally Sarah. "You'll do," she announced when she had finished. "Good Luck."

The group made their way to the Flash Point room again in the company of Nurse Judith. At the end of the Flash Point transfer was to be the first checkpoint so the four joined hands in the chamber and Albert signaled to the operator that they were ready.

The unfamiliar sensation of the flash transfer almost made Sarah sick and Jonathon could tell instantly that the experience had not been pleasant for her. She responded to his concerned look however with a weak smile. The checkpoint operator again checked their transponders and asked if they were all right and wanted to continue. He explained that if the group wanted to back out of the exercise they could remain at any checkpoint and they would be collected by Skycart. Jonathon looked at Sarah with concern but she joined in with the rest of the group in assuring the operator that they wanted to continue.

The flash transfer had deposited them on a remote mountaintop and the view was spectacular. Jonathon managed to whisper to Albert and Angelina that they were to fly close to each other and below him and Sarah. The air was cold enough to make Albert grateful of the warmth of the flying suit and he was sure that the others felt the same.

At the second checkpoint Sarah flew down to check in and the operator insisted despite her protests that each of them check in individually. This added to Angelina's worries about the third checkpoint where only two of them would approach.

The four stopped on a mountain ridge about 15 minutes later. This rest stop had been carefully put into their flying plan to reduce the difficulty of the flight and to allow the four to have a brief chat before separating.

"Sorry about this, you two, but it looks like you are going to be cold. I am going to need your flight jackets" Jonathon had taken out two weighted strings from his pockets as he spoke. He attached the strings to the end of an extendable rod, which he extracted from his trouser leg through a hole in his pocket. Accepting the flight jackets and their fixed transponders he tied each to a spare end of the newly constructed structure. "Swap you," he said as he took Albert's Jacket and handed him his Cloaking device. "You might need this and hopefully we won't." He indicated Sarah who was handing her cloaking device to Angelina.

"Be careful, you two." The concern in Sarah's voice was obvious through her efforts to mask it.

"Walk in the park," quipped Angelina as she and Albert left to the South.

Jonathon attached the laden rod to his belt and when he indicated that he was ready, he and Sarah left flying west.

Angelina and Albert's flight to the hotel was uneventful. They kept just below the mountain ridges where any people were very unlikely and where they wouldn't present a silhouette against the sky. As they approached the hotel after about 15 minutes Angelina signalled that they should activate the cloaking devices and the couple disappeared from living view.

Albert waited behind a rubbish skip while Angelina flew into the hotel through the door that was open in the summer sun. Her passage noted only by the slight refreshing breeze of the sweep of her wings, but the clerk just enjoyed the breeze without associating it with a passing Angel.

Her quick survey of the hotel done she returned to Albert five or six minutes later. "There is no obvious hiding place but then for something the size of a camera it might not be obvious."

"Grafton would not want an alarm so he would put it where it would spread around the complex quickly," replied Albert. "This place must have air conditioning vents just to keep it cool."

"I noticed quite large vents in the ceilings but they would be difficult for Grafton to get to unnoticed."

"We have to find the central cooling unit. The device would need to be somewhere close to that so that the effects would spread over the whole complex."

The hotel complex had effectively disguised its inner workings behind a pleasant façade it had also kept the large and noisy cooling and heating plant away from the living quarters some small distance behind the back of the Hotel.

The two Angels found the plant after a further five minutes search and noted the large duct which disappeared underground as it went to feed the hotel with either cooled air in the summer or heated air in the winter. At the point that it disappeared underground the duct was around two metres across and a hatch was evident which was secured with two screws on one side and hinges on the other. A pair of rings was held together by a padlock but investigation showed that the lock was damaged and no longer operated. A small piece of thread was caught in the hinge, which Albert recognized as being the same colour as Grafton's jumper when he returned from his trip and went through customs.

A nearby maintenance shed had a door slightly open and the unmistakable sounds of work being carried out within. Ensuring his cloaking device was working, Albert peered through the door. Slowly he pushed the door further open hoping that if the movement was noticed that it would be put down to the wind. A man called out from within "Who's there?" The sound of footsteps approached the door and a bearded face pushed through the gap. "Come on, who's there?" the voice insisted and the face was followed by the attached muscled body of a maintenance man. The man took some effort to try and find the assumed intruder but could see no one and after a couple of minutes disappeared back inside the shed to continue his work. Luckily for Albert he left the door mostly open as he went.

Albert slipped inside and spied a screwdriver suitable for his needs lying on a bench. 'Risky,' he thought,'but I have no choice.' Picking his time he reached out and secreted the screwdriver under the operating cloak. The maintenance man caught a movement out of the corner of his eye and spun around. Albert froze. Not daring to move or even breath realizing that the cloaking device would stop him being seen but would not cover any sound he might make. The screwdriver was now invisible and the man not being able to find a reason for his disquiet shortly shrugged and continued with his work on a damaged door lock. Albert moved silently and smoothly out of the building.

Angelina was waiting by the hatch. "We have to hurry we have taken too much time and still we have found out absolutely nothing." The screws holding the hatch closed yielded quickly to Albert's manipulation of the borrowed tool and the hatch was soon open.

"Wait here and keep a lookout," said Angelina. "I am better at flying and the size of the duct means that I should be able to fly for some distance."

Albert did not like the thought of Angelina alone in the duct but saw the logic of the move and nodded. Angelina flew quickly into the duct switching off the cloaking device to save power and followed the duct in the direction of the air flow towards the hotel, the cool air actually feeling refreshing compared to the hot air of the summer outside and the air helping her towards her goal. A small light which she had brought with her strapped to her wrist meant she could see quite easily.

Angelina flew past the steel rungs that were set into the duct as it went down into its underground hiding place. The bend as it leveled out was no problem and didn't even cause her to pause. The flight upward at the other end meant again passing a series of rungs that would have allowed conventional access was taken more slowly as she expected to find the device fairly quickly as the ducting reached the hotel.

Angelina carefully but quickly searched an area where the duct split into three smaller pipes, without finding anything. The pipes reminded her of the passages in the flying test, which would be forever strong in her memory. 'Albert would have found flying in such confined space difficult,' she thought as she ignored the pipe, which traveled upward. She explored a pipe, which ran further into the hotel. This soon split again into pipes which she would have had to crawl along. Angelina thought that searching these pipes would take too much time and she knew that this was a commodity that was lacking. Retracing her steps, which took more time as she was now flying against a stream of air for which she created a partial dam. When she reached the junction she went down the other horizontal pipe and at a point where this also split into smaller channels she found an object.

The device was a little smaller than a camera and had more than one battery powering several electronic panels. A glass vial, surrounded by a metal cage like structure, which was part of the device, was held in clamps close to both ends and Angelina could see through several wires a metal tube positioned above it. A magnet fixed the whole device to the steel of the duct and attempting to move it would be out of the question even if no anti tamper circuits had not been included by the builder, a fact that could not be determined in the time that Angelina felt she had to spare. Taking a stub of pencil from one of her pockets she quickly sketched what she could see and with a sigh flew back to the hatch which should offer her release into the sunshine and the now urgent flight back to join Sarah and Jonathon. The fact that the hatch was closed did not trouble her as Albert would have closed it to avoid suspicion should anyone pass by, but even a hard push did not cause it to yield. Angelina was trapped in the duct.

Angelina had disappeared into the ducting and Albert had closed the hatch as soon as he was sure that the light that the entrance gave would no longer be of use to her. A sound behind him had warned him just in time of the approach of the maintenance man in time for him to engage the cloaking device but not in time for him to disguise the sound of the closing hatch as it closed the last two inches. The maintenance man was instantly attracted to the sound and came to investigate. Albert now crouched in shadows with his cloaking device off to save power but with his finger poised on the activating button in case it should be needed, watched as the man examined the hatch. Albert was close enough to hear the man whisper under his breath, "I have you now," as he reached into his pocket and extracted a new padlock with which he proceeded to lock the hatch. After testing the lock he strode off towards the hotel. Albert waited a few moments before leaving his hiding place to check the lock himself. The lock seemed very secure and Albert doubted that he could break it even with the aid of the large screwdriver that he still held in his hand. Because of the danger of anyone returning it was in any case pointless to try until there was some chance that Angelina was waiting on the other side and she had only just disappeared into the ducting. Albert waited.

The wait seemed interminable but in reality was only a few minutes, and then things happened all at once. First Albert, watching carefully saw the slight movement of the hatch against the restraint of the padlock that announced that Angelina was waiting. Albert went to move towards the hatch but the sound of voices speaking made him withdraw deeper into the shadow. The maintenance man and another came into sight walking directly towards the hatch.

"I think I trapped them inside," said the maintenance man.

"Well they can't get very far and if they don't come out now then they will soon get hungry." Albert could see from his hiding place that the newcomer was wearing a badge, which announced that he was the Assistant manager, and below that, was his name, but Albert could not quite make it out. The maintenance man removed from his pocket a bunch of keys and proceeded to apply one to the lock. The lock was quickly undone and the hatch now free of encumbrance was pulled open sharply. The Assistant manager peered inside using a torch provided by the maintenance man and swept its beam down the ducting. The slight distortion caused by Angelina's cloak was not noticed and the duct was pronounced empty. "You down there," boomed the manager's voice. "We know you are in there. Come on out or we will be forced to call the police." The Assistant manager waited for a response in silence but heard nothing. Turning to the maintenance man the manager whispered, "You sure there is someone in there?"

"I heard the door close and there was no one this side. No one could have moved away fast enough not to be seen unless they were invisible."

"There doesn't seem to be anyone in there now."

"Your decision," said the maintenance man, "but I shall make sure it is locked and screwed down properly if we go."

Albert was beginning to panic. Angelina had had no chance to leave the duct because the one of the two men had always been in the way.

"Lock it up then," said the assistant manager after a pause "but check on it in an hour or two. Perhaps again in the morning as well" he continued after a further pause. The manger withdrew himself from the hatchway so that the duct could again be sealed and Albert started to laugh. Albert had moved further away under cover of his cloaking device so that the point from which the sound came was just a little out of sight. The maintenance man lost no time at all and in seconds had moved to a position where he assumed he could have seen the laughing interloper. He of course saw nothing. The assistant manager had followed much more slowly but the distraction had been enough. Albert noticed the slight haze of the cloaked Angelina leave the duct and fly upwards however the two men were now too close to him and any movement might alert them to his presence. Albert stood still and held his breath the two men, side by side, not more than three feet from his position.

"Where is the terror?" The maintenance man almost screamed, "He must have been around here and he couldn't have got away that quickly."

"Perhaps he was further away than we thought, there can sometimes be a strange echo around here." The assistant manager had never actually heard a strange echo around there at all but he didn't want to look as foolish as he felt. "Who ever he or she are they do seem to be having some fun with us."

"Fun!" the maintenance spluttered, "Fun! I'll find the little blighters." And once more the man advanced towards the hopelessly trapped Albert. The Assistant manager moved with him getting closer with every second his badge glinting in the sun.

A stone clanged against the open hatch of the duct and both men turned and ran back the way they had come. Albert dropped the screwdriver that he still held and flew directly upward in pure relief and joined the waiting Angelina.

"Thanks, Ange," said Albert, "I thought I was a goner then."

"I certainly would have been a goner if it wasn't for your distraction," said Angelina, "We need to fly. I know the others would have taken their time but we have taken much too long over this trip. The pair increased their speed towards the rendezvous with Sarah and Jonathon.

CHAPTER 11

The trouble with checkpoints

ANYONE CHECKING THE POSITION OF the four flyers on the monitors would have seen nothing amiss, Jonathon's device which trailed the transponders of the two missing Angels caused enough variation in the wind to mimic the variations in position of natural flight. The group had been careful to fly reasonably slowly up to the point where Angelina and Albert had left and Sarah and Jonathon continued the slow progress.

Jonathon made meticulous notes as he flew. Every significant landmark was noted. Every notable piece of scenery was included. "The others will need to be able to describe this scenery if asked about it," he said.

The next checkpoint which was on the turn of the loop eventually crept up on them and at a convenient remote mountain top Sarah and Jonathon stopped to rest and talk.

"This is as close as I go," said Jonathon. "The next bit is up to you."

"I'm not worried," Sarah lied. "We planned this resting place to be close to the likely checkpoint and they can see all of the transponders still working and in the place where they should be. Why should they ask to see us all in person?"

"I will do the occasional loop with a mixture of the transponders in tow so that we won't be noticed just sitting and waiting. The checkpoint is just beyond that ridge sufficiently far off to be awkward to call for all of us but it should not be too bad a flight for you."

Sarah was now an accomplished flyer but the trip was the longest that she had attempted and she was feeling tired though she had no intention of showing this weakness to anyone else. Jonathon's words of encouragement had helped and she set off without saying anything more to the man that she now knew she wasn't fooling.

The flight itself took less than five minutes and in itself was uneventful. The position of the checkpoint was found but there did not appear to be a checkpoint. Sarah flew around a little looking but still could not find the elusive checkpoint. She checked her transponder, which had a readout of her position. She was in the correct position it was just that the checkpoint was not there.

Flying over an outcropping she noticed an old goatherd and quickly dived out of sight nestling in the deep shadows of a crevasse. She did not think that she had been seen. The presence of the living in such a remote spot was an unexpected complication and she reached for the operation switch for her cloaking device before remembering that she had given it to Angelina. 'What do I do now?' she thought to herself. 'I am trapped in a crevasse from which I certainly cannot escape from without risk of being seen while looking for a checkpoint that isn't where it is supposed to be.'

She peeped above the rock and was dismayed to see the old goatherd heading directly towards her. She was sure that she had not been seen. Could she have been mistaken? The old goatherd had been looking down when she had seen him and a hood covered his head, as she had been above him surely it would have been impossible for him to have seen her. Sarah sank back further into the shadows. The old goatherd continued towards hers with a purposeful step. He stopped no more than three feet from her hiding place. "Hello," he said. There was no one else around so the goatherd could only be speaking to her. "Don't be afraid," he continued, "The use of your cloaking device would be a much more effective way of hiding than sulking in the shadows." The goatherd was obviously more than he appeared.

Sarah stepped out from the shadows. "It was bothering me and I gave it to my friend, Angelina," she said, at least partially truthfully.

"I am Sean," said the goatherd, "A volunteer from the final year to man this checkpoint."

"I couldn't find the checkpoint," said Sarah, "Where is it please?"

"The trouble with checkpoints is that if they can be seen easily by you so they could easily be seen by chance from over flying aircraft."

"Are aircraft common around here?"

"No—very rare indeed, but we were warned that we should not be seen. I tracked you coming in by monitoring your transponder. I thought that all of you were supposed to check in."

Sarah thought things through quickly—this guy was obviously a stickler for the rules and if she put up a big show about going to fetch the others he would probably insist on all of them checking in. Better to play it quietly. "They are all resting on a nearby ridge. It seemed pointless us all coming down as we would be flying close to the ridge on the way back, and we were told that only one of us need check in as the others would still be showing on the monitors." Sarah paused to let the explanation sink in watching his reaction carefully and then continued, "I could go and fetch them if you like but if I do, do I have to come back as well?"

Sean seemed to be weighing up the options. "I was told I was to check each of you in individually. Nice of them to keep us informed when there is a change of plans."

"We were told that it would be OK but we were also to follow your instructions."

Sean thought some more and then shrugged, as much as to say it was too much bother. "Doesn't matter," he said. "I'll clear up here and then perhaps I could go back with your group."

Sean joining the group would of course be disastrous. She smiled and shrugged her shoulders to gain a bit of thinking time. "It wouldn't be much of a navigation exercise if we had you to help us," said Sarah, selecting what she hoped would be the best way of preventing this unwanted company.

"I suppose you are right. You go and continue your exercise. Make sure that you have your cloaking device with you at all times, you could have been in serious trouble without it if I had been one of the living."

Sarah hoped her relief didn't show as she quipped, "If you had been a goatherd you wouldn't have seen me anyway." Stretching her wings she used an updraft to assist takeoff and flew towards the waiting Jonathon.

Jonathon had just been on a quick flight wearing just Angelina's transponder and then as Sarah rested he mounted his transponder on to his trapeze device and then wore Angelina's. Her jacket was much too tight so he left it undone. "I thought that it would look better if we weren't always in the same formation so if the two girls flew together for a while it might allay any suspicions if someone checks. Sarah nodded and did not voice the thought that it was probably a waste of time as no one would ever be that interested.

The two flew towards the meeting with Albert and Angelina.

CHAPTER 12

The Virus Bomb

THE FLIGHT BACK TO SARAH and Jonathon was exhausting even for Angelina. The pair had lost too much time and even with the delays at the checkpoint Sarah and Jonathon were waiting at the agreed hilltop when they got there. Albert could have done with a rest but to do so would have meant a questionable amount of time with the transponders effectively stationary. Ensuring that each Angel had their own flying jacket they flew on to the next and last checkpoint before the Flashpoint that would take them back to school.

Sarah and Jonathon had to give the others a quite detailed description of the scenery that they had flown over so that they could give a reasonable account for the debriefing. Jonathon's detailed notes making sure that nothing serious was missed.

On getting back the four were advised that a de-briefing would be required which would take about 30 minutes and that they were to report to Soarelle's office three quarters of an hour before class on Monday morning. The flight had been long and for now the recognized need was rest. All four retired to their rooms without further ado.

Early on the Sunday morning the four got together. The emphasis on Sundays was rest and no formal activities were ever planned. Jonathon and Sarah went together to Albert's room and Angelina joined them there shortly afterwards.

Jonathon was the first to speak. "Well, did you find anything?"

Albert looked at Angelina and after a pause started to speak. "The hotel is supplied with both heating and cooling through a large duct which is fed from a huge air conditioning plant at the back of the Hotel. The plant is a little distance from the hotel so that the noise will be minimized for the guests. The duct goes underground which helps minimize cooling or heating losses due to weather and for maintenance purposes the duct has an access hatch before it disappears underground. The lock for the hatch was broken and the screws showed recent signs of being undone. At least it made it easy to undo a second time. I stayed out of the ducting on guard and Angelina hasn't told me if she found anything yet." Jonathon gave Albert a strange look but Albert missed it as he continued, "We had a little trouble and then we were late to meet you we just had to fly. I think we could have done with more time but if we had taken longer we would have aroused suspicions."

Jonathon looked at Angelina and she began to speak. "I insisted that Albert stay on guard," she said having caught Jonathon's earlier look, "And it was a good job to because we would otherwise have both been trapped in the ducting."

Albert and Angelina's mission was then recounted in detail and Angelina's sketch of the device she found was spread out on Albert's desk.

"A good drawing," exclaimed Sarah. "How did you get so much detail in such a short time?"

"I always was good at drawing," said Angelina, "But it's a very complex device and it's the detail I missed that is important not the detail that I recorded. It was magnetically attached to the ducting but on looking at my sketch before coming here, it seems that the switch on the right might have disengaged the magnetic clamp and I could have removed the device and brought it home."

"Too difficult an assessment to make in the time you had," said Albert.

Jonathon who had studied the drawing carefully and said nothing, spoke, "Angelina, you have drawn a wire here." He indicated a wire on the right, "But it doesn't seem to emerge anywhere. Could you remember where it went to?"

Angelina looked at the indicated portion of the drawing and then searched her memory to find the requested information. "I'm sorry I can't remember but it does seem to be going to that part of the device that looked like a silver blob in a tube."

"I think you have done a good job with the drawing, Angelina," said Jonathon, "but I will need to be sure of its accuracy before I could make any assessment."

"What can we do about it then?" said Angelina. "I don't see that we have got anywhere. We know that a device has been planted and where and we can describe it but how can we say anything without getting into serious trouble and without alerting Phurus that we are on to him and Grafton which will simply make them more careful next time. I doubt that Grafton has left a trail and we know that Phurus erases any trace of his contact as he goes along."

"The fact that we know where it is located is useful," said Albert. "We should be able to use the Omniview to study the device at least."

"Brilliant," said Jonathon, "The Omniview can only lock onto known markers or living people. The fact that you two have recently been there and can identify someone there will mean we can use the Omniview to give us a fix and then we can roam the site to look at the device directly. We might have to risk leaving a marker to find it again but after that it should be easy to find. What was the name of the maintenance man, Albert?"

"Sorry, I don't remember him ever being called by a name." Albert paused, "The assistant manager had a name plate but I couldn't quite make it out and I didn't think it would be important."

"Well we should be able to trace the place from the nearest town and then follow a car to the hotel or something we might get lucky," said Jonathon, "but we could have done that without you two taking any risk at all. Otherwise without knowing actual markers in the region it would be easy to miss the place in the mountains."

"We should go to the authorities with what we know," said Sarah, "We now have evidence of the threat because we know where the device is physically and they would find it and disable it somehow and everything would be alright."

Jonathon touched Sarah on the arm in a comforting manor. "We would get in an awful lot of trouble, all four of us, and we can't even mention Phurus as we can't prove a link. We can mention Grafton but we can't prove that link either. Although we can't let that many people die and we must go and tell Seraphus if we can't do anything else but it would only be a temporary solution as the perpetrators would be alerted and as Angelina said would be more careful next time."

"We should go to the Library and see if we can find the place," suggested Angelina, "We should do some more work for our living group study anyway. We are a little behind."

"It's Sunday," replied Sarah, "So no one will be in the Library anyway. Why don't we book two Omniview rooms and Jonathon with Albert can look for the hotel, as Jonathon is best with the controls and Albert should know the flight you took, while we do some work on the living group. We have to produce some sparkling work for class to explain the amount of time we spend in Omniview rooms."

This suggestion was instantly agreed by the four and only minutes later the search began. Time passed rapidly for the two teams of viewers.

"We know our flight path," said Jonathon sitting at the control panel in Omniview room Five, "The trouble is that the Omniview works with references and we don't have any of those."

"Can't we just fly the same route?"

"No, that won't work. The Omniview is difficult to control simply moving across the countryside. I tried the name of the hotel but the reference has not been added to the machines in the Library yet."

"I bet that it has to the one in Corrections, though," replied Albert, with just a hint of bitterness in his voice.

"Corrections is linked to the main administration centre and they get all the up to date information but these test machines get updated rarely. If we had a name, as long it wasn't a baby the system would be able to find them."

Albert forced his mind back to the time when the Assistant manager had arrived and concentrated hard on the badge that he was wearing, forcing his memory to try and decipher the name but the badge was too far away and the name escaped his detection.

Jonathon watched his friend and saw the shrug as Albert gave up the quest. "Did they ever call each other by a name?" he suggested, "or perhaps some time when they were closer."

'Closer,' thought Albert. Of course, when he had so nearly been discovered before Angelina's distraction they had only been inches away. Albert forced his memory back to that moment and tried to ignore the memories of the fear he had felt and concentrate on the approaching assistant manager's badge. He could remember the person standing there but he had not looked specifically at his badge at that moment but the information had to be there, somewhere amongst the image within his memory. Albert forced his memory to find the image and concentrate on the badge. Beads of sweat began to appear on his forehead as he concentrated. Jonathon watched in fascination and silence.

Suddenly Albert could see everything in his memory. The picture of the two men advancing towards him and the fear that he felt knowing that to move would mean certain problems and not to move would mean certain discovery. He remembered the distraction created by Angelina. And his eye caught a full close up view of the nametag worn by the Assistant manager, the name clearly visible.

"His name was Peter Percival," said Albert gleefully. "I remembered it from when he came really close although it had not registered at the time."

"Peter Percival. The system should be able to find him quite easily although it probably isn't a very rare name," said Jonathon. "Not too many in that general area though I wouldn't think."

The search found the Hotel Assistant manager quite quickly, however the man was on a day off and unfortunately did not live at the hotel.

"I will find him quite easily without a tab on him," said Jonathon. "The search is not so urgent that we cannot wait until later to find the place and it would be very time consuming just to look around. We will spend a little time familiarizing ourselves with the area perhaps we will get lucky."

"I will do a little more research on the hotel," said Albert, moving across to one of the computer type terminals that would give him access to the Earthly Internet.

Jonathon worked quickly at the controls of the Omniview while Albert found a website about dam construction and from there another which talked about the new dam. An article on the hotel took him to that web site. Reading through the information describing the excellent facilities at the hotel Albert found a passage which explained that the conference facilities were second to none and the remote location of the site meant that any conferences would not be disturbed. A helicopter transfer from local airports could be arranged but failing that a 40-minute taxi ride along the metalled roads constructed originally for the dam traffic made for a pleasant journey to the hotel. The hotel prided itself in superb service and boasted almost as many staff as the number of rooms most of which had a panoramic view over the reservoir. Any wishes that a guest had should be communicated with the Assistant Manager Mr Peter Percival or the manager himself, Mr. Timothy Townsend.

"Jon," called out Albert. "The manager's name is Timothy Townsend. Try to locate him, perhaps he is at the hotel."

A twist of a knob and a flick of a switch found Timothy berating firmly a cleaner for some minor item left out of place in the foyer. "I don't expect this to happen again." The manager's voice held the attention of the cleaner despite being only a whisper and inaudible to anyone else in the room. The cleaner assured him that this was an unfortunate oversight and that it would not, of course, happen again.

The watching Angels never did find out what had annoyed the manager so. However the hotel had been located and the coordinates had been duly written down so that they could be found again instantly.

Under Albert's directions the view on the Omniview screen changed, tracking out of the door and along a wall to the back of the hotel. From there a bit of trial and error found the air conditioning ducting. Angelina's instructions had been precise and detailed so finding the device was simple from that point. The views allowed using the machine included cross sections and Jonathon explored the device carefully.

"Look at that trigger," said Jonathon. "Any attempt to move it would certainly have triggered the device. There are so many booby traps on this that I doubt that the person who created it could disarm it once set."

"We have to disarm it," exclaimed Albert, "Too many people will die if we don't."

"I don't think we can," said Jonathon, "The device is well protected. If we could alert the living somehow, it is likely that they would trigger it just trying to move it. They might not even evacuate the hotel first and then we would have done Grafton's job for him."

"We have at least five days to come up with something," said Albert, "The conference starts in six and I doubt that it would be triggered until all the delegates are likely to be there."

"You have a point there. We have a little breathing space."

While he talked, Jonathon added some detail to the excellent drawings Angelina had made earlier and then created a couple of new ones giving the position of hidden triggers and mechanisms which had been shown up by the Omniview.

The drawings that Jonathon produced were incredible. His eye for detail and his ability to make the pencil follow every line accurately was astonishing. He created several drawings some of the cross sections with notes to show the origin of wires and likely trigger mechanisms.

"The timer is already set," said Jonathon, "Because it is electronic I cannot tell how long it is set for but the device will go off with no further input from anyone at some time. The trigger is remarkably simple. The vial can be broken by the impact of this falling weight." Jonathon indicated a weight in one of his drawings. "The weight is entirely enclosed in a metal tube and the only reason I can see it is because the Omniview can take a cross section. The tube guides the weight onto the vial less than a millimetre below the tube. It is possible that any heavy-handed movement in the ducting could set it off. Lucky that Angelina was flying."

"Lucky it was Angelina at all," mused Albert out loud, "I doubt anyone else would have been flying in that sort of space." Thinking a little more clearly Albert spoke again. "So if we can stop the weight falling the device would be safe?"

"Sorry, Albert, the timer is linked to this small charge." Again he indicated an area on his drawing. "The force of the explosion itself would shatter the vial and almost certainly release the weight as well if that was needed by then." The charge was shaped around the inner side of the glass vial not touching the glass but leaving about a two-millimetre gap. "The gap is there to allow the explosive gasses to build up speed before impacting the glass and makes the destruction more certain," explained Jonathon. "I don't see any way of disarming this device, any movement would set it off, even rough movement around it might do the job. If Angelina hadn't been flying it might already be too late." Jonathon put his pencil down. "I have done all I can for now. I will study this drawing and find out what I can. After all there must have been some way that Grafton crawled away from this and maybe there was a delay pin for the weight that could be reinserted."

"The weight is only one of the triggers," said Albert feeling very helpless.

"Yes, but if we could stop the weight trigger at least arranging somehow for the living to discover it would at least allow them to get close to examine it."

"If there is nothing more to do we should join the girls," said Albert thinking hard "We need to be up to speed on the work they are doing as well for class tomorrow."

Albert and Jonathon carefully checked that they had left as little evidence of their investigations as possible and headed for the other Omniview room. Sarah and Angelina had amassed a wealth of information and were now packing up.

"We will go through this lot in my room" said Angelina, "I'd rather not be caught in the Library if avoidable. You two had better have good news. You have been hours."

Albert glanced at his watch. Nearly three hours had passed. He wondered where the time had gone and then wondered what if anything had been achieved.

CHAPTER 13

Ransom Demand

ALBERT AND JONATHON WERE BOTH strangely missing over the following days. Both seemed permanently tired. Class work was taking more time but even when they weren't working on that they were not able to be found in their usual haunts. Sarah could find Jonathon. Jonathon was normally in his room pouring over the drawings he had made and his nose in engineering and electronics books that he had borrowed from the Library. His demeanor dwindling with the passing days as he seemed to get more and more frustrated.

Albert was tired all the time; his mood determined and dark. He attended classes and then disappeared refusing to let anyone know where he had been muttering once that it was best that they did not know. Angelina was worried and spent some time unsuccessfully looking for him. She knocked at his room door late on the Thursday night and got no answer and assumed that he was at last sleeping but the following morning he was obviously more tired than ever.

Jonathon whispered to Sarah during a period where Nurse Judith was distracted helping another group of students during the afternoons comforting class. "We need to get together tonight. Can you pass the message to the others?"

Albert had left the room some time back to go to the toilet but had not returned though it had been some time and Angelina had gone to look for him before he got into trouble and she had also been missing for longer than was sensible. In any other class except Nurse Judith's, both would certainly have been in trouble long ago. Nurse Judith was always gentle and was everyone's favourite teacher but even she could be strict when she needed to though this was rare as no one took advantage of her. Undoubtedly she had noticed the absence of Albert and she was sure to have noticed the tired and haggard look about him when he came in, though to both she had said nothing. The nurse would also be aware that Angelina would have gone to look for him and Jonathon knew that nothing would be said even if neither of them returned. As it was Angelina returned without Albert well before the end of the class and nodded to Sarah's mouthed enquiry as to whether she had found Albert.

At the end of the class Albert had not re-appeared. Angelina who had been working with Jade Jones for most of the class told the curious pair that she had found Albert so tired that he had simply been wandering the corridors seemingly not knowing where he was. "I have taken him to my room and he was asleep before I left."

"Jonathon wants to get together tonight," Sarah told Angelina as they walked out of the comforting class.

"I suppose we should," Angelina stopped a little way down the corridor and waited with Sarah for Jonathon who had stopped to talk briefly to Bradley.

Jonathon came running up. "Sorry about that," he stated, "I discovered that Bradley was a electronics whiz before his death and I needed a few questions answering." He looked at Angelina, "Where is Albert?"

"I hope he is still asleep in my room." She paused "I think perhaps we should go there, but quietly I would rather he slept as long as possible and when he awakes we can have the talk that you wanted and perhaps we can find out why Albert has been missing so much lately." Angelina looked at Jonathon and asked, "You don't know what he was doing do you?"

"No," said Jonathon. "I have been a little busy myself trying to study the device you found, trying to find a way to disarm it."

The three friends had been walking as they had talked and the conversation had taken a lot longer than it has taken to read due to pauses when other students or members of staff had been in possible earshot. They arrived outside Angelina's door. She put her finger to her lips and opened the door. Peeping around the door she was pleased to see that Albert was still asleep. Jonathon found a book and sat in an easy chair to read quietly and the girls sat on study chairs and conversed quietly.

About two hours later Sarah and Jonathon went to the canteen to pick up some food for the four of them and Angelina sat in silence watching Albert's sleeping form wondering what dark secret had left him in such a state. She wondered why he had not confided in his friends and just before the others came back she noticed him stirring. The tiny knock on the door or her movement to open the door for the others was the signal for his eyes to flicker as Albert awoke.

"Welcome to the land of the living," said Jonathon as he noticed Albert awakening, and then giggled as he noticed that his statement wasn't very accurate.

Sarah asked how Albert was and then Angelina suggested that they eat before anything else was discussed.

The meal finished, Jonathon was the first to speak. "I have been studying the device that Angelina found at the HydroVista Hotel." He paused. "Disarming this device is difficult but may be possible but to do this we need more information which we are unlikely to get. It is certain that we were lucky when Angelina originally went to look for the device because if she had crawled or walked on the ducting she might have set the device off. The device has extremely sensitive anti-tamper devices. It would be impossible for the living to even approach the device without setting it off and unless we can convince the living off the seriousness of the threat then it is unlikely that they would evacuate the hotel before at least taking a look. I believe however that I can stop the electronic triggering of the device by cutting certain wires but these are very close to other wires which will, if damaged will cause immediate activation." Jonathon looked up and scanned his eyes across the faces of the others. "The problem with this is that the wires being cut will alert the authorities and then Grafton to interference. Inevitably the trail will lead back to here through Phurus as no human could approach the device to disarm it." He paused again, "In addition I don't have the skills. It would need extreme precision and that would need practice and we don't have the time."

"I can do it," said Albert quietly. "I have been practicing for many hours over the last week. I didn't want any one with me because if we were found with the key anyone with me would be in very serious trouble. I was hoping to be able to surround the whole device with a shield so that when it went off the virus would be contained within the shield."

"We couldn't hold the shield for long enough," said Angelina. "We would have to remove the device and the holes in the ducting would be worse than cut wires."

Jonathon was deep in thought "Albert, you said you could cut the wires, do you really think you could, there is less than a millimetre clearance for some of them and they have to be cut in strict order?"

"I can put a shield up to a fraction of a millimetre," said Albert, "and the shield itself can be used to cut the wires."

"Can the shields be created in irregular shapes?" asked Jonathon thoughtfully.

"It is a little more difficult," replied Albert, "Why?"

Jonathon pulled a sheet of paper from under his gown which proved to be a copy of the detailed drawing of the insides of the device. "Can you create a shield which can surround the vial at the point under the weight and another to protect the vial from the blast of the charge?"

Albert looked at the drawing and shook his head. "I can't create two shields at the same time. It is probably possible but I don't know how."

Angelina took the drawing from Jonathon's hands and looked at it carefully. "The vial is held so that if a shield can be created to cover the whole of the top and side and covers this part of the clamps it could protect both areas at the same time."

Albert took the drawing from Angelina and looked at the drawing carefully, his hands shaking from the tiredness that still filled his body. "It looks possible," he said cautiously.

"But not if you don't get a good night's sleep," Angelina pointed out noticing the shake.

"We will need to have the shield in place as the device is triggered, then we can remove the shield slowly enough to allow the weight to rest on the vial without breaking it and of course the charge will be spent. There will be no evidence of tampering at all. It will look if as if the vial just failed to break." continued Albert almost as though he had not noticed Angelina's interruption.

"Right," said Angelina, "Albert gets some sleep and we will take it in turns to look for some close indication as to the time that the device is to trigger."

"I will investigate the conference timings, that will give us some ideas as to when a man as evil as Grafton would want to create the most trouble," said Sarah.

"I will take the first shift to watch Grafton," said Jonathon. "Albert go to bed. We will fetch you if we think that anything is likely to happen."

Angelina escorted Albert to his own room and gave him a hug at his door. "Thank You, Albert. It was nice of you to do this on your own to protect us from the potential backlash." Her hand brushed his and she was gone.

Jonathon found Grafton in his office with the usual crowd.

Anne Brown was looking superb in a velvet dress that fell to the floor and although it covered her completely her attractiveness seemed to be enhanced. "The microphone has been set up," she said. "An echo effect as well as a digital effects unit should disguise your voice beyond all analysis."

Lights placed behind Grafton's desk were currently dark but seemed to have been deliberately placed. A high quality professional video camera at the back of the room was being setup by a man in a brightly coloured shirt. Jonathon could not see his face.

"Have you got that set up yet, Barry?" sneered Grafton. "I know this isn't that urgent but a ten year old could probably do it quicker."

Barry, the man in the coloured shirt, probably wisely, did not answer but instead leaned down and flicked a switch which resulted in the lights behind Grafton's desk shining brightly. The effect was to completely remove any detail of Grafton or his desk from anyone standing by the camera.

After no more than a few seconds Barry stood up properly behind the camera. "Ready. Let me know when you are."

Grafton almost pushed Anne away from the desk "I am always ready," he announced, his voice bearing a mixture of his usual sneer mixed with a hint of anger. "Start recording."

"Good morning leaders of the world. This recording will be delivered via the Internet to television stations around the world simultaneously. The time, by the time you receive this, will be a little after three in the afternoon at the Hydrovista Hotel in the country of China. I suggest that those people in America go and wake their President for what I am about to say I am sure that he will want to hear." Grafton sat in silence for a couple of minutes the recording still running. "I think that should be enough time. At precisely three o'clock local time today during a major conference all the people at the Hydrovista Hotel, which is part of the new hydroelectric dam, were exposed to a fatal virus. Over the next few hours they will find it impossible to speak and painful death will inevitably follow. The virus, which caused this tragic event, is short lived in air and will be harmless in about 12 hours. Until then I suggest that no one goes to investigate or they too will also fall victim to the plague that has been released there.

I expect that each of the governments of America, The United Kingdom, France, Germany, Russia, Japan, China, Singapore, India and Brazil, to pay into the accounts the details of which I will arrange to have made known to you the sum of 100 million US Dollars. This list has been compiled from the countries in the top 20 for foreign currency reserves. If any of these countries believe that this is not money well spent then I suggest that the laboratory, which some weeks ago denied having been robbed, is approached for information on the infective capabilities and the longevity of the second batch of phials that were removed from their possession. The money will ensure that one of these phials is not accidentally broken in their country. Of course should one of these countries fail to pay I would suggest that you close your borders. You wouldn't want infected people from their country bringing the problem into yours. I will contact you again in ten days' time when you have had time to investigate the carnage at the dam and arrange for the money to be awaiting the accounts to credit. I will assume that Switzerland will maintain its usual banking secrecy and efficiency or it may find its own population a little annoyed."

Grafton signaled to Barry to stop the recording. Turning to Norma who was in her usual place on the settee, he said "Take the recording and get it ready to send over the internet at six tomorrow, which is three at the Hydrovista Hotel. Ensure that the origin is untraceable." Norma nodded but did not say a word.

By pure luck Jonathon had now all the information that he required. The bomb would go off at three o'clock local time so Albert would know what time to set up the shield.

CHAPTER 14

The interference panel

ANGELINA WOULD NOT ALLOW ANYONE to disturb Albert and tell him the good news. He was to sleep as long as he could and Angelina suspected that this would be for a fair period because of the amount of sleep he had lost during the previous week. Jonathon had booked Omniview Five for the period 7:30 to 9:30 corresponding to 1:30 to 3:30 local time at the dam, so that they should be able to use the machine undisturbed. Sarah had discovered that the keynote speech for the conference was scheduled to start at 14:45 and last for about an hour. Most of the engineers if not all would therefore be in the hall at the time that the bomb was scheduled to activate.

The three friends discussed options for a while and during the discussion Albert stirred and awoke to join in.

"If Albert can't put the shield in place we can still contain the whole unit and fetch the authorities," said Sarah. "I know it would get us into a lot of trouble but we can't just let those people die. I wonder if it wouldn't be better anyway we now have the evidence to prove we are not completely mad"

"But we have no evidence of either Grafton's or Phurus' involvement so the threat would simply be delayed. said Angelina

"As a last resort." Jonathon held Sarah's hand in a gesture of support.

"It will not be a problem," Angelina's voice sounded more confident than she felt. Such a lot would ride on Albert's skill with a machine that he had only a week to practice with.

"I think we should work together on our living group for a while," said Albert. "I don't want to have to hold the shield in place for longer than necessary because the longer the panel is open the more chance we have of being caught."

"How long will it take to put the shield in, do you think?" said Sarah.

"Well I have never tried anything as complex as the shield to protect the phial but if I can't do it in 40 minutes then I probably can't make it at all. I can't hold concentration for much longer in one go. I would say that normally it should take about 20 to 30 minutes."

"About quarter past eight we will turn the machine over to Albert, then," said Angelina. "Let us know if there is anything we can do. If we haven't got the shield in place by 8:55 then we will use the machine crudely and simply surround the whole device to contain it."

The four friends entered the Omniview room just a few minutes before the 7:30 booking time. No one had booked the room before them and therefore they did not have to wait.

The work on the living group went rather well despite the fact that everyone there was nervous in anticipation of the task to come upon which the lives of several hundred people would depend. The clock in the corner passed the hour of 8 o'clock and the tension rose even more in the room.

"It's time," said Jonathon.

Albert reached into his gown for the key for the interference panel and had just placed the key in the lock when the door opened to admit Seraphus. As he entered he was turning to some guests that were following him. "I was hoping one of the Omniview machines would be in use this morning so you could see it in action."

Jonathon had not yet moved the view from the groups living subjects and his hand moved subtly to simply adjust the angle of view rather than the big jump across the world that he had been preparing to make. Angelina saw the start that Albert made which pulled his hand away from the Interference panel door. She noticed the key was still in the lock and shifted to put her body between the entering Arch Ardon and the panel. The movement also blocked Albert's view of the Angel's entry and he moved to find out more about what was happening. From his new position he could not have reached the key and to have moved quickly back again would have been unnatural and would be certain to be noticed and cause suspicion.

"Good morning," said Sarah, getting up from the chair at the back of the room where she had been sitting.

Going the long way around the machine she walked towards the entering group as if in greeting and tripped. Using the Omniview machine as support she caught herself as Seraphus also stretched forward to catch her. The incriminating key had disappeared, secreted in her right hand and by the simple action of brushing her hand across her robe to dislodge some non existent dust the key fell to the floor where Albert managed to cover it with his foot. Any sound of the falling key was covered by her actions and Albert's small foot movement would have seemed natural to anyone who had been watching.

As Sarah had been the one to offer greeting, Seraphus directed his next statement to her. "I wonder if you could explain to my guests what you are doing today?"

"As part of our course, sir, we are observing a group of living individuals and will write a report of their activities for presentation to the rest of the class. The report is to include all aspects of the training so far including the effects of morals, their need for comfort, success and companionship. All of this observation is done with full regard to the Angel law and rights of the living individual."

Sarah then directed what was being seen on the screen and Jonathon skillfully followed her directions noting that when the group split, she deliberately followed David and Jewel, the couple most likely to get amorous should they be left alone. The guest unfortunately seemed interested in the project and kept asking questions of the group. About 20 minutes past until David at last got Jewel out of the sight of the rest of the group and turned to hold her in his arms.

Jonathon switched the view off. "I'm sorry, sir, the rights of the individual mean we should not view moments of intimacy." Jonathon was aware that a hug and a kiss was not strictly what was in the rules but he needed to get these people out of the way quickly it might already be too late.

Seraphus, who undoubtedly knew precisely the meaning of the rules, simply accepted it and thanked the friends for their explanations and time before ushering out his guests to continue their tour.

The instant that the door closed Albert dived for the key still residing under his foot. Sarah continued her interrupted passage to the door to check that all was indeed clear and Jonathon who had not waited even for the last of the departing Angels to clear the door had already dialled in the memorized coordinates of the hotel and its deadly device.

Albert took his place at the interference panel and quickly using a dial and pencil like wand created the start of the shield alongside the phial. Seemingly ever so slowly he expanded the shield along the glass, starting from the bottom and forming the shield between the explosive charge and the deadly virus load. The other three Angels watched as the shield slowly grew under Albert's guidance. No one however was watching the clock. The whole group noticed the flash as the device triggered and Albert was still working. Albert noticed the shake as the explosive device tried to breech the shield that he had put in place but the shield held. Angelina watched and during the next split second the Omniview showed the weight quiver and start to fall, the shield had not covered the top of the phial. The weight fell towards the delicate glass of the phial and seemingly ages passed as the group held its breath. They had failed there would be no time to surround the device with a shield some of its deadly cargo would disperse into the wind of the air conditioning duct and people would die. Then a fraction above the glass the weight just stopped.

When the device exploded Albert had still be working extending the shield little by little and the shake had caused an unintended spike in the shield. The spike protruded just enough to impede the passage of the weight out of its enclosing tube towards the glass.

Albert's breath was audible throughout the room. "I thought," was all that he managed to say. No one else said a word. Two or three minutes passed.

Jonathon broke the silence "Albert, we need to finish up and get out of here."

Albert shook himself and gradually used the shield to lower the weight onto the glass beneath it, and then with extreme care he withdrew the shield completely. Closing the Interference panel Albert once again pocketed the key. The device had been neutralized and they had left no evidence of their presence except the unlikely occurrence that neither the explosion nor the weight had actually smashed the phial.

"There will be major fallout for this," said Jonathon. "I would love to be a fly on the wall when Grafton finds out that the device has failed."

"Grafton's video tape should now be delivered to the various media around the world, and I doubt that they will sit on it for long at all," said Angelina, "We could watch what is happening on terrestrial television. It would take the Omniview system to watch Grafton himself of course but I don't think we should be using those at the moment."

There was no one in the Library as they left and Sarah adjusted the times of entry and leaving so that the records would show that when the device triggered that they were not there. "If anyone knows differently and we are challenged then I will simply claim to have misread the time" As it happened no one knew differently and Sarah's foresight saved them a lot of trouble.

By the time the four had reached the common room, where terrestrial television was often on, the news was the hottest item. Grafton's video had been broadcast without question by one news agency and more responsible broadcasters had then been forced to follow suit or be left behind. Warnings were broadcast that the information was unverified and that the unknown source was being investigated. Someone had contacted the hotel and discovered that the person who answered the phone had no idea that the hotel had been targeted in any way what so ever. One news bulletin reported that a biohazard team had been dispatched by helicopter and roadblocks had been erected to both keep people who might try to leave the Hotel in, as well as keep the inquisitive out. One channel had a live feed to a cell phone of one of the engineers at the conference who informed the world that there appeared to be nothing wrong at the conference and that the keynote speech had been delayed because of the amount of trouble that the video had created. This of course meant little as the effects of the virus might not appear for a few hours.

By the evening the news reports were treating the whole thing as a hoax as no one had even been taken ill at the hotel and no reports of any deaths could be found. Biohazard teams had checked the rooms of the hotels and tested the air and had found no reason for concern. Delegates of the conference had however been told that the conference would have to be cancelled as a more thorough check would have to be made. The organizers argued that as none of the delegates were being allowed to leave the hotel the conference might as well continue but the authorities simply asked the delegates to remain in their rooms. Some enterprising journalist had found a report that minute traces of explosive fumes had been found and managed to get that fact to his editor before being arrested and silenced. Explosive, however, meant that the threat had to be taken much more seriously.

Explosives should not have been there and this meant that the police were contacted and the whole hotel became the focus of a concerted investigation. During the course of the investigation the manager and all the staff were interviewed over a period of the next several days.

The assistant manager had promised the authorities every help possible and he organized for each staff member to meet the police in one of the hotels meeting rooms during work time. He himself was interviewed on the first day. "I don't see how I can be of help at all," he said. "It seems that the whole affair was a hoax anyway."

"Then how do you explain the small quantities of explosive residue in the air that was discovered?" said Inspector Ravash.

"I have no idea, but I suppose that something may have been disturbed and let out a pocket of gas from when the dam was built. A lot of explosive was used during construction.

The inspector was dubious but decided to ask forensic if that was at all possible. As no damage to any part of the Hotel had been found to explain the residue, it might just be possible. "I would like to know if there have been any suspicious people around during the last—say three or four weeks."

"This is a hotel inspector" stated the assistant manager, "We make a habit of being discrete and if we took notice of all the strange people in a hotel, especially during conferences, then no work would get done at all. In addition to that we still entertain people who simply want to tour the premises to check on the facilities that we provide. This is still a very new location and we need to promote it as much as possible."

The assistant manager had failed to mention the incident around the maintenance shed. He had forgotten it and even if he had remembered he might not have mentioned it as he still felt that nothing had been seen and no harm had been done.

The maintenance man himself was forgotten. He was a part time person, who had stayed after the rest of the British construction specialists had gone home and preferred to keep himself out of the way most of the time, preferring the relative solitude of the shed at the back of the hotel. There was little work to do, as the hotel was so new that not many things were yet breaking, but old enough so that most of the small teething troubles had already been fixed.

The forensic scientist agreed that it was possible that the explosive residue could be a result of the dam construction but he didn't think it was very likely. "I haven't been told of any landslips close by or any other seismic activity." The scientist shivered thinking about the consequences of earthquakes this close to the dam. "If that was the cause you would expect that the residue would have been found generally not just within the hotel complex." He paused. "It was a small trace however, even if it had been a recent explosion it would not have been more than a few tens of grams of explosive."

The hotel was losing money while the investigation continued and after two days Inspector Ravash was now being pressured to allow the hotel to re-open. People who had been detained wanted to go home and new people with bookings needed to be accommodated. Deep in thought he walked out of the front door and around the back of the building. Wandering aimlessly his thoughts on the investigation, he did not concentrate on the direction he was taking. He passed without noticing a screen of transplanted trees and rounded a small knoll and stopped. The small workshop and the air conditioning plant looming before him. 'I didn't know about this,' he thought. He wandered forward this time the movement was very deliberate, heading for the partly open door of the workshop. The dusty track on which he had arrived made little sound to give away his approach and he stepped inside without having to touch the door. The room was not small but the view was obstructed by several rows of shelves containing various materials that would have been used in the construction of the hotel and might be useful for repair. Inspector Ravash moved further into the room stepping between two shelves and walked almost silently along them. A further turn saw him almost at the centre of the room. He had not been trying to be silent but he had made little noise. The noise made as the door to the workshop slammed shut and a key turned noisily in the lock caused him to jump.

"You ain't getting away this time," said a voice from the general direction of the door.

"What makes you think that I would try?" answered Ravash, "Who are you anyway?"

"Don't matter who I am, I am supposed to be here and you ain't," said the voice.

The direction of the voice had changed slightly and Ravash decided that the unknown man was trying to get to a point of advantage without being exposed. Ravash decided that the best place to be was in the centre of the room where he would show no threat and at the same time would have the most warning if the unknown man should decide to be aggressive. "I am Inspector Ravash from the city police."

"You should have some kind of identity card then," said a man coming from behind a plywood stand. The man was lowering a metre long piece of wood as he appeared. However he did not let the improvised weapon go.

Ravash pulled from his top pocket a wallet and flicked it open to allow the man, who had stopped about eight feet away, to see the warrant card that it contained.

"Sorry sir. Didn't know you wanted to see me," said the man.

Ravash stuck his hand out to be shaken. "I like to see everyone." He didn't see any advantage in letting the man know that up to now that he had no idea that anyone had been here.

The man took the offered hand cautiously "Bill Brady. Maintenance," he said.

The words that the man had already used after closing and locking the door were replayed in the inspector's mind. "Tell me about the last time that you had a problem back here"

"Last time was just strange," said Bill. "Nothing really happened, well, not that I can't put down to imagination. I thought someone was around but never saw anyone. I thought someone had gone into the air ducting but we never found anyone and we secured the duct and that has not been disturbed since so if anyone was in it they would be dead by now. That day was the second time that my screwdriver had gone missing and was found on the ground outside and I am convinced that I had been using it in the workshop within a couple of hours of finding it so I couldn't have dropped it myself." Bill paused, "Perhaps I could have caught it on my overall and dropped it from there."

"Possible," said inspector Ravash. *'But I doubt it,'* he thought.

Inspector Ravash spent some time with Bill chatting away and placing simple questions occasionally in an attempt to not only put the maintenance man at ease but to extract any relevant fact, but apart from a more detailed account of the incident gained no further information. He requested urgently that a forensic team check out the air conditioning ducting.

The police found the evidence that someone had been in the ducting but the forensic team said that this was unlikely to have been as late as the incident that the maintenance man had reported. However, as a result of this finding, the ducting was searched and the device located. The Hotel was immediately evacuated. This time the media decided that "No comment" was not evidence of a hoax and the helicopter bringing back specialists in bio-protection suits was reported quickly on the world's television.

The authorities had really no choice; some statement had to be made.

Various heads of governments had hurried phone conversations and an agreed response was released in many countries at the same time.

A device has been found which could have released a biological agent at the HydroVista Hotel. The device failed to operate correctly and has now been completely disarmed, removed and is under further investigation. The liquid found as part of the device has yet to be analyzed, and it is currently unknown whether this was a significant risk.

This fueled speculation and rumour and soon the contents of the phial was reported as being a virulent plague with horrible death certain for all that came in contact with it. The authorities did not comment on this at all. Only a few knew that the rumors had got very close to the truth. One paper obtained a leaked report, which noted that investigators had found a sophisticated trigger and anti tamper system and that it was a miracle that the device had not been found early as any attempt to disarm it would probably have failed. It was a miracle that no one had investigated any intrusion into the air conditioning system as such an investigation would probably have set it off and a major miracle that the device once triggered had failed to break the phial. Another paper picked up on this in America and their headline spread across the world—*A Plague of Miracles*.

CHAPTER 15

The Fury of Phurus

Phurus had lost no time at all speaking to Grafton. He had heard Grafton's broadcast video and he was pleased that the vengeance that he had been seeking was to be executed.

Grafton's threat of an even more virulent organism did not surprise him either though he was unaware that the more virulent strain actually existed. The failure of the attempt on the engineers however did not please him at all.

"Perhaps I could get one of those lousy engineers to do your job. Perhaps they could engineer a trigger that would work." The furious and sarcastic voice echoed through the anteroom of Grafton's office.

"The device has not yet been found. When it does it would not surprise me that it was one of your lot interfering." The sarcasm had not been lost on Grafton, the fury had been noted but Grafton was not one who could be cowed.

"No one up here interfered. Do you think that I had not checked? There is no record of anyone even checking on your operations. Tell me where the device was and I will look for any interference."

"It's in the air ducting where it splits to go to the conference rooms. Precisely where you told me it would be most effective," replied Grafton. "Perhaps it just doesn't go anywhere from there."

Phurus was not in the mood to banter words with Grafton and did not answer but spun the Omniview dial to look at the Hydrovista Hotel. Quick and accurate use of the controls meant that within seconds he was looking at the device itself. Phurus noted the weight resting on the top of the glass and the residue of the explosive charge but could find no trace of any cut wires or any other problems. Returning the Omniview to Grafton "It would appear that you chose too strong a glass phial. Too scared to travel with a reasonable one in case it broke in transit."

"That phial would break easily if either of the triggers where operated," said Grafton.

"All evidence to the contrary," said Phurus his contempt dripping from every word, "Both triggers have been operated and neither has broken the phial. The weight is resting on the top of the glass and the explosive has definitely exploded."

"WHAT?" Grafton almost shouted, "No way. Either was plenty to break that phial."

Phurus was glad to have seen Grafton's momentary loss of calm exterior. "Apparently not," he said in a condescending tone pitched low as if he was simply arguing with a child.

Grafton was not going to allow his concern to show again. "You could trigger the device yourself now if you wanted but it will achieve my purpose anyway. When they find the device they will know that I have the capability and they will have to take my threats seriously."

Phurus' tone softened but seemed to contain double the menace. "It will not achieve my purpose and I assure you that me, as an enemy, will certainly not achieve your purpose."

Grafton allowed not any of the fear he felt to show or enter his voice. "I will get to your engineers later. I will probably need another example group anyway."

"Ah, then you have more of this particular organism then. I thought that you had used it all at Hydrovista."

"You don't know everything I do. I always have a backup plan and I never make idle threats."

"I expect to hear your plan to rectify this problem shortly." Phurus did not wait for a reply he had other things that he wanted to do.

Grafton picked up the phone. "Barry." The silence on the line confirmed the identity of the person on the other end. "Perhaps you can explain the failure of your device."

"Can't see how it could have failed," quaked Barry, even over the phone he found Grafton very scary. "I would have to have a look at the unit to see why the explosive didn't go off."

"I have it on good authority that the explosive did go off and that the weight fell but both failed to break the phial."

"Not possible, boss. I know you said that you didn't want too much noise but a quarter of that much explosive would have shattered that phial into tiny pieces."

"Find another way. I will not tolerate another failure." Grafton did not wait for a reply and slowly replaced the receiver.

Phurus had seen the device and could not understand why the phial had remained intact. First he went to his office and by using the access he had to the records checked again that no one had interfered officially anywhere throughout Heaven. He checked the logs of the machines in the correction faculty to ensure that no one had done anything from there. Next he checked all interference panel alarm records from all machines to ensure none were in use at the time the virus bomb should have exploded. Next he checked all the bookings for the Library machines, not that he expected to find anything as none of the alarm records had shown an interference panel had been opened. The booking sheet showed nothing had been in use at the correct time.

The forensic laboratory examined the device. "The weight should have shattered the phial inspector, even if the explosive had not already done the job."

"It didn't or the world would be short a large number of hydro dam engineers. Any other ideas."

"The only explanation is that it wasn't meant to go off. The weight must always have been touching the glass so that it could not fall to shatter the glass."

"So why did the explosive not do the job?"

"It is possible to shape explosive so that the whole blast goes in one direction which appears to be what happened? Certainly the force appears to have warped the device in the direction away from the phial only. Another explanation is that the explosive was triggered before the phial was put in the device either way the device was not meant to trigger."

"Can't see any point to that," said Ravash.

"Could be that the person has a heart. He wanted us to know that he could if he wanted to but is hoping that the threat was enough. The bio boys tell us that the virus in that phial would have wiped out the people in that hotel and anyone that had gone near that day."

"I hope that is no more of that then or we could lose a lot of people."

In a laboratory work was being done on the phial in a bio secure room. The phial was being handled by remote arms in a completely airtight area. Various tests were in progress and several people were sitting on and around a desk in the corner with worried looks on their faces. A computer printout rattled in the corner and a laboratory assistant moved towards it.

"I'll get that," said a man from the desk. His uniform sported insignia and gold braid indicating a high rank. Retrieving the paper the serious expression on his face went even more serious. "This is the modified phial, used to develop vaccines. This phial would be ineffective two days after release. The other phials that were stolen are fully virulent. The guy has an organism which could kill anyone and would keep spreading to anyone who had not been vaccinated."

"How much vaccine can you produce?"

"Very little, and then who would you give it to? The time is now. The vaccine, to be effective has to be given at least 10 days before infection. The virus is so infectious that contact with an infected person will transmit the infection to forty percent of people and death is then certain. The only protection is to isolate. If this becomes a reality then the world will become a multitude of small isolated communities. In communities where the infection is found everyone will try to leave and communities which are infection free will kill rather than let anyone in."

"Surely the perpetrators of this would also risk death as well."

"There are several problems with assuming that they would not release because the risk to themselves is too great. Firstly there is no guarantee that they know what they are releasing. Secondly they are already prepared and can take precautions where the rest of the world could not be warned without mass panic and thirdly they could be protected as a quantity of the vaccine was stolen with the virus."

"And if they are one of the idealistic extremist groups they simply may not care. The situation is indeed very grave."

In the Whitehouse, five world leaders were in conversation and several others where participating in the conversation on a secure video link.

"We have confirmed that the virus stolen is just as infectious as the madman claims. A dozen samples were stolen so he does have the material to carry out his threat," said the American President.

"And hold on to some for some other play later on," said an unidentified voice from a video link screen.

"I don't see him carrying out his threat," said the Singapore spokesman.

"Possibly not," said the German delegate, "But can we afford to take the risk?"

"The man has been very careful to choose countries that could if they were so inclined afford his ransom demand. A cool billion US without being too greedy should be easy among the countries he selected. However there is nothing stopping the man simply coming back for more," said the British spokesman, "I don't see how we can pay this ransom it simply shows us as weak and gives us nothing permanent."

"We have to be agreed on the action to take," said the American President, "It should be all or nothing. I see no value in some of us paying and some of us not. The infection will spread if released anywhere."

"He had the chance to kill those people at our dam," said the Chinese via a video monitor, "and he didn't. I don't think he will this time when the time comes."

"That was simply to prove he could if he wanted to," said another voice, "And it was a miracle that he didn't."

"We are running out of time," said the President after several minutes of discussion. "We took six days to get to this point because the device was not found very quickly. Can we take a poll of those who consider that their countries should pay the ransom?"

The count proved that only four countries would pay the ransom and only one of those said that they would pay even if no one else would.

"We must leave this to the individual countries but I suggest we meet back here in three days to see if any of us have changed our minds. In the meantime there is nothing we can do except to redouble our efforts to find this man and the missing phials of virus," said the President.

One by one the video links were closed down with various grave comments and slowly the President was left on his own to ponder. 'If only one country did not pay then it would be the world at risk including those that had paid,' he thought. 'But I still cannot see a way of recommending that we should be one that pays.' He returned to other paperwork on his desk which somehow seemed pointless after the discussions that he had just been part of. The world could be at the mercy of a disappointed and angry madman with the ability to basically destroy the world.

CHAPTER 16

The Meeting

As the deadline approached the world held its breath. News releases had confirmed a half-hearted rumour that a low level biological weapon was likely to be available to the terrorist. The true nature of the threat had been played down to prevent mass panic. The people of the world in the main had reacted well with most believing that their government would sort it out somehow. Discussion in the streets was split with the majority agreeing that the various governments could not bow to a terrorist's demand. Some claimed that they would do it secretly. Some had blind faith that the terrorist would not use a biological weapon anyway and some thought that the combined efforts of the world were bound to uncover the perpetrator. All however, secretly were scared to some degree.

Albert's small group knew more than most and also knew that Grafton would not hesitate. They knew that there was no ounce of compassion in his makeup.

"Do you reckon that they will pay up?" said Sarah who seemed more scared than the others.

"I don't see how they can," said Jonathon, "To pay would simply delay the time when someone else would do the same thing, and that is even if you could trust Grafton not to keep going back for more or releasing the virus anyway".

"Even he wouldn't do that," exclaimed Sarah.

"I wouldn't put it past him," said Angelina, "I think the time has come to contact the authorities so that at least official Angels could be watching and foiling the plot."

"And when you went to the authorities who would you tell and would they believe you?" said Albert, "We still have no proof."

"I agree with Albert," said Jonathon, "I heard a group of Ardons talking about this the other day. They seemed to think that as the perpetrator had arranged for the first bomb to fail, that he would not actually release the virus later. I am afraid that our untraceable interference has lent credence to the possibility that the perpetrator is soft."

"Grafton soft!" exclaimed Angelina.

"Surely someone is already looking into the incident officially," said Sarah.

"Oh yes," sneered Jonathon, "But then they came in too late and they don't know what we know and I suspect that they will be being fed small items of untraceable misinformation courtesy of Phurus."

Back in Grafton's office Barry had once again set up the video equipment and prepared for the conclusion to the ransom demand.

"The video will be sent direct to the British, Americans and the Chinese via a scrambled Internet link," said a sultry voice.

"I assume that I can rely on the impossibility of any trace back to this office. I don't like failure." Grafton looked at the back of Barry's head as he said it.

"I have tested that design several times since you said it failed," said Barry. "I don't get any failures even at half the weight and a tenth of the explosive. For it not to completely smash the phial would have been a miracle."

"I have it on good authority that there were no miracles available that day," sneered Grafton.

"Anyone would think you have a direct contact in the ever-after," chimed in Anne Brown her ginger hair shaking with laughter. A laughter which was immediately silenced with a simple glance from Grafton which also extinguished her infectious smile. An infection against which Grafton was obviously immune.

"In the other devices I have doubled the explosive charge," said Barry. "There will be nothing left of the whole device except pieces when the unit is triggered, not that I expect that to be a worry to anyone here or anywhere else for that matter. The only problem is that the device is significantly larger and the larger amount of explosive would have been more difficult to get past airport security measures."

"I take it then, by your use of the past tense that you have solved that particular problem." Grafton's voice was neutral.

"I used one of our mining companies and shipped the devices as part of consignments of explosive," explained Barry. "The security services had the correct licenses with them and they never checked for bomb making parts, not that they would have found them if they had. All the devices are now available in the countries that you have nominated."

"Very good, Barry." Grafton seemed to hold momentarily a tone of congratulation, "But had the devices been found then a trace back to us here would have been possible, more care is needed in the future."

Three days later the video that Grafton had produced was simultaneously transmitted to the three countries mentioned. Actually it had been in transmission in encrypted form for several hours being switched back and forth between various world wide servers before finally triggering a process to de-encrypt it and being transmitted to the three locations.

The twelve world leaders had already set up a meeting, which had been in session for several hours when the transmission was delivered. This time the transmission was directed specifically to the government departments involved and not meant for broadcast but it took almost no time to be communicated to the meeting.

"We now have instructions as to how and when to pay," said the American President. "They were transmitted to us via the Internet as last time. Our investigators are attempting to trace the source however this is likely to be a complete waste of time as the last transmission proved impossible to trace. The instructions however are more specific about the deadline. We have until midnight GMT to have the money clear into a specific account. That gives us just over 18 hours. We have asked the Swiss government to allow us to trace the money through their banking systems which they are allowing discretely but they have been threatened with the same fate as the rest of us if they co-operate and are a little reluctant to get involved."

"I can see their point," said the Singapore spokesman, "But is anyone here inclined to pay anyway? I can see no guarantees no matter what decision we come to and no end to paying if we decide that this is the best thing to do either."

"We are going over and over the same ground that we have been going over for the past few hours," said Henry Messenger, the British foreign minister. "The advisers say that the threat has a time limit of about four months unless the organisms are removed from the phials they were stolen in and cultured. Culturing them would require fairly expensive laboratory facilities and we should be able to watch most if not all the known labs with the correct facilities. Our madman may not know of this limitation so delay may be a reasonable tactic, if dangerous. On the other hand it also means that if we should decide to pay up it is unlikely that we would have to pay again."

"At least not to this madman," said a face on a video monitor, "but to the string of other idiots with a similar threat of world wide disaster."

"I am afraid that we are of the same mind," put in Henry Messenger. "The British cannot support payment of this demand."

"Release of this organism anywhere in the world would lead to almost certain worldwide contamination," said a scientific adviser from the corner, "Containment would mean all worldwide borders closed for several months."

"Our economic advisers have told us that the cost of allowing even one release of this organism would be almost unlimited. It would be cheaper to pay the ransom," chimed in the Germans.

"Is Germany inclined to pay the money then?" asked the American President.

"Actually we are against it, however we are prepared to go with the majority on this matter, with the condition that the eventual action is the action taken by all. We can see no point in paying if even one of the targeted countries decides not to pay."

The meeting continued, the arguments going around in circles. Eventually the President called a halt. "We have been here for several hours and now have less than 15 hours in which to respond. I would like to take a poll of those countries who are currently prepared to pay."

Only one country was prepared to pay, several would pay if everyone paid. Four countries would not pay under any circumstances and two had yet to make a decision.

"Bit late not to have a view at all," said a voice from a monitor bitterly.

"Given the gravity of the situation recriminations are pointless," said another voice.

"I propose that we simply do not respond," said Henry Messenger. "I don't think we could be worse off as not all of us will pay anyway and it may give us more time to investigate and find the villain. When he gets back we could claim we require more time and we could possibly help the one us who wants to pay do the transaction and hope that we could then trace the payment."

"What if he simply releases the virus?" said the German representative.

"Then he simply removes any chance of being paid at all," continued the British foreign minister. "I very much doubt that he will be that eager to take away his own bargaining power."

"Make a decision not to make a decision as usual," someone muttered though no one was sure who said it.

"I didn't say that," said Messenger. "We still need to decide what we will do when he does eventually come back to us, but it might buy just a little time to find this idiot."

"I don't think we should underestimate this man," said the Brazilian representative, "The bomb certainly was sophisticated enough and he is clever enough to hide from a combined world effort to find him since the demand was broadcast. In some ways perhaps we should be thanking him if we come through this in one piece. There has not been this amount of cooperation across the world at any time in history."

"I see your point," Messenger replied, "On the other hand does he really think that he can get the whole of 10 countries to pay this sort of ransom?"

"He has at least got those ten countries talking about it," said a nameless voice.

"America will not pay the ransom under any circumstances," put in the President. "I couldn't get the money past Congress without a major leak and America will not be seen as that weak."

"I can see no point in any of us paying if we all are not going to pay. This virus anywhere will spread to us all."

"Perhaps a token would be enough," suggested a voice from a conference screen.

"What would you consider to be a token?" asked Henry, "More important what would he consider to be a sufficient token? I suggest we take another poll. Who amongst us will not pay this ransom under any circumstances?"

"Aye," the word echoed around the room four times.

"Who amongst us is prepared to pay at this point?"

"Aye," said one lonely voice.

"The majority therefore are still undecided as before," continued Messenger. "We need to resolve this before we leave despite the fact that we have agreed not to respond to the deadline."

"I missed that decision," said the French representative.

Henry Messenger looked at the notes he had been making on the pad in front of him. "I'm sorry. That didn't go to the vote, did it?"

The discussion rambled on for another hour and one by one representatives left the conference leaving their final decisions to be counted later. Eventually only Henry Messenger remained with the President.

"Where are we now, Henry?"

"Well, Mr President, we will not respond to the deadline at all. We have no way of contacting him directly anyway and even if we wanted to pay getting the various decisions though the various government procedures would be impossible in the time we have to do it."

Grafton had asked Norma to keep him informed of what money had been entered into the various accounts that had been set up and her silence had not worried him. 'Governments would be likely to hold on to the money for as long as possible,' he thought.

The deadline passed and Grafton was expecting a call from Norma imminently but no call came. It still did not enter Grafton's mind that the payment would not be made. The weapon that he held was so terrible. Unstoppable. The very fact that he had it and they knew it should be enough. His hand went out to the telephone. "Norma?" was the only thing said the question obvious in his voice, the menace suggested in the tone showing that he had not liked being the one to make the call.

For some reason this slight weakness amused Norma but she kept her smile to herself. "I checked 30 seconds ago. There were no transfers to any of the accounts. Nothing at all.

Computer Networks can take a little time but the banking systems take priority because of very fast dedicated lines. I would say that they are all just not paying."

"I suppose the failure of Barry's device has made them think I am soft," thought Grafton and a chuckle at the other end of the line made him realize that he had spoken his thought aloud.

"They obviously don't know you at all." The smile in Norma's voice was almost visible over the telephone line, "You should have given them some way of communicating with you as I suggested." She knew that she had gone too far as she spoke, but it was too late now.

"I don't need you to point out what you consider to be flaws in my actions. I don't give you enough information to think." The old sneer was in Grafton's voice. His mood had run from anticipation to fuming anger through confusion and surprise in a matter of minutes. He knew now he should have created a communication channel. He knew that he had made an error and in this mood Grafton was a very very dangerous person. He replaced the receiver without another word, his actions deliberate and thoughtful, fury coursing through his veins.

He pressed a button on the phone and dialed using a quick combination of three numbers leaving the phone on "hands free". There was no danger of any one hearing as the building was empty apart from him. "Anne, who do you consider is the least likely to pay my demands?"

"I think America might without letting anyone know. Some of the others are bound to eventually though they will ride the coat tails of the others as a group for a while but of them all Britain is the most likely just to say no."

"Thank you, Anne, my thoughts exactly." Grafton pressed the button again twice and quickly dialed another combination of numbers. "Barry."

"Yes, sir."

"Is the device in place in the British Library in London?"

"Yes, Sir."

"And it will not fail this time?"

"No, Sir." Barry paused. "There won't be much left of the device but dust this time," he continued.

"Thank you, Barry."

Grafton once again pressed the button twice. This time he dialed a lengthy international number in full. "Goodbye, Britain." He said aloud to himself.

Albert and Jonathon in Omniview room Five listened incomplete disbelief. Albert recovered quickest and reached into his pocket for the interference key. "Quick British Library, London," he snapped.

Jonathon awaking from what seemed to him a stupor quickly located the Library while Albert unlocked the interference panel. The Omniview showed dust swirling around inside the Library. Certainly the device had already exploded in the centre of the room there lay face upward the body of a security guard not yet dead but squirming in agony.

"That could have been caused by the explosion," said Jonathon, "But that guard has probably been infected and dying so it would not matter."

"So will the rest of Britain if we don't do something." Albert's mind was working overtime studying the pictures on the screen of the Omniview. "The explosion wasn't big enough to break the windows." he exclaimed, "The Library contains old delicate manuscripts and has a controlled environment. We learnt that on a school trip. The virus may not have got out of the Library yet."

"It will if anyone comes to investigate though," said Jonathon, "See if you can contain the building."

"That's easy," said Albert, his hands moving quickly over the controls, "There is a method to do that quickly but now we have it contained, what do we do?"

"Burn it," said Jonathon. "The explosion could have started a fire and it should cause the air to get hot enough to kill the virus."

"How about any people inside?" agonized Albert.

"Any people in there are already dead or will be within hours and so will a lot of others if you release that containment screen before those bugs are taken care of."

Albert used the panel to start a fire in the enclosed building. He wanted to build up the temperature and he did this using a fireball created by the Omniview machine. The Omniview machine fed the fire directly with fuel and as the fire burnt the temperature rose sharply. The picture got brighter and brighter as the building began to burn and the heat caused books to catch fire. With the temperature high enough in the building to kill anything living, Albert allowed the fires to die down and they quickly went out as the oxygen needed to feed the fire was used up. The heat had finished of the virus—at least Jonathon thought that this was likely and there was little else that they could do but watch. They didn't have to watch for long as people came to investigate the explosion and the fire whose glow could have been seen through the windows.

"Can you let anyone through the screen but still keep it intact, Albert?"

"I think so. Why?"

"We need to know whether the virus is gone before you let the screen go."

"I could be condemning someone to death!" Albert exclaimed, "Isn't there another way?"

"Not unless you want to stay here forever or simply take the risk and let the screen go. Come on, Albert. I know it's difficult but we have no choice."

"Go and get Seraphus," said Albert. "He'll know what to do."

"And while I'm gone you get a visit from Phurus and then all the evidence will be gone and probably you as well and the screen will have gone as well. Let someone in."

Albert wrapped an extension to the screen around a passing runner who was investigating and released a door in front of him and allowed him to enter the building. Using the screen he pushed the door closed behind him pushing in some external air with him. Albert and Jonathon knew that the virus when concentrated could produce difficulty breathing and great pain in seconds. The runner stopped to take in the scene of devastation around him and turned to run from the heat. Albert held the door shut forcing the runner to take gulps breath in an effort to break free. For as long he dare hold him there without serious injury, Albert kept the door shut. The runner fought harder and none of the symptoms of the deadly bug were apparent.

"That should be enough." Jonathon tapped Albert on the shoulder and Albert allowed a fireman to break down the door and released the screen.

CHAPTER 17

Fire Investigation and Hidden Secrets

ALBERT AND JONATHON WENT BACK to the dormitories and Jonathon went to fetch the others. Angelina was the first to arrive opening the door on the first knock without waiting for a reply. She caught the tears in Albert's eyes and immediately sat on the bed beside him wrapping her arms in comfort around him without a word.

"I killed him," said Albert wiping away the tears which he wished she had not seen.

"I doubt it," said Angelina softly the back of her hand wiping away some of those tears.

"Then I used someone else as a test I could have killed him as well".

"But you didn't and I am sure that it was necessary. Tell me what happened.

"He was incredible, a major hero" The door opened to admit Jonathon trailing Sarah. Sarah had obviously been told the story in brief as they travelled.

The story was then explained to Angelina by Jonathon. Albert interrupted almost not at all, plainly upset with what he still saw as killing the guard.

Angelina never let him go, her arm comforting him all the time. When the story was finished she leant over and kissed him lightly and tenderly on the forehead. "He would have died in pain and misery anyway even if the injuries from the explosion had not been enough to kill him, and you could have saved millions of people."

The meeting in the Prime minister's study the next day was only attended by four people—Henry Messenger, William Harrington, the Prime minister himself, and a home office pathologist. A video link had also been set up to the American President.

Henry spoke first. "Could you explain to all those listening your findings?"

"I am Osbourne Green," said the pathologist, "and I am chief pathologist at the main London Laboratories. I was running near the Library last night and went to investigate a fire at the Library. The fire, I think you can confirm from the Fire chief, was strange in the extreme however I have asked that the chief allows only those who need to know see any report or be allowed inside that building."

"He is to report directly to me and no one else," interceded Henry.

"As Henry knows I was part of the British team which was investigating the incident 11 days ago I thought that perhaps this was the start of the attack and you ought to know. I have ordered that all those that were near to be put into immediate isolation. I don't believe that the virus escaped, if that was the purpose of the explosion, which I am assuming it was, but it will keep our madman guessing and explain why there are no reports of deaths." Osbourne Green continued, "The fire so I have been told must have reached a fair temperature because some books actually caught fire because of heat but apart from that very little actually seemed to have been burnt. The fire claimed only one victim the guard or night watchman if you prefer. Strangely he was killed by suffocation as the fire sucked all the oxygen out of the air." He paused to collect his thoughts before continuing running his fingers through graying hair. "I noticed lesions in the mouth and throat which would not have been caused by the heat so I had the body sealed in a safe manner and then taken directly to the laboratory." He paused again this time for effect but everyone just waited for him to continue, "Gentleman, if the lack of oxygen hadn't killed him or the heat then he would have died in pain within the following couple of days anyway. He had been exposed to some exceptionally potent organism. Not only that, I believe he was exposed to a massive dose of that organism and therefore its effects where almost instant. In smaller doses it would take several hours to create any symptoms and then possibly one or two days more to die. I have not seen anything like this before. The body is now in isolation and there is a blanket silence imposed on all information."

Then a voice on a video monitor asked, "Where to from here?"

"We are flying one of the laboratory experts from where the virus was stolen, to look at the body as quickly as possible" said the Prime minister. "It won't be comfortable as we are using a military jet for speed but he should be here soon. He will be able to confirm that the man was infected."

"I have requested the fire investigator to be discreetly brought here as soon as he has reached any conclusions at all," said Henry.

An intercom bleeped on the desk. "A fireman here to see you sir. He says you are expecting him."

"Send him in, please."

The door opened and a tall man with a briefcase entered. "Actually a fire investigator. Used to be a fireman, but that was some time ago now." The big man smiled, "Tom Cleveland, pleased to meet you."

"Thanks for coming, Tom," said Henry. "What can you tell us about the fire?"

"The fire was strange, sir. I have never seen anything like it before."

"How strange?" questioned the face on the video monitor.

"Sorry, Tom. I should have mentioned we have a connection with the American President."

"No problem. As I was saying the fire got very hot very very quickly. There was evidence of spontaneous combustion of some of the books though some were started before the fire really got hot. For a fire to get that hot that quickly there had to be accelerant used but I could find no residue at all. And then there was the lack of ash." He paused. "Let me explain when anything burns there has to be something left, combustion products, but I found nothing. There was simply not enough fuel burnt to create the heat. Then the fire extinguished itself. I have known fire do this in the past in sealed rooms but this was not sealed enough for that. There should have been a steady stream of oxygen at least enough to have allowed some small fire but the fire was completely out by the time Mr Green entered."

"Could this have been set up deliberately so that the fire would behave as you describe?" said the Prime Minister.

"I don't know how unless someone was a magician. I wouldn't know how to set this one up even leaving a pile of evidence behind but to hide all the traces as well." His voice trailed off but then continued, "Nothing short of a miracle that the fire stopped so quickly. Those books could have made a difficult fire to control."

"Thank you, Tom. I look forward to your written report as soon as you can get it to me. You can assume that any mention of the fire or its investigation is classified," said Henry.

After the fire investigator had gone the Prime minister spoke first. "I think we can assume that this was a real attack and some yet unexplained circumstance has saved us from serious consequences. I don't believe we can take this madman's threats as anything but deadly serious after this."

"I don't think this was meant to be a warning. Right now he is thinking that Britain is dying," said Henry.

"Strangely however Britain is probably now the safest place," said the President. "I doubt that he had two devices in any country so Britain can be regarded as relatively safe. I think the others should be told of this incident, confidentially of course, and I think that we can expect another communication shortly."

Grafton got over his fury quickly he had lost a cool hundred million which both he and Anne reckoned that he stood little chance of getting anyway. They had also given a massive wake up call to the rest. Deaths in Britain could only be covered up for so long and the heads of the other governments would be kept informed anyway. Acting quickly he had asked Barry, Anne and Norma to come to the office. They arrived within 20 minutes. "Barry, set up the equipment please. We will later speak to a few world leaders. I would like them to able to see and hear enough detail to be sure I am not bluffing but not enough to be able to make any identification."

"I will put in a digital voice filter and with some clever lighting you should get the correct effect," replied Barry.

"I do not need to know the details, Barry. Norma, can you get ready to throw a link to some private networks? When we get given the IP addresses and passwords I would like to stream video direct to the world. Anne, watch any attempts to trace the links. I don't even want them to get as far as to trace the country."

"Bit optimistic expecting them to give you IPs and passwords direct to international leaders, isn't it?" asked Barry.

"I think they might just be accommodating. Norma, when you are set up, can you set up a link to some government departments and a dummy secure e-mail account so they can give us a way in? Then close everything down so that in two hours we can flash the information down for the links to talk with some nice accommodating world leaders. That should give them enough time to soften up."

The communications which arrived in various government offices in various countries were of course immediately traced. All of them appeared to have come from somewhere completely trustworthy. One of them appeared to have come from the same government office that was trying to trace it. The messages contained within them where quickly communicated to the relevant government heads. Each e-mail requested direct access to government private networks with passwords sufficient to stream video. Several high ranking officials wondered about giving away such sensitive information but orders came down from the top to comply. When Norma flashed down the replies two hours later the correct information from all nine countries was available. The e-mail address to which the replies were sent was monitored so that a trace could be made of any attempt to pick up the emails. It was noted by eight countries that the e-mails were being accessed. The speed with which any trace information was stripped off and dumped surprised some of them and only two managed to get a trace on the line quickly enough to track the information to a server, one managed to get to the next server but then the speed of the transaction left them behind and by the time the trace had got to the third server the line had gone and a trace erase program had already deleted any further possibility of continuing.

Grafton was happy to let the leaders of his target countries stew for a while. He was actually enjoying the thought of panic amongst the leaders of the world. He smiled as he thought of the people now dying in Britain certainly that would make everyone else sit up and take notice. The time gave Anne and Norma time to set up links and ensure that no trace could be successfully completed.

In the so called "free world" things like this cannot go unnoticed for long and the press picked up on the right people being in the wrong place, the quarantined people being held in London was correctly attributed to the previous threat of the virus. The press however could not get to any of the quarantined people and incorrectly assumed that they were seriously sick. This latter assumption was just what the British wanted as it also kept their adversary in the dark. The British official word was a mixture of "Just precautionary" and "No comment" which just left the press to make up stories.

In many countries of the world, not just in those threatened, hotlines and conferences were set up. Links were forged so that several countries could listen if any of them were contacted. This last precaution turned out to be completely unnecessary as the communication came through to all of them at the same time.

Grafton's voice held a menace which was unmistakable. "I am about to say something and despite the fact that this is a two way communication I would suggest that interruption would be foolhardy. By now you will be aware that I have the means to infect countries should I require to. You should be in no doubt that I will use these means if there is any further unauthorized delays. It is just before 10 in the morning in Britain and some probably a large number of that country's population is now in various stage of dying. It is unfortunate that Britain will not be contributing to the fund however I suspect that despite quick and extensive quarantine efforts, that they will shortly have a country of very sick people on their hands and will need their 100 million to cope, plus quite a bit more. I would suggest that you all close your borders to anything that comes from Britain—of course that will hit your economies considerably but then not as much as allowing that infection to spread to your countries would. I have noted the lack of seriousness which you attached to my previous ultimatum and suggest that you do not make the same mistake again." Grafton's voice had lowered to almost a whisper. "I trust you are all paying attention." Grafton paused. No one said anything, not that Grafton expected a reply. "I will expect the full nine hundred million dollars to be in the accounts in 12 hours' time. There will be no further warnings. I will not accept banking hours or any other excuses. If your banks are closed then wake the executives and get them open. I will not accept the excuse that you require permissions from your various government bodies for the expenditure. That is not my concern. You have had plenty of time to get it prior to this point. Are there any questions?"

"How do we contact you if we have any problems?" said the American President.

The sneer in Grafton voice was so strong it was almost visible "Use the same email that you used before. We will randomly monitor its content but I suggest that you find that any problems are solvable within the next 12 hours. I will not accept any excuses."

The silence that followed seemed to last for ages yet the time that passed was easily less than a minute.

"I suggest, then, gentlemen, that you have work to do." The link went dead and Grafton was gone.

The President looked glanced at a technician in the corner who was working hard at some electronic gismo. "Sorry, sir. The trace kept hitting a block point and going around in circles. The encryption changed every few seconds. Whoever set the link up knew what they were doing. I couldn't even tell you which continent they were on let alone a close location."

"Thank you, anyway," said the President, as he turned to the other people in the room, "We need to get the money ready and we need to speak to Congress in secret session."

"Yes, sir," said several people in unison.

The slow workings of nine countries suddenly tried to get into high gear in secret while the rest of the world ran its normal course.

Meetings of world leaders by videophone and in person met with few decisions being made. Most world leaders could have authorized the expenditure in an emergency but each recognized that to do so was political suicide and still they searched for a method in which they could win in such an impossible position. Emergency sessions of parliaments were set up behind closed doors. In each of nine countries $100 million was prepared and held with the hope that it would not be needed but awaiting the decision to transfer it should that decision be made.

World leaders however had received the information that Britain thought that it had completely contained the threat. No one had been infected. World leaders always seemed to think that they could get away with anything and the knowledge that Britain had done so meant of course that they could do so as well. World leaders of course had no idea that a small group of trainee Angels had been taking such an interest and only their intervention had contained the outbreak and that had been a very close thing. World leaders decided eventually that they could not pay to terrorists and that they couldn't pretend not to pay the terrorists, as they couldn't hide that kind of money. World leaders decided not to pay and that the threat was a bluff. World leaders as usual were wrong.

Grafton was sure that the money would this time be forthcoming. Grafton was sure that infection would shortly be reported as a fact in Britain and was sure that this time nothing could go wrong. Grafton unusually was also wrong.

CHAPTER 18

The world according to the view from Omniview room Five

THEIR CLASSES HAD FINISHED AND in Omniview room five, four friends talked softly. They, unlike, the press could watch the people held in quarantine and knew that the only thing wrong with them was boredom together with a growing anger at being held for no reason against their will.

"This is completely out of hand," said Angelina, "We should tell the authorities what is going on."

"I agree," said Sarah, nodding her head looking at the boys who surprisingly did not say anything at all.

Albert eventually looked up straight into Angelina's eyes and nodded. He was still feeling the effects of the strain of events and the passage of a few hours had left him still depressed and worried.

Angelina got up and gave him a quick hug. "Sarah and I will go and report to Seraphus. He will know what to do."

Sarah and Angelina left the room on the way to Seraphus' office. Jonathon spun the dial of the Omniview to Grafton's office, not really knowing why.

Grafton was sitting on the edge of his desk, which was unusual for him. His attitude showed a tenseness, which neither of the friends had seen before. On his desk was a stack of pictures and a small box on which a single red light was blinking.

"Look," said Albert in a whisper as if he was afraid that Grafton could hear.

Jonathon looked where Albert was pointing on the screen. The top document was a list of ten items and one had been crossed out with a scribbled bold line.

"Zoom in on that," said Albert.

Jonathon zoomed in on the document, which could now be seen as a list of countries with an address and what looked like a telephone number for each of them. The address which had been crossed out was almost illegible but the word Library could still be seen.

"The locations of the virus bombs," breathed Albert. "Quick, write them down."

Jonathon picked up a pen and across a page of his report book he began to write as Albert read out the information on the list. The two friends worked quickly but accurately and soon had the information copied and were able to listen to Grafton finishing his conversation.

"Norma, please monitor the e-mail in swift bursts."

"They cannot trace it even if we left it open all day," replied Norma.

"Nevertheless I don't want it left open for any significant time." His voice suggested that Norma should be careful with anything that could be construed as questioning his requests. "I don't expect to have to use this list," he said and turned to point at the document. His eyes spotted the blinking red light and he swiftly covered all the documents on the desk and almost shouted "OUT! All of you."

When all of the others had left the room Grafton's sneer returned in full force. "Still checking up on me my feathered friend," he said apparently to no one at all. To the idle watcher it would be unsurprising that he received no answer but this just seemed to annoy him more. "You only gave me this thing so that I knew when you wanted to speak to me, so what game are you playing this time?" Still he received no answer. "OK, play your little games and don't worry I will get your precious hydro engineers."

The two watching Angels suddenly knew that Grafton was speaking to Phurus but that Phurus was not answering probably because Phurus wasn't even aware that he was being spoken to. Jonathon and Albert together realized at the same time what the box with the blinking light was but Jonathon voiced it first. "An Omniview Detector."

Jonathon spun the dial of the Omniview so that the view changed randomly. The box on Grafton's desk stopped its blinking but by now of course the two could no longer see this.

"Those things are not supposed to exist," said Albert, "and they are not supposed to work in view mode anyway."

"This is going to make things even more risky. If Grafton reports this to Phurus then he will know for sure that someone was watching Grafton this afternoon." Jonathon paused. "And I don't see him not reporting it to him even as just a way of getting to him."

"Perhaps he will think it was just a random chance overview by some other Angel somewhere else," mused Albert not even convincing himself.

"I think we got the important information anyway," said Jonathon.

"Don't you think it was strange though," Albert said thoughtfully, "the way he covered up all those documents when he thought the Phurus was watching as though he didn't want Phurus to have that information?"

"Which must mean that Phurus doesn't know his plans. I wonder just how much he does know."

"I wonder just how much he doesn't know." The question in Albert's voice was obvious but no reply was possible as the girls burst in a little breathless as they had come as quickly as they dared without raising any suspicions.

"Is Seraphus coming?" said Albert looking at Angelina who shook her head.

"We couldn't tell him," Said Sarah.

"He wasn't there," put in Angelina. "He has gone to Skyhouse and may be gone several days."

"And worse," continued Sarah. "Phurus is in charge while he is gone."

By now the girls were calming down after their rush back to the Library.

"Tell us the story but it's not safe here," said Jonathon. "We will explain later but we need to be somewhere else, almost anywhere else".

Moments later the four left the Library and hurried to Angelina's room. The boys told their story first and when they had finished Angelina whistled.

"Have you amended the Omniview booking sheet so it looks as though you weren't there?" said Sarah.

"Luckily I forgot to book it in the first place," replied Jonathon. "Not that I expect that that will save us this time as Phurus, when he finds out will be doing a very good job of investigating. Still can't be changed now. Tell us what happened on your trip to find Seraphus."

"When we left here Sarah was a little panicky because things were getting so much out of hand."

"I was!" interrupted Sarah.

"Ok we both were," continued Angelina, "so we hurried up to the office and rushed in having knocked once and not waited for a reply."

"It was a hell of a shock to see Phurus sitting at Seraphus' desk," said Sarah.

Angelina glanced at Sarah as if to say that the interruption was unwarranted. "As Sarah said it was quite a shock, but we now had a problem of explaining why we would rush in on Seraphus obviously excited and of course we could not tell him the original reason why we were there."

"I didn't have to fain surprise. I said sorry and said I wanted to see Seraphus and apologized again for bursting in."

"Phurus said that entering without knocking was not to be encouraged and explained that as Seraphus had been called to Skyhouse to advise what should be done about some threat on Earth he had been left in charge. Any school business was his to deal with and anything should therefore be discussed with him."

"She was brilliant," said Sarah, her grin being the first smile that the boys had seen recently.

"I am not sure that Phurus bought it," continued Angelina. "But I told him that I had this idea about a end of year flying pageant which could involve several students and some of the Ardon's as well and that the idea if it was to be done needed to done quickly as it was getting close to the end of term and it would take a lot of organizing. He seemed to think it was a good idea and asked that I create some more detailed plans and then bring them to him in the next few days. In principle it was a good idea but the students must do most of the work and he reminded us that the end of term exams will be an important drain on the time of the people involved and that they should come first. I am afraid that I have landed us all with even more work."

"We have no choice then to do this ourselves," said Albert. "None of the resources of the school are likely to be available to us but I don't see how we could do all this ourselves I don't know enough about the Omniview's capabilities and it took several minutes to neutralize the bomb in London. We need to have some idea of what time we have to prepare and without going back to Grafton's office."

"I will pop into the Library and use Omniview three to have a look in on the Whitehouse. They are bound to be having some meeting there and a few minutes listening should tell us all we need to know about any new deadlines," said Jonathon.

"Good idea not to use O5," said Angelina, "Keep anyone who notices guessing a little longer."

"You go and run the errand in the Library, Jon, and we will meet later after dinner," said Sarah.

Jonathon left the room and headed to the Library.

Angelina spoke up. "If you have any spare time or can't sleep then have a few thoughts on the flying pageant. I am going to have to create some sort of plan for Phurus within the next couple of days."

"We could use any of the more famous stories from the Bible," put in Sarah, "There are plenty of popular stories from there."

The three friends sat and discussed ideas for a few minutes and Sarah actually had her hand on the door handle when Jonathon knocked on the door quietly but urgently. "I don't think we will be getting much sleep." He paused, a little breathless. "The deadline is now midnight our time."

"I suggest we return here around 10 then," said Angelina. "Try and get some sleep. We are all tired and we may need to be alert. Anything could happen tonight."

CHAPTER 19

World in Danger

ALBERT FOUND IT DIFFICULT TO sleep but lay down and tried anyway. He could have sworn he didn't sleep at all but he was nevertheless surprised to find the clock reading only minutes before he was due to meet the others. Jonathon had not even tried to sleep but instead had returned to the Library, borrowed an Tourist guide and returning to his room spent some time finding keywords of the various locations on the list that the Omniview machine would be likely to recognize. He looked for locations with unusual names so that if the machine found more than one for each name the list of possibilities would be shorter. He had thought of entering the coordinates into the Omniview machine and leaving markers so that the machine could return to each location instantly but this would have risked being discovered. The friends should have time later before the deadline ran out to set the markers.

Albert was last to get to Angelina's room and the others were ready to go to the Library and Omniview room Five. Albert simply held the door open for the others and they all went down the corridor together.

Not a word was spoken as they travelled the short distance to the Library. The Library should have been in darkness but a light made them all suspicious.

"No one should be here at this time of the night," said Angelina.

"Including us," responded Albert in a whisper.

"We don't have time to wait around out here and we must get to the Omniview room Five shortly or many people could die on Earth," said Jonathon.

"I could go in on my own," said Angelina. "If someone has just left the light on then I could come and tell you. If it's simply some other students than that would be fine as well. I will leave the door slightly ajar. I would have to close the door softly for it to remain open as it is a self closer but that is easily explained by not wanting to make a noise late at night."

"What if the person is Phurus?" Sarah pointed out the fear that was in all of their minds.

"Then I am doing research on flying rules for the flying pageant." Angelina pushed gently on the door handle and quietly opened the door. Looking around she at first thought that no one was in the Library until she noticed the sliver of light that was coming from under the door of Omniview room Two. Retracing her steps she reported this to the others.

"Every time we know that Phurus has contacted Grafton Ree he has used Omniview room Two," said Jonathon, "and who else is likely to be around at this time of night except someone who is up to no good?"

"I would like to think that we are up to some good," mused Albert, "and we are around at this time of night."

"We have no choice anyway," said Angelina. "At least if Grafton knows that Phurus is looking on the Omniview detector will already be on and that will mean that he won't know that we are looking in as well. I think if we are quiet we should be able to slip into O5 without being heard and then if we block the light at the bottom of the door before we switch the light on. It would be difficult to see that we were there if Phurus left."

Jonathon was very thoughtful "I think that Phurus looking on could be a very good thing." All the others looked at him strangely while he paused. "If you remember the way that Grafton covered up when we were watching and that we speculated that Phurus had not been let in on the whole plan. This might mean that while Phurus is watching Grafton will have to delay any reaction to the result of the deadline."

"Do you think therefore we should wait until he has gone before going to O5?" said Sarah.

"Oh no," said Jonathon, "Once he has left there will be nothing to stop Grafton wrecking havoc anywhere in the world. We should spend the time setting up the Omniview machine to all the locations that we can and if possible finding all the bombs so that we can neutralize them quickly as necessary."

The four friends then moved slowly and silently through the Library door and across the red carpet and reaching the relative safety of Omniview room Five without incident. The door was closed and while the small click as the door latched made all of them start the sound would not have been heard through the closed door of Omniview room Two. Angelina laid her cloak across the bottom of the door to stop light giving away the fact that O5 was in use.

"I will start by trying to find all the places on Grafton's list," said Jonathon. "It should be fairly quick as I have created a list of recognizable keywords for the Omniview search systems."

"Once we have them all loaded then we need to look at each in detail to see if we can find the devices," said Albert. "There is one thing that I am worried about and that is that I can only hold a screen around one device at a time, what if Grafton operates two devices?"

"We need to find a source of heat to kill the virus before we release the screen," said Jonathon. "Although contained by the screen the explosion itself may be enough."

"Could we take that risk?" asked Albert of no one in particular.

"The Omniview system can introduce heat," said Albert, "much as we did in the British Library, but we had more time then."

"We could try the heat and open the screen perhaps underwater to stop the spread of the virus," suggested Sarah.

"Good idea," said Angelina, "See if you can make a note of any local areas of water when we look at each location."

"We would be found out pretty quickly but I can take the intact screen straight though walls if necessary," said Albert, "It would make a hell of a mess of the wall but it would also save a lot of time."

"Once we start doing that we could use another Omniview Machine and use two at the same time. Alarms would of course go on everywhere but by then I suspect covering up would be too late anyway."

"We would need another key to do that, said Albert.

"If I can make one copy I can make two," said Jonathon reaching into his pocket. "Obviously I am not as practiced as you but I have been watching and learning."

"It might be useful to use as many machines as possible to search for the devices," put in Angelina, "I will go to Omniview room Four with Sarah. Jonathon could use Omniview room Three, while Albert stayed here."

"I don't like the idea of being split up," said Sarah, "It increases the risk of being spotted."

"OK, I will go to O3 and Sarah and Jonathon can work O4," said Angelina.

Sarah began to protest that she wasn't personally scared of being caught when Angelina cut her short.

"We don't have the luxury of time to find these things, and a few minutes before the deadline we also need to be monitoring Grafton so that we know what he is doing so that we can react correctly."

"These things are not likely to be easy to find anyway. They are all hidden in public places where they have been undetected for weeks," said Sarah.

"I agree," said Albert, "All the locations are public places such as art galleries, Libraries and museums. I have been thinking that the devices must have been delivered to their locations openly otherwise at least one of them would have been discovered by now and the probable disaster would have been common knowledge. The only things that could have been so openly placed would be some works of art such as pottery, sculptures etc. We should be looking for these sorts of things which have been recently donated or lent to the institutions. The Omniview machines can look through pottery walls and things like that but it still won't be easy to spot and the fine movements required will take a little time to master."

"We had better get going," said Jonathon, "I have made copies of the list of locations."

"I'll take the top four locations," said Albert. "I am more practiced with the Omniview than any of you and so I should be quicker. Angelina take the next three and the last two are yours, Jonathon."

After a warning from Angelina to remember to mask the light from the bottom of the door three of the friends left Albert already using the Omniview controls.

The Art Gallery, which was Albert's first search, proved to be easy. Only a few items in the gallery were big enough to contain the device and Albert found it on only the second item he investigated. The item was a large pottery vase which appeared to have a cork jammed in the top. Next was a museum and that proved much more difficult, but now Albert knew what size the device was likely to be and that meant many more things could be bypassed as either too big or too small. Forty minutes later Albert had found all four of the devices at the locations he had been assigned. Once he knew what he was looking for the search had proved relatively easy.

Angelina walked in just as he was writing down the last precise coordinates having finished the three that she had been assigned. "The controls are much like flying," she said as she quietly closed the door. "I think having watched you before that I could operate the screens to enclose the devices fairly easily."

Jonathon was finding the controls a little more difficult to deal with, much to his surprise, however he found the two that he had been assigned well before the deadline passed. Albert had by this time been watching Grafton in his office.

The Omniview detector winked out its warning. Albert couldn't know whether this was due to Phurus watching as well or only to the fact that he was watching but Grafton ignored it.

Grafton's office once more had the usual people in it. Norma, seemingly more tense than usual, was sitting upright on the settee along the wall. Barry looked as though he wished he wasn't there and Anne was sitting typing on a computer keyboard in the corner. Grafton wearing his usual supremely confident expression watched a space somewhere on Anne's back expecting her to tell him that the bank accounts were now a lot healthier than they had been last week.

"You seem to be taking a long time to check those accounts, Anne," said Grafton.

"Just doing a quick recheck," came the faltering reply.

"I would have thought that even you could have read a few figures from a computer screen without having to have it spelt out to you," Grafton sneered, "No matter how many zeros they happen to have."

"I have to check all three collection accounts and the two transfer accounts. It has to have some complexity otherwise it wouldn't be safe," replied Anne, "In this case there aren't that many zeros to consider. Only five. That is one from each account. All the accounts are empty."

The faint smile that had been playing on Grafton's lips completely disappeared and Barry got up and left the room making some excuse about needing to go to the bathroom.

Grafton fought hard to hold on to his composure but for all those in the room and watching the only outward sign was the missing smile and some did not even notice that either. "We will wait a short period before any reaction. Anne, is there a time lag between deposits and them showing up in the accounts?"

"Nothing of any significance," replied Anne from the computer. "A few minutes at most."

"I will let this development sink in for a while and see if this is a temporary setback before any reaction. You may all take a break back here in 15minutes." Grafton wanted to be alone and the occupants of the office did not need a second hint. The office emptied very quickly.

"Well done, Mr Ree. I did not think you were going to hold on to your cool mask. Things yet again not going to plan." The voice did nothing to help Grafton with his composure. However, this still did not show.

This was the confirmation that indeed Phurus was watching via another Omniview machine and explained why Grafton had ignored the blinking light on the detector.

"A mere setback, Mr Pathos. A temporary setback. I am sure that they will realize the error of their ways and the fact that they have very little choice. Perhaps this will give me the excuse to deal with the hydro engineers."

"I am pleased that you had not forgotten the outstanding part of our deal. I will look forward to reading all about it in the Earthly press."

"Oh I am sure that any action I take will make all the relevant media." Grafton's sneer and playful smiled had returned for Phurus' benefit.

"I will leave you to your plans then," said Phurus. "I do not expect to be disappointed again."

"I will make the event newsworthy," said Grafton picking up some papers from his desk.

"Goodbye," said Phurus.

A knock on the door announced that one of the others had arrived back from the break and Grafton threw the papers gently across the desk where they gently toppled a further pile of papers. "Come."

"OK, to come in?" said Barry.

Barry had been out of the room when Grafton had dismissed the others, which explained his early return. "Thank you, Barry. I want the communication equipment set up in five minutes. Ask the others to come in will you, please."

Barry left the room without really entering. Anne and Norma arrived less than 15 seconds later giving no time for Grafton to do anything else or even realize that a few sheets from the toppled documents now covered the Omniview detector.

"Norma, we are about to make another broadcast will you set up so that we cannot be traced please. Anne, could you monitor the bank accounts and let me know if there is any change of status?"

Barry returned with a camera and lighting set as Norma went out to collect her equipment. Albert watched through the Omniview machine as the office became very busy. The lights and camera together with Norma's communication links to the Internet were set up in record time. Grafton was not a person to be crossed at any time and the workers correctly assumed that Grafton would not currently be in a good mood.

"Ready when you are." said Barry.

"The links will be active as soon as you ask." confirmed Norma.

"Anne?" said Grafton.

"No change." said Anne after checking each of the five accounts again.

Grafton nodded to Barry and the lights came on and a red light on the camera indicated that it was also running. A further nod to the watching Norma caused her to flick a switch on her control board and nod back again. Grafton started to speak.

"Gentlemen, I am disappointed that you haven't taken my threat seriously. Perhaps I had forgotten to emphasize that the payment is not optional. We have noted a few communications earlier which we regard as transparent delaying tactics. Perhaps I forgot to emphasize that excuses would not be tolerated. I am not a completely heartless man so I may be prepared to give you a little more time let us say 30 minutes in which to complete the formalities for payment. I am disappointed that my demonstration in the UK and the people who are almost certainly dead or dying there despite your somehow managed news blackout did not convince you how serious were my intentions. As I said I am not a completely heartless man and so I have decided that my next demonstration will also be an island to allow you to contain the disease so long as you act quickly to close the borders of Japan. Shame about the few million people who live there but then that is the consequence of not accepting my demands. I will leave you with that thought as I believe you should now be busy with your own arrangements." Grafton nodded at Norma who instantly cut the link.

Grafton reached out a hand and picked up a mobile phone and started dialing a number.

The Japanese maritime museum had been one of the locations that Albert had searched and he had previously put a marker on. Selecting the marker Albert returned to the museum almost instantly and without a moment's hesitation he surrounded the vase containing the device with a force field. Albert had reacted without thinking. The decision to switch to Japan had been instant. Once there he had worked accurately and quickly but even so the screen was barely in place before the flash of the detonation occurred. Albert did not stop there. He needed to get back to see what Grafton was doing. Forcing the screen and its deadly content directly through the wall of the building, he submerged the screen tens of metres below the surface of the nearby Pacific Ocean. Using the Omniview machine to feed fuel into the protective screen and ignite it he increased the temperature massively before releasing the screen slowly allowing any escaping gasses to seep slowly to the surface through the water, safely cooling as it went.

"Wow," was all that Sarah could say. The flowing motion of Albert's actions had taken about four or five minutes to complete. Four or five minutes of frantic activity, during which all of the four friends had been totally silent.

"That will put the cat among the pigeons," said Jonathon, "The hole you punched in the wall of that building will cause some serious questions to be asked."

"Not to mention a vase disintegrating in a blinding flash of light," put in Sarah.

"No one would have seen the vase disintegrate as the museum was closed. Just after seven in the morning. There would however have been many who saw the hole appear in the wall, but what else could I do?" said Albert already switching the Omniview back to Grafton's office.

"Not a lot," said Angelina. "That was incredibly quick thinking. The world is safe in your hands."

"I don't think so." Albert's face showed the concern he was feeling "If Grafton sets of more than one of those devices." Albert paused, "all he needs to do is dial a number. It took me something like 10 minutes to deal with that one. I could never keep up"

"I think Albert is right." Jonathon paused, "Albert dealt with it quicker than that but still we couldn't hope to keep up even using two machines if they were detonated one after the other."

"Then we have to hope that Grafton does this one or two at a time," said Angelina.

"We don't have much time," said Jonathon, "We need to make sure that markers are placed on both machines that we wish to use for all the locations. Albert only contained the last device because he could go directly to it. Any slower and the virus would already have been out."

"We also need a third machine to watch Grafton's moves. If he detonates one after the other then we need to know which one to go to next—if we are to stand any chance at all," said Albert.

"We should be able to use any of the machines as Phurus has gone now," said Angelina, "but as we only have two keys, I suggest that Albert and Jonathon man two machines with Albert taking the first of any devices and Jonathon used only if necessary. Me or Sarah could watch Grafton on another machine."

"You were quicker than me, Angelina, in the search and speed is going to be important if we need the second machine," said Jonathon, "I think that you should take the more active part."

Angelina looked worried but after a small pause nodded.

"I will get on with using Albert's notes to place the location markers in O3," said Angelina passing her notes to Albert so that he could do the same on the machine he was sitting at. "Once

Albert has got your locations in, Jonathon, get Sarah to bring them to me."

"OK, then I will use O4 to monitor Grafton and, Sarah, you join me there to act as messenger should anything happen."

By the time the friends had finished setting up the extended deadline had almost expired. The view in Grafton's office showed that little had changed. The players still were they had been when the four had last looked but all except Grafton showed signs of uneasiness.

"Grafton thinks he has just killed millions and is as unconcerned as if he had just squished an ant," said Angelina her anger rising inside her. "That guy is going down."

"Anne?" Grafton's use of her name was simply to find out if there had been any activity in the accounts.

Anne played her fingers across the keyboard in front of her and watched the results on the screen. "We have one hundred million," she said after a pause. "I will be able to trace the source in a few minutes."

"One player from eight." Grafton's statement was just a thought voiced aloud. "That I am afraid simply isn't good enough."

"Is the payer America?"

"No, the source is somewhere in Europe," replied Anne.

"Good enough. I think we need further communication with the world."

The communication system was quickly set up and silhouette of Grafton once more spoke to the world leaders. "I see that only one of you has thought fit to treat my demands seriously." Grafton paused and the world leaders listening could not see the smile which further angered Angelina when it was reported to her by Jonathon. "I have run out of islands, unless you count Singapore. Still there should be plenty of time to close the borders with China and Russia. They are such large countries. I suggest that you don't try my patience again. You have ten minutes to comply. The communication was cut and Grafton reached for his phone.

Sarah had reported that China was the next target before Grafton had finished speaking.

Working quickly Albert had a screen around the device from the display at the Museum in Beijing before Grafton had started to dial and the device with its enclosing vase was already out of the building when the flash of the detonation showed on Albert's screen. Using the power of the explosion with the fuel that he had already started inserting into the enclosed space the temperature soon disposed of the virus and once again Albert immersed the whole into a nearby lake before allowing the screen to slowly release any remains into the water.

Angelina had had more time to deal with the Russian target which was dealt with in a similar manner. Despite the extra time Angelina only just managed to contain the deadly device. On opening the interference panel an alarm had sounded. Angelina had silenced the alarm by placing a piece of tape over the activating switch but she didn't know if anyone had heard the brief blare of sound. Actually nobody had heard the sound but a light blinked insistently in the monitoring panel in the office of Seraphus. Luckily no one was currently there to notice it. The light however was not reset as easily as the sound.

The four friends met briefly in Omniview room Four. Angelina was almost in tears. "It was so close. I almost didn't get the device enclosed before it went off and then I nearly accidentally released it before I had the temperature up high enough. I could have killed millions."

Albert quickly tried to calm Angelina "To start with even if you had failed to contain the device it would not have been you that had killed millions it would still have been Grafton. Secondly you made it. Feel very very satisfied that you have just saved millions."

"Jonathon, you ought to deal with the next one. I am simply not quick enough."

"Angelina, you did well. I doubt I would have made it. Albert is the quickest but he has had more practice you would be quicker than me as you proved with your manipulation of the controls when we were searching for the devices earlier."

"If Grafton detonates all the devices then I won't stand a chance. Albert will take the first and I might control the second but even if Albert gets the third I won't have finished with the second to catch the fourth."

"Then we had better hope that Grafton slows down a little," said Sarah.

"Jon and I will get back to monitor Grafton while Albert sets up to take the first device and we will give you, Angelina, as much time as possible in O3 to take the second."

The four split up again with Angelina returning to O3 to prepare to do what she could, convinced that she would probably fail. She opened the door which she couldn't remember closing and made her way to the machine. Her back was to the open door.

The picture on Omniview room Four's screen still showed Grafton's office and Anne was typing away on the console in the corner. Grafton waited for the news that the money was being credited to the accounts but Anne said nothing. The new deadline was fast approaching and Grafton was this time sure that the governments of the world would be so scared that they would be rushing to meet his demands. News from Russia and China could be expected to take some time to be public however the world leaders would be better informed and the expected deaths in Japan would shortly be a major news item. Grafton turned on the radio.

"And finally in Japan a few minutes ago a bright white light punched a hole in the wall of a maritime museum and then disappeared into the Ocean taking with it a recently donated work of art. People who witness the event said that the bright light caused a plume of steam as it disappeared under the water. We will now cross to the weather desk for the forecast."

Grafton was under no illusion "Leigh," he said. "Your doing."

The three people in his office looked at each other. Grafton had forgotten momentarily that they were there. Recovering he said, "Well, Anne. Are we richer?"

Anne turned back to her screen and after a second or two said, "Sorry, there have been no more transactions at all."

"Then they have had enough time and I will carry out my threat."

Barry went pale. "You can't detonate all the devices. The infection would spread and we will be killed as well."

"The injection that I administered three days ago was a vaccine. You should not be affected." Grafton paused slightly picked up the list from the desk, noted as he moved some papers in the process that the red light was blinking on the Omniview detector. But by now he didn't care. He smiled. "I think I will start at the top and work down." His hand picked up the phone and Sarah rushed out and told Albert that the detonations are to be top to bottom on the list shouting to Angelina the same instructions as she went past the open door.

Albert quickly contained the first device knowing that Angelina would be working on the second but Grafton was moving too quickly and Albert barely got to the third and knew he wouldn't be clear to catch the fifth. Albert was beginning to panic but he carried on working as fast as he could.

Albert working on Omniview five had just managed to get the fifth device in view when he saw it detonate. "Missed it," he cried out in agony. Then he noticed that the device had been contained. A screen had appeared on the instant of the explosion. Noting this unexpected event, Albert thought quickly and quickly switched to device six, succeeding in placing protection around that device moments before the flash of light that announced that it too had been triggered.

CHAPTER 20

Unexpected help

ANGELINA STARTED WORK ON THE second device and surrounded it as it detonated and knew that the fourth device on the list was not going to be covered. 'HELP,' the thought was almost screamed out loud in panic as she thought of millions that would die as she failed. "Those poor people," again the thought was voiced as she worked. The sound of her outcry had however masked the sound of the room door closing behind her.

A hand passed her shoulder and pressed a button on the panel and a voice said, "Ignore that one and start the next." Angelina started. The voice was not one of her friends but was a voice that she recognized. She half turned and looked straight into the eyes of Phurus.

"You don't have time to stare," he said quietly, "I will help you here but you must give me time to leave unhindered when I have finished, say 30 minutes." Phurus was now using both hands on the controls, his arms effectively holding Angelina in her seat as he worked.

"This whole mess is your fault," said Angelina when she again found her voice.

"While I am not without blame in this matter I think that my involvement only allowed things to come to a head quicker than they would have anyway. I was unaware that Grafton had a more dangerous virus as well as the one that was used in the HydroVista Hotel." Phurus paused working quickly to contain the fourth device. "I doubt that your friends will get to device five. We need to work quickly. Do we have a deal?"

"I will not tell anyone for that time if we manage to stop all the devices, but my friends will probably know and I can only ask them to do the same. I cannot guarantee their actions."

"Good enough," said Phurus moving to one side into a better position to work the machine. "Press that button, third from the left top row." Angelina did as she was told. "That will hold the containment until you can deal with it properly." Phurus worked with practiced speed, much faster than Albert as he surrounded device five. "Take over, Angelina, please. Your friends will cope with the others and I have work to do. You will need to take care of the other screens, which we have left simply hovering in limbo. Press that button to return to the first and that button to return to the second." Phurus indicated two buttons on the control panel. Looking for confirmation that Angelina had understood he stepped away from the console. "I suppose it was you that stopped my revenge on the engineers. A very slick job"

"Albert," said Angelina.

"I will deal with him later. If that had gone ahead I would have known before this that Mr Ree had been up to something more and been able to solve it all myself."

Angelina cursed herself for letting Albert's involvement out of the bag. She wondered what Phurus meant by dealing with him later. The thought was interrupted by Phurus

"Remember 30 minutes."

Angelina nodded "Thank you," she said.

Phurus said nothing as he opened the door and slipped out almost silently.

Jonathon was still watching Grafton. "He doesn't seem too worried about the fact that he has killed millions of people," he said to Sarah who after delivering the necessary messages had thought it best to leave Albert and Angelina to concentrate.

"I hope the others have managed to stop all the devices," said Sarah turning as the door opened to admit Albert, who looked drained.

"Get them all?" asked Jonathon.

"I didn't," said Albert, "But someone did," he continued noting the look of panic on Sarah's face.

"So who got to it?" said Jonathon.

"I don't know," said Albert, "I thought it must be Angelina but she would have had her hands full with the others."

Suddenly a voice was heard through the speaker. "Mr Ree, I would suggest that in future you keep me well informed of your plans. I am not accustomed to being used. I will speak to you shortly."

Jonathon looked at Sarah "Phurus".

"I wonder how much he knows," said Sarah.

"Angelina not back yet?" asked Albert. "I will go and see how she is."

Angelina was disposing of the last of the devices as Albert entered the room.

"OK?" said Albert.

"Tired," replied Angelina.

Realizing that Angelina was dealing with one of the earlier devices Albert walked over to see how she was doing it. "I didn't know you could hold screen without them being in view."

"Neither did I until I was shown," said Angelina, "Phurus was here."

"Phurus!" exclaimed Albert.

"He helped me contain the devices, Albert. Without him I would have stood no chance."

"We must tell the authorities now—speak to Soarelle we can't let him get away."

"I promised him 30 minutes," said Angelina softly. "Help me keep my promise, please."

Albert looked shocked then realized the amount of strain that Angelina had been feeling, the drained look which showed what it would have done to her if either of the friends had failed to contain even one of the devices. Albert wrapped her in his arms and held her until some minutes later Sarah quietly opened the door.

"Sorry, you two, but all hell's breaking loose out here. Several people in the mortal world have seen balls of light and fire hanging in the air then diving into bodies of water. This has made news all over the place and the authorities here are asking questions about who authorized such a demonstration. We picked this up off the Angel channel but it won't be long before there are Angels everywhere asking questions. I suspect that the sources of such miracles can be traced. I think our secret is out. I think that eventually you two are going to be heroes."

"Thanks, Sarah," said Albert. "It was a team effort without all four of us we would be listening to tales of death and disease from the Earth and Heaven would be a little overwhelmed to worry about us. We will simply let it come to us and see how long it takes."

Sarah closed the door behind her softly and returned to Omniview room Four where Jonathon had just returned from retrieving the key from Omniview room Five.

Angelina remained, Albert's arm around her shoulders arms with the occasional sob showing the strain she had been under and the fear she had felt of failing.

CHAPTER 21

Seraphus' Return

THE DOOR OPENED WITH A bang and in stepped Soarelle obviously in a bad mood. "Which one of you two was it that performed unauthorized miracles?"

Soarelle surveyed the scene noticing the shake of Angelina's shoulders and became a little more conciliatory. "The alarm shows that the interference panel has been opened in this room and the amount of flying lights and fireballs report means that someone is in very deep trouble." This surprised Albert until he realized that the Earthly press would have seen the work he and Angelina had done but not realized the significance or the danger that had been averted.

"It was necessary," said Albert simply. This simple statement took all the blame off Angelina as Soarelle assumed that he had been the perpetrator.

"I would suggest that you make your way immediately to Arch Ardon Seraphus' office. We have received word that he will be returning shortly. I am sure that he will want to think very hard about the punishment that is to be meted out for this unforgivable breaking not only of school rules but also Angel Law."

"I don't think that will be necessary," said a voice from just beyond the door. "I think that Angelina, Albert and their friends should go and rest a report can be made later."

"But I don't think you understand, Arch Ardon Seraphus. A major and serious breach of Law has occurred here," said Soarelle. "A very serious breach."

"I understand perfectly, Soarelle, and I suspect you will have a different view on the story when you have been acquainted with all the facts. We owe these Angels a major debt but first we should let them rest." Seraphus turned to someone behind him. Please run to the hospital and let Nurse Judith know that four Angels will be joining her in a private room. Tell her they are to be monitored but not disturbed. Ardon Charina please, collect the other two from the other Omniview room and we will escort them to their rest."

The four friends were escorted to a private ward in the hospital wing and allowed to rest. Seraphus obviously knew most of what had gone on, despite the fact that he did not interrupt the accounts of the four later when he came to their room.

The Earthly newspapers had reported the phenomena as a real Plague of Miracles but either the news of the deadly devices had been suppressed or had been unknown to the reporters as this was not mentioned. Several world leaders knew how close they had come to disaster but they weren't saying anything either.

The end of term exams were run as usual. Angelina and the three friends actually arranged a flying pageant in which Angelina flew an amazing display.

Seraphus found Albert on the last day before the holiday. "I hope that next term will be a little less eventful."

"I expect so," said Albert. Then as an afterthought he asked, "If you don't mind, sir, what happened to Phurus?"

"He has, I am afraid, escaped to Earth and has taken with him several items which will help him elude detection and make his life a little easier. It doesn't matter. Your intervention prevented any harm."

"The intervention was a team effort, sir, without any one of us we wouldn't have been able to do it."

"It would however have been better to report it to the proper authorities," said Seraphus.

"We did if you recall and it was passed to Phurus to cover up."

"Ah, well, so you did. He is gone now and we won't hear from him again."

Albert was not so sure of this last statement. Angelina had reported Phurus' last words and Albert knew that Phurus was not known for idle threats.

Albert wondered about next term. Would it be such an uneventful time he hoped so. He would like to have someone to talk to about it but virtually all the angels he knew would be going away for the holiday. Angelina was going on a flying trip for which Albert wasn't yet qualified. Jonathon and Sarah were going off somewhere together and obviously going with them would be out of the question. Albert had got some reports and projects to do so he didn't think he would be bored.